THE QUEEN OF DREAMS
A
VOYAGE THROUGH AIR

Peter F. Hamilton was born in Rutland in 1960 and still lives in that county. He began writing adult science fiction and fantasy in 1987 and since then has sold over two million books in the UK alone and is the UK's bestselling science-fiction author. He has two young children who inspired him to write for a younger audience. *A Voyage Through Air* is the final instalment in the fantastic The Queen of Dreams children's fantasy trilogy.

Also by Peter F. Hamilton from Macmillan Children's Books

The Secret Throne
The Hunting of the Princes

THE QUEEN OF DREAMS
A VOYAGE THROUGH AIR

PETER F. HAMILTON

ILLUSTRATED BY ROHAN EASON

MACMILLAN CHILDREN'S BOOKS

First published 2017 by Macmillan Children's Books
an imprint of Pan Macmillan
20 New Wharf Road, London N1 9RR
Associated companies throughout the world
www.panmacmillan.com

ISBN 978-1-4472-9116-9

1 3 5 7 9 8 6 4 2

A CIP catalogue record for this book is available from
the British Library.

Printed and bound by CPI Group (UK) Ltd, Croydon CR0 4YY

This one is for Sophie and Felix,
who in real life are far more awesome than
anything I've written about them in here.

CONTENTS

Prelude: The Vital Message   1

1   Secrets New and Old   5

2   History in the Annexe   13

3   The Letter   32

4   Preparing for War   39

5   Visitors   52

6   Dawn Departure   63

7   The *Angelhawk*   80

8   The Enchantments of Deceit   93

9   The Voyage Begins   100

10   Gone Surfing   111

11   The Isle of Banmula   127

12   Isle Ho!   133

13   A Long-Ago Voyage   145

14   The Heirs   160

15   Into the Fourth Realm   176

16   Betrayed   187

17   A New Ally   199

18   The Sea Globe   214

19   Battle Stations   228

20   Monsters of Air   248

21   Where Nobody Wants to Be   265

22   The Resting Place   275

23   Rothgarnal Once More   284

24   Truths Revealed   294

25   Party Time   306

PRELUDE

THE VITAL MESSAGE

The lands and seas of the First Realm formed the inside of a sphere many thousands of miles across. Right at the centre, far above the air and clouds, a little sun burned brightly, its golden rays stroking the rambling emerald forests and expansive meadows in a warm haze. This solitary sun was surrounded by the heavy weave of multi-coloured streamers that the First Realm's inhabitants called moonclouds, which cast thick nightshadows across vast swathes of the sphere's surface. Cities and towns glimmered like jewels among the darkness.

Captain Feandez of the Second Realm's Blue Feather regiment stood on the prow of the *Lady Katherine*, watching keenly as the ship approached a small island just offshore. The helmsman was steering them into a rocky inlet where the stark cliff walls on either side rose higher and higher, growing narrower as they did so. A huge waterfall tumbled down the far end of the inlet. Captain Feandez tried not to appear nervous at how fast they were approaching the thundering torrent of water.

'Most august Harrolas,' the schooner's bosun called out behind him. 'We request passage to the Second Realm,

I

and ask that you kindly grant us this privilege.' The bosun held his fist out over the gunnel. Captain Feandez saw a glint of coins tumbling into the water. He imagined that the inlet's floor must be a thick blanket of gold and silver by now, as for century after century captains made their respectful offering to the Great Gateway.

The addition of a few more coins seemed to appease the Great Gateway. With the prow now only metres away from the vertical spray, the waterfall began to part, revealing only darkness behind. A fast swirl of droplets, half-spray half-rain, drenched Captain Feandez. The schooner sailed into the gap – and immediately emerged into another, very similar, fjord to the one they'd left behind in the First Realm, with a waterfall divided on either side of the ship like a liquid curtain being held open.

Captain Feandez let out a relieved breath, and started shaking out his pale blue shirt, whose ruff neck and wrists were completely sodden and limp. The wonderfully familiar hot sun of the Second Realm warmed his skin. It would dry him out soon enough. Instinctively, he patted the little leather purse hanging round his neck, containing the very special bullet which had been entrusted to him by the Queen of Dreams herself.

It was his mission to ensure the bullet was presented to the War Emperor himself, thus exposing the full treachery of the Karrak Lords and Ladies. If the armies of the War Emperor, armed only with their usual mage-enchanted swords and arrows, came up against modern machine guns they would be slaughtered. The fate of so many people depended on him accomplishing that one task. It was a heavy responsibility.

Reassured the purse and its precious bullet was still around his neck, Feandez scanned the horizon beyond the end of the fjord. The sea into which they were sailing was relatively calm, and there was a good wind blowing.

'How long to Shatha'hal?' he asked.

The bosun made a show of sniffing the air. 'Half a day, maybe less.'

Captain Feandez let out a long breath of relief. Soon now, and a terrible disaster would be averted.

The *Lady Katherine* cleared the fjord, and swung round to sail parallel to the coast. In a short while they would reach the estuary of the river Zhila, which led inland to Shatha'hal. Gulls wheeled high overhead, squawking loudly. An extra set of sails were unfurled on the mainmast, and they picked up speed, cutting cleanly through the water.

It was the fall of silence which made Captain Feandez realize something was wrong. He turned to see the bosun staring anxiously up into the sky.

'What's the matter?' he asked.

'The gulls,' the bosun replied.

Captain Feandez glanced upwards. The swirl of gulls which had accompanied the *Lady Katherine* since she had emerged from the fjord had abandoned them. 'There aren't any,' he said as orders were given to furl the sails.

'Yes,' the bosun agreed with a grunt. 'All gone.'

3

'Why?'

'We don't know. That's bad.'

Sailors were scrabbling nimbly up the masts. The big white sails flapped loosely as they were furled. Then there was a shout. Arms were raised, pointing.

Captain Feandez squinted up into the sky where so many fingers were jabbing. A lone black dot was visible in the bright azure sky. It grew fast, resolving into a big bird.

An eagle, Captain Feandez recognized with growing unease. *A big black eagle.*

Captain Feandez didn't know much about birds, but he was sure eagles didn't normally fly over the sea. He hurriedly put on a pair of revealor glasses; crafted by the anamages of the Second Realm, they showed up any spells as a glowing light.

At first he thought he was looking straight at the sun, so bright was the eagle shining with magical power. His hand automatically went to his sword hilt.

A destruction spell stabbed out from the eagle to hit *Lady Katherine* amidships. The explosion blew a gaping hole in the hull. Chunks of smouldering wood spun through the air like scythes. Captain Feandez ducked—

1

SECRETS NEW AND OLD

Lorothain, the capital city of the First Realm, was on the edge of an approaching nightshadow. As the vast border of shade drew closer, tiny sparks of bluish lightstone illumination began to prickle the windows of the exuberant domes and elevated towers of the grander mansions, while the neat streets of terraced houses glowed a rich sapphire from the wakening streetlights.

In the private wing of the capital's royal palace, Jemima Paganuzzi, the Blossom Princess of the First Realm, got ready for bed. 'I'm so tired,' she told Taggie, her older sister, and the First Realm's Queen of Dreams. 'Do you think Dad will mind if I don't do my teeth?'

'I'm sure he won't mind you missing one night,' Taggie told her. 'Hang on, I'll shut the curtains.'

As the Blossom Princess, Jemima was entitled to her own suite of rooms in the palace. They were rather sumptuous for a twelve-year-old, with ornate furniture and marbled floors and gilt-edged paintings.

'I'll do them twice tomorrow,' Jemima promised unconvincingly as she climbed into her huge bed and pulled the duvet up.

Taggie grinned as she walked over to the tall window. 'There's probably a spell for teeth cleaning,' she said as she pulled the long velvet curtains shut.

She smiled to herself. It had been an incredible day for the two of them, ending in a thrilling and at times utterly terrifying showdown with the Grand Lord's forces in London's docklands. Their ordeal had proved worthwhile, for they'd found Lord Colgath, the one Karrak Lord who might be able to help them prevent the coming war between the Grand Lord and the War Emperor.

Outside, the moonclouds were expanding across the entire First Realm. Taggie nodded in satisfaction. As Queen, her magic controlled the First Realm's nature, of which the moonclouds were an important part. Normally only half of the First Realm was in darkness at any one time, but these weren't normal times.

'If that's a real spell, Mum will know it,' Jemima said drowsily. Their mother was a Third Realm sorceress, who seemed to know just about every sort of magic.

'When she gets back, we'll ask her,' Taggie said.

'Do you think she'll be back soon?'

'With any luck, she'll be able to leave the Gathering as soon as Captain Feandez hands over the bullet to the War Emperor.'

'I hope so. I really miss her, Taggie.'

'Night, Jem,' Taggie said, and leaned over the bed to kiss her sister.

Jemima's eyes were already closed. 'Are you going to dream tonight?'

'Of course I am,' Taggie said. 'I'm the Queen of Dreams, it's what I do. And tonight I'm going to reassure everyone about the war.' Whenever she slept in the First Realm, Taggie would drift into the dreams of everyone else, soothing away their troubles and offering all the comfort only a truly kind heart could.

'Oh good.'

Jemima dreamed, as did everybody in the First Realm that strange all-encompassing night. In her dream she walked through the halls and corridors of the palace she'd grown familiar with in the year since she and Taggie had overthrown the Karrak Lords and Ladies who had tried to usurp the First Realm.

But in this dream, on this unusual night, other people were walking through the palace with Jemima. Holvans with their four arms, giants with their green hair, ordinary men and women and children, the folk who were almost spherical, a few centaurs, some hearty trolls. Much to Jemima's delight there were even elves sharing her dream, tall and ebony-skinned with long plumes of hair reaching all the way down their backs.

Thousands upon thousands of people streamed into the throne room, which in her dream was much bigger than it was in real life. Yet Jemima along with everyone else was standing close to the dais which held the shell throne. Taggie sat on the purple and scarlet silk cushions of the throne, watching serenely as every dreamer appeared before her. When Jemima waved excitedly, she didn't notice.

Taggie stood up and looked round the dream throne room with its weirdly insubstantial walls. 'I cast this night across the First Realm because I have something to tell everybody who lives here.' Her voice carried clearly across the room. 'A War Emperor has been anointed once more. He has summoned together all the armies of the realms so he may lead them into battle against the Grand Lord. Well, I will not be ordering any soldier of the First Realm to fight in this war. We have fought the Karraks in a conflict which has lasted for generations. This has to end. Too many have died already. There has to be another way. I intend to devote myself to finding a peaceful answer to the conflict between our kinds once and for all.' She inclined her head at the massive audience. 'Thank you for attending. May the Heavens guide us all safely.'

Jemima saw many smiles of gratitude and relief among the crowd. As she started to walk out of the throne room she caught sight of a dark motionless figure. It was an old woman in a black dress made of some stiff fabric. A veil covered her face, which instantly made Jemima curious to know what she looked like.

Everyone else was flittering away from the dream like ghostly moths, but the old woman remained still and solid.

'Hello,' Jemima said.

'Dear Blossom Princess,' the old woman replied in a

thin voice. 'How
nice to finally meet
you.'

'Who are you?'

'A messenger.
Your mother asked
me to seek you out.'

Jemima looked
round frantically
for Taggie, but her
sister was nowhere
to be seen. 'You
know Mum?'

A chuckle
emerged from
behind the veil. 'A

very long time ago I was her nurse. Now I'm just a simple
seer, helping out where I can in these troubled times.'

'Gosh, really?'

'Your mother wants to know if you are all right.'

'Yes, tell her we're fine. Tell her we're going to stop the
war.'

'I will. She'll be so proud of you. And she asked me to
say she thinks she may have found a cure for the curse
which turns Felix into a squirrel.'

'*What?*' Jemima squeaked. 'I thought only the Karraks
can lift that curse.'

'The sorceresses of the Third Realm have studied

Karrak wizardry ever since the Dark Lords and Ladies first emerged through Mirlyn's Gate. It is not easy, but some sorceress mistresses now believe they can cure their evil curses. It is one of these academy mistresses that your mother has sent for.'

'Really? Mum can do that?'

'You are very fond of Felix, are you not?' the old woman said in a sympathetic voice. 'I heard he single-handedly saved you from the gols in Shatha'hal's docks.'

'Well, yes, he did. What did Mum say? It would be so fantastic if we could cure him. I can't imagine what it must be like to live like that every day. I so want to help him,' Jemima said eagerly.

'The sorceress mistress is on her way to your mother, and should arrive quite soon. Will you be here? These sendings are difficult for me, especially if you're moving around.'

'Er . . . Taggie said we might be travelling again soon.'

'Oh, perhaps you could let me know where you are,' the woman said smoothly.

'Well, it's kind of a secret.'

'I understand. I'm sure Felix can wait until you get back.'

'No, wait!' Jemima said, desperate for the chance to help Felix. It was just that she didn't want to do anything that might cause a problem for Taggie's quest. She tried to think of a way round it. 'I can cast a wardveil that will let you sight me,' she said slowly. 'But you must promise not to tell anyone where we are.'

'Your mother will want to know. She's desperate for news.'

'Well of course you can tell Mum,' Jemima said, slightly indignant.

'All right then.'

'And you'll give us the cure as soon as you get it?'

'Absolutely.' The stooped old woman bobbed about anxiously. 'It is not my place to tell royalty what to do, but if I can give you one word of advice, Blossom Princess?'

'What?'

'Don't tell Felix that your mother is trying to find the cure. If it doesn't work – and by all the stars in the Heavens let us hope it does – he will be so bitterly disappointed.'

Jemima could well imagine that. Poor Felix. She couldn't stand to raise his hopes only for them to be broken. 'I understand,' she said earnestly. 'This'll be just between you and me.'

The woman bowed slightly, her black dress rustling. 'You are so honourable, Blossom Princess. I consider myself fortunate to have met you. Goodbye, my dear.'

'Goodbye.'

'Goodbye?' a familiar voice asked.

Jemima sat up in bed. One of the palace maids was pulling the curtains back. Brilliant sunlight shone in through the tall arched windows.

Felix, the white squirrel, stood on the bottom of the bed. He was about the size of a Labrador today – some days he was bigger, some smaller; there never seemed to be any pattern to it. His fur was so soft and fluffy it was always hard for Jemima to resist the urge to stroke it.

'Pardon?' she said.

His nose twitched as if he was on the scent of something. 'You said "Goodbye". Are you going somewhere?'

'It must have been a dream,' Jemima said, suddenly feeling guilty, though she wasn't sure why. She wanted to blurt out that she knew a spell to cure him – or at least knew there was such a spell.

'A good one?' he asked politely.

'I don't remember.'

'Ah well. Who does, come morning? I'll wait outside while you get dressed for breakfast.'

HISTORY IN THE ANNEXE

As dawn broke across Lorothain, the royal palace started to bustle with its usual activity. The night guard was replaced by the day guard, horses were brought out of their stables, and cooks prepared various meals.

Inside the ancient collection of battlements, towers, halls and courtyards, three people made their way along the broad corridors to the Dalswath wing on the eastern side of the sprawling palace which housed the royal library.

Taggie Paganuzzi, the Queen of Dreams herself, pushed open the high double doors and marched straight in. She always enjoyed the library which occupied a nice warm hall with two balconies running round the high walls, allowing scholars and historians to reach the highest shelves that covered every wall from floor to the vaulted ceiling.

Following behind Taggie was Prince Lantic from the Second Realm. The third, and most unusual member of the group (at least from Taggie's point of view), was Lord Colgath, a Karrak Lord. He stood an easy head taller than Lantic, with a smoke cloak constantly swirling round his body to protect it from the excessive light that pervaded the universe. Unlike the dense black cloaks of his brethren, his was flecked with small wiggling ripples of phosphorescence, which cast a weird aurora in the darker corridors of the palace.

Mr Blake was the palace's chief librarian, a quietly spoken scholar who had devoted his life to shepherding the knowledge gathered in the library's books. He rose from his desk to greet his unexpected visitor, blinking behind his glasses. 'My Queen, welcome.' He bowed deeply. Then his mouth dropped open in alarm as he caught sight of the Karrak Lord behind her. 'Ah, Majesty?' poor Mr Blake stammered in confusion. 'Your, er . . . that is, you have . . .' Yesterday afternoon the palace had been alive with the rumour that the Queen of Dreams had brought a Karrak Lord back to the First Realm. As the news had filtered its way to the library via maids and footmen, Mr Blake had shaken his head in dismay and told his assistants to stop gossiping. Now it seemed he might have been hasty.

'I know,' Taggie said in sympathy. 'Mr Blake, this is Lord Colgath. He is helping me to prevent the war that is coming between us and the Karraks.'

The librarian polished his glasses with a small piece of cloth. 'I see, Majesty.'

'And this is Prince Lantic of the Second Realm.' Taggie tried to keep her voice neutral, but it was difficult for her. She'd grown close to Lantic during their adventure to find Lord Colgath. She considered him a friend as well as a useful companion (*and nothing else*, she told herself sternly).

Lantic, a gangling fourteen-year-old with floppy dark

hair, gave the flustered librarian his best smile. 'Hello.'

'Your highness,' Mr Blake said formally; he still couldn't take his gaze from the imposing Dark Lord.

'We are going to need your help, Mr Blake,' Taggie said.

'Of course, Majesty. How may I assist you?'

Taggie kept her face expressionless. 'I need to find Mirlyn's Gate,' she told the librarian.

Mr Blake turned away from the Karrak Lord to gawp at the young Queen of Dreams. He saw a charming thirteen-year-old girl with straight auburn hair that came down over her shoulders. Her eyes were very brown, and looking at him so intensely that he knew she wasn't having a joke at his expense. 'That may prove difficult,' he stammered in what may have been the biggest understatement of his career.

He led them through a narrow archway at the far end of the library, the stone lintel was inscribed:

IN HONOUR OF ALL THOSE LOST
AT ROTHGARNAL

It opened into a hexagonal annexe that was nearly half the size of the library itself. 'Queen Layawhan had this section of the palace built after the Battle of Rothgarnal,' Mr Blake explained. Just like the main library, the six sides of the annexe were all lined with ancient leather-bound books whose gold lettering was almost faded from age. 'These books list all those from the First Realm who gave their

15

lives during the war. They also contain the tales of every survivor who chronicled that time, along with official records and accounts from many other Realms.'

Taggie looked round the shelves. She couldn't begin to count how many tomes were there – probably thousands. 'So the answer could be here?'

Mr Blake pulled an unhappy face. 'Majesty. The search for Mirlyn's Gate has essentially been going on from the moment that the War Emperor and the Grand Lord left the battlefield together taking it with them. It is one of the greatest mysteries in all the realms.'

'What can you tell us?' she asked.

'Very little outside the basic history every child learns before their tenth birthday,' Mr Blake said.

'Then we'll start there,' Lantic said.

The four of them gathered around a reading table next to the annexe's fireplace, where flames burned brightly in the grate. An assistant librarian brought a tray of tea and cakes while Mr Blake began the story of Mirlyn's Gate.

'The Universal Fellowship of Mages was formed during the First Times,' he told them as the logs crackled and tea was poured for everybody. 'They forged the Great Gateways between Realms, allowing travel and trade to enrich everyone. But Mirlyn, the greatest mage of all, went further; he opened his gate into the Dark Universe. To begin with, everyone on both sides celebrated, for the wealth and enlightenment which had bloomed as the realms were opened to each other by the Great Gateways was nothing compared to the hopes of two universes mixing. But it soon became clear that there were fundamental differences between the two universes, and they proved most disagreeable to anyone who crossed over.' Mr Blake glanced at Lord Colgath, seeking confirmation.

The Karrak Lord's perfect silver eyes set in a skeletal head reflected tiny copies of the old librarian. 'That is true enough,' he said in his deep voice. 'I find this universe too bright, it is too hot, its very fabric torments every cell in my body. Each living moment I spend here is a punishment. So it is for all of us who came through. But we all had such magnificent dreams for the future when Mirlyn's Gate opened. The opportunities for our growth appeared limitless. Our magic is stronger here, there were vast uninhabited lands we could claim for our own. At first, we thought we could shelter ourselves from those ill effects, so we persevered. It was a foolish delusion born of arrogance we gave to ourselves. We tried to change the nature of the world around us, to make it less hostile. Some of us succeeded to a small extent – the dawn of yet another false hope. And of course those changes were inevitably hostile to the natives of this universe. That was the start of a conflict which pride and stupidity on both sides quickly helped to escalate. A struggle which culminated in the Battle of Rothgarnal.'

'Unfortunately, yes,' Mr Blake agreed, now relaxing a little in the Dark Lord's presence. 'As the Battle of Rothgarnal ended its ninth day, both the War Emperor and the Grand Lord admitted the price both sides had paid in lives was too much. They made a blood-bound agreement that would end the fighting. The War Emperor gave his word his forces would withdraw from the Fourth Realm. In return, the Grand Lord gave his assurance that the folk of the Dark Universe would not leave the Fourth Realm.' Mr Blake gave the brooding Karrak Lord a nervous glance. 'Regrettably, those promises have not been well kept down the centuries.' He shrugged. 'But we are concerned with Mirlyn's Gate, as were the War Emperor and the Grand Lord. It is the only opening that exists between the two universes. Both leaders were desperately worried that the gate would permit invasion in either direction – those were sad warlike times, remember, full of suspicion and mistrust. Rumours were strong that there was a similar conflict raging in the Dark Universe as people from this universe fought against its nature as we did here.'

'Ha,' the Lord Colgath purred. 'No rumour to me,

librarian. I was there that day when my father and the War Emperor stood side by side and bound Mirlyn's foul Gate.'

'You were there?' Taggie asked in amazement. 'At Rothgarnal? But that was . . .'

'A very, *very* long time ago,' the Karrak Lord agreed. 'I was a youngster then, of course. The truth is that Rothgarnal was fought purely over possession of Mirlyn's Gate. The gate was bound shut because both sides feared it might be used to wage war on the other universe. Before it was, I looked though with my own eyes and witnessed a battle just as savage as Rothgarnal being fought on the other side. Death was everywhere that day, and it was terrible in its magnitude. When the truce was declared, my father decided to sacrifice our future here in order to protect our home universe. He offered me the chance to return home before it was closed, but I would not desert my brethren. I chose to stay, to share my fate with those I loved and fought with.'

'This might sound odd,' Taggie said, 'but I'm glad you did. I'm glad you're here. It gives us a chance to put things right.'

Lord Colgath inclined his head respectfully.

Lantic put his empty cup back on the table. 'So how many times have people tried to find Mirlyn's Gate?'

'There is no recorded number, Prince,' Mr Blake said. 'Though I know of six major attempts by Kings and Queens of various realms. Numerous adventurers and explorers have also quested down the centuries. Not to mention every seer that has been born since. All to no avail.'

'And my brethren, too, have searched,' Lord Colgath said. 'With equally empty results. It would seem the War Emperor and my father were very determined and extremely clever.'

'Then if nothing else, you can tell me where not to waste my time searching,' Taggie told the librarian.

'The Gate does not reside in the Fourth Realm,' Lord Colgath said. 'Of that you may be certain.'

'Could they have brought it here?' Taggie asked.

'No. It is not in the First Realm,' Mr Blake told her. 'The very shape of this realm means we have no hidden places.'

Taggie pursed her lips. 'I don't think it could be in the Outer Realm, either. Every square inch of land has been photographed from air and space, there are no secrets left there.'

'There are several theories among scholars who study the mystery,' Mr Blake said. 'Given Mirlyn's Gate has remained lost for so long, the disaster theory is the strongest. So it goes that the War Emperor and the Grand Lord were on their way to an agreed hiding place when they were overtaken by some unexpected tragedy. Mainly that their ship sank in uncharted waters. If so, there is simply no point in attempting to find it. The same goes for the two great endings theories.'

'What are they?' Lantic asked, intrigued.

'Legend says there is a waterfall at the end of the Sixth

Realm's sea,' Mr Blake said. 'None have ever returned with proof one way or the other, for it is a vast sea which has so far defeated even the boats of the elves in their voyages to find a far shore. But if the War Emperor and the Grand Lord did indeed sail through the sunset and over the waterfall into the everlasting abyss, then Mirlyn's Gate would be truly lost to this universe.'

'That's as bad as a shipwreck,' Taggie said. She'd known it wasn't going to be easy, but with barely an hour of a real historian explaining the problem she was starting to lose heart.

'Indeed, Majesty,' Mr Blake said. 'The second great endings theory is that Mirlyn's Gate was somehow taken over the wall.'

'The wall? What wall?'

'It circles the Seventh Realm,' Lord Colgath said. 'No Karrak Lord has seen it.'

'The wall is at least a two-year trip from the central lands where most Seventh Realm folk live,' Mr Blake said. 'The wilderness is inhospitable at best, and full of wild creatures, but with a large well-equipped caravan of determined people, it is possible to reach the wall. The Holvans have mounted at least nine successful expeditions in the last seven hundred years. One of them was sent by their King Usaran to see if there was any sign of Mirlyn's Gate. They found nothing, of course.'

'What's on the other side of the wall?' Taggie asked.

Mr Blake didn't quite manage to hide his smile. 'Why,

nobody knows, Majesty. Common belief in the Seventh Realm is that it holds back the Realm of the Dead. We'll never know, of course, for the wall is fifty miles high. It is impossible to climb over and discover what lies beyond.'

'So what does that leave us with?' she asked.

'There are two lesser theories,' Mr Blake said, clearly enjoying the attention he was being given.

'Go on,' Taggie said, knowing she'd probably regret asking.

'One is that they travelled to the Realm of Air where they took it on board a ship, and sailed into the sun.'

'If that's right, then the Gate would have been destroyed,' Lantic said.

'Indeed,' Mr Blake agreed.

Taggie looked at Lord Colgath. 'Would your father have agreed to that?'

The Karrak Lord stirred uncomfortably. A shoal of red flecks swept across his smoke cloak. 'It is unlikely. However, he was the most honourable among us. If there was no other way, he would likely sacrifice himself thus. Such a selfless act would befit a Grand Lord.'

There was a long pause.

'And the other lesser theory?' Taggie prompted.

'Perhaps the most simple and elegant of all,' Mr Blake said. 'The War Emperor and the Grand Lord called out to the angels, who – alarmed by the number of souls slain in the Battle of Rothgarnal – broke their promise to the gods and came down from the Heavens one last time. The angels took pity on the two war-weary leaders, and carried Mirlyn's Gate into the Heavens, where it sits somewhere amid the stars, forever beyond mortal reach.'

'Ha!' Lord Colgath sneered. 'That is nothing but a simple child's fable. If it were true, then my father would have returned. He did not, and neither did your War Emperor. That is not how Mirlyn's Gate was lost.'

'What do you remember of the actual day they left?' Taggie asked Colgath. 'Did your father say anything to you?'

The Karrak Lord's silver eyes appeared momentarily tarnished. 'After the binding, he bade me and Amenamon farewell, and told us he would return when he could. That was the last I saw of him. When morning broke, he and the War Emperor had gone.'

'So now what?' Lantic asked.

Taggie looked at her friend, and found she had nothing to say.

Sophie the skymaid turned up with the assistant librarians, all of them bringing lunch trays into the annexe. Taggie was delighted her friend was going to help, as so far the morning had been fruitless. Sophie gazed at all the books as she hovered above the table, her big wings a blur in the air. Long fronds of her red hair were waving about indolently, making it look as if flames were leaping around her head. Like all skyfolk, her skin was almost translucent, and her slender frame made her appear almost fragile –

though Taggie knew just how wrong it was to make that assumption: Sophie was one of the toughest people she knew.

'Any progress?' Sophie asked.

'None,' Lantic complained.

'Good job I'm here to help then,' the skymaid announced, and landed on one of the stools at the table.

Taggie slid a pile of ledgers over to her. 'You could start with the Light Guard's official inventory. If we knew what they took with them when they escorted the War Emperor, it might give us a clue where they were heading.'

'Oh great,' Sophie said with a great deal of irony. 'My favourite.'

Taggie grinned, and returned to the accounts of the last day of the battle. She was still reading the ancient journals two hours later when she caught a strange motion in the corner of her eye, a flicker similar to Sophie flapping her wings. Earl Maril'bo sauntered into the hexagonal annexe. Taggie let out a happy squeal and ran across the room, heedless of the surprised looks that earned her from the others around the table.

'Maril'bo,' she exclaimed excitedly. She held both arms out to the seven-foot-tall elf, and grinned up at him.

Earl Maril'bo was dressed in his usual loops of rainbow-shaded cloth, with firestar pouches and a couple of broad, curving daggers buckled on. His mirror board was slung over his back, where his lengthy plume of jet-black hair constantly flicked against it.

'Yo, little Queen.' He grinned back and took her hands in his. 'Good to see you again. You've grown a couple of inches since last year.'

'Yes, but I'm never going to get to your height, am I?'

He chortled. 'Give it a couple of hundred years, you never know.'

Sophie flew across the reading table, and stayed airborne so her head was level with the elf. 'Yo, Maril'bo.' She held up a hand, and he high-fived her.

'Sophs! I heard about the fight in London. You *v.* a helicopter, huh? Major league, *awesome*.'

'Oh, it was nothing,' Sophie said in a casual fashion that didn't fool Taggie for a moment.

'Why are you here?' Taggie asked. 'Uh, not that I'm not glad to see you.'

Earl Maril'bo smiled down at her, white teeth shining bright amid his midnight-black skin. The kindness shown there just made him look even more handsome. 'Been hearing about you, little Queen. The wind is full of very strange songs.' He turned to stare at Lord Colgath, and nodded ever so slightly. 'Dude.'

'Earl Maril'bo,' Lord Colgath acknowledged.

'So it is, like, true,' Earl Maril'bo said almost to himself.

'And this is Prince Lantic of the Second Realm,' Taggie said to divert his attention; it felt as if he and Lord Colgath were getting ready to fight each other.

'Earl,' Lantic said, and there was a definite note of sourness in his voice.

'Lord Colgath has agreed to help me,' Taggie explained to the elf.

'Help you do what?'

'Find Mirlyn's Gate.'

Earl Maril'bo laughed for a long time. 'Man oh man, that is something else, little Queen. Only you could come up with that one.' He glanced over at Prince Lantic. 'What does your father say about this?'

'He hasn't been told yet,' Lantic said. 'Captain Feandez should arrive in Shatha'hal soon. We're hoping what he has will make my father reconsider the war.'

Earl Maril'bo pulled thoughtfully on his lower lip. 'That'd be cool. But this invasion the War Emperor is planning is something that can't be stopped by hope alone. No offence, little Queen.'

'None taken,' Taggie assured him. 'I'm starting to appreciate how difficult this task is going to be. Do the elves have any ideas as to where Mirlyn's Gate is?'

'Not really. We have few songs about Mirlyn. Us elves, we kind of take it for granted that the War Emperor and Grand Lord sailed over the waterfall at the end of the Sixth Realm and fell into the abyss.' He paused and gave Lord Colgath a curious look. 'But if you're going to be serious about this, we don't even know how big Mirlyn's Gate was, if it would even have fitted on to a ship. Most of the Great Gateways certainly wouldn't.'

Taggie pulled a face, annoyed she'd never thought to

ask even that simple question. 'Lord Colgath? You saw Mirlyn's Gate.'

'I did,' the Dark Lord replied with a low murmur. 'It was a big circle of stone perhaps four or five metres in diameter, but made from hundreds of smaller blocks of stone.'

'Five metres?' Lantic said. 'The Zanatuth we saw in the Fourth Realm wouldn't have fitted through a hole five metres wide. They were huge animals.'

'Indeed,' Lord Colgath admitted. 'But that was after it was subdued and bound by my father and the War Emperor. I also saw it open – then it was much larger. My father had seen it larger still, he claimed. Our lore masters believed it could expand to whatever size was needed. That was one of the reasons my father was worried about an invasion.'

'But when it was taken from Rothgarnal it was five metres across?' Lantic persisted.

'About that, as I recall, yes.'

'Difficult to move, but not impossible,' Lantic said. 'A large cart could carry it.'

'So where's the nearest Great Gateway to Rothgarnal?' Sophie asked.

'They didn't need a Great Gateway to take it away,' Taggie said. Her hand went to the large leather bag hanging round her neck, which contained the dark gate that used to belong to Lord Golzoth. She was getting used to the strange magic which ran through it now, though it was very weak. The best she could hope for was to open it a couple of times more – and she only needed one, to bring Mirlyn's Gate back. 'The Grand Lord had a personal gate.'

'Really?' Mr Blake asked in fascination.

'Cool,' Earl Maril'bo murmured.

'My father gave my brother his gate before he left,' Lord Colgath said. 'It did not go with him.'

'There must be others,' Taggie said.

'Five personal gates were brought with us from our universe,' Lord Colgath said. 'All are accounted for. My brother has one. Two have perished. You now have one, Queen of Dreams. And Lord Drakouth has the last, though I believe it is close to extinction.'

Taggie wanted to stamp her foot in exasperation. 'So you see, we're not making much progress. If there's any way you can help . . .' she appealed to the elf.

'Of course I'll help, little Queen. For a start, I'll be coming with you.' He winked.

Just then Dad and Jemima arrived, with Felix behind them. Jemima let out a happy whoop and flung her arms round Earl Maril'bo. 'You came!' She sighed happily. 'How's your band?'

'All good, little Princess.'

'Are you going to take me surfing?'

Earl Maril'bo patted his mirror board. 'Soon. We just need some rainbows, and we can curve the indigo together.'

'When we get back, Jem,' Taggie said irritably. 'We have to find Mirlyn's Gate first.'

'Any progress?' Dad asked sympathetically.

'Not significantly,' Mr Blake admitted.

Sophie gazed round at all the books on the shelves, then the ones sprawled across the reading table. Her long hair floated gently around her with the motion. 'The answer has to be in here somewhere. This is everything we know of Rothgarnal.'

Jemima gave the big hexagonal room a puzzled glance. 'What is this place? I've never been in here before.'

'Didn't you read any of the histories I told you to?' Dad asked in dismay.

'Daddy! History is so boring.'

'Clever people always learn from history, Blossom Princess,' Mr Blake said in a slightly hurt tone. 'It is the reason this tower was built. An old story of love and the hope it brings.'

'Huh?' Jemima grunted.

'This part you are in now is a memorial,' Mr Blake said. 'Queen Layawhan had it built to honour her consort, the Prince Salaro. Sadly, he never returned from Rothgarnal. Yet she never gave up hope he would come back as he promised.' The librarian lifted his gaze to the vaulting ceiling above them. 'Above us is the tallest tower, not just in the palace but in the whole of the First Realm. For the rest of her reign Queen Layawhan ordered a fire to be lit at the top every night, so it would provide a light to guide him home to her. For sixty years the flames burned brightly there. Every morning she asked the captain of the palace guard if he had come, and every morning the captain would have to tell her no. She became known as the Mourning Queen, so great was her sorrow.'

'That's awful,' Jemima said, looking dismayed.

Taggie gave the librarian a baffled look. Something about the story was puzzling her. She couldn't quite figure out what.

'Her daughter, Queen Canarie, never allowed the brazier to be lit after the death of her mother,' Mr Blake went on. 'She said she didn't want her father's soul to come back to the palace, she wanted the two of them to find each other out among the Heavens as true lovers always do.'

'That's very romantic,' Sophie said wistfully.

Taggie narrowed her eyes as she scanned all the volumes yet again. 'But why didn't Queen Layawhan know her prince was dead? Mr Blake, you said this annexe contains a complete record of all nine days of the battle. Didn't they find his body?'

'Oh, he didn't die at Rothgarnal,' Mr Blake said. 'He was a member of the War Emperor's Light Guard. He accompanied Mirlyn's Gate to wherever it was hidden. That's why he didn't come back.'

Very slowly, Taggie turned to stare at the earnest librarian as her skin turned strangely numb. 'What did you say?'

'He accompanied the War Emperor and the Grand Lord,' Mr Blake said, smiling nervously under his Queen's intense stare.

With her sight still fixed unwavering on the librarian, Taggie said 'Jemima!' from the corner of her mouth.

'What?' Jemima said.

'Prince Salaro is our ancestor,' Taggie said. 'He's family.'

'Yes. So? Oh!'

'Mr Blake,' Taggie said with her heart in her mouth. 'Are there any effects of Prince Salaro left today? Something physical, something that Jemima can touch?'

The librarian was polishing his glasses in rapid movements. 'I, ah, that is . . .'

'The Royal Archive!' Dad said firmly. 'There must be something there. There simply must.'

3

THE LETTER

'I don't get it,' Lantic said as they all trooped down the spiral stone steps to the cellars below the palace's privy council hall.

'Jemima is a seer,' Sophie told him. 'She's almost quite good at it. If she ever practised properly she'd be brilliant.'

'I heard that,' Jemima's voice floated up the stairs.

Sophie grinned. 'I was here when she found the dungeon the Karrak Lords were holding Prince Dino in.' She managed to avoid a guilty glance at Lord Colgath who was several steps ahead of them.

'Right,' Lantic said cautiously.

'A family blood bond is the greatest link there is,' Sophie went on. 'The War Emperor and Grand Lord cast a wardveil around Mirlyn's Gate, the best there's ever been. But if there's something down here that was precious to Prince Salaro, Jemima might be able to use it to sight where he went.'

'And he was with the Gate,' Lantic said, nodding as he suddenly understood.

'Exactly!'

The crypts at the bottom of the stairs were all supported by huge pillars that extended away into the darkness; the chamber they were in was bigger than a football pitch. With her heels echoing off into the emptiness, Taggie walked over to a wall from which protruded a small worn stone carved with the crowned shell emblem. She put her hand on it, and spoke the opening enchantment. The stones in a circular patch of the wall turned to phantoms, and she walked through.

'I didn't know we had an archive,' Jemima muttered as they all followed Taggie in.

Dad sighed.

The vault containing the Royal Archive was comprised of several brick-lined cellars with arching roofs. The air was musty but dry, and a lot cooler than it was upstairs.

Three of the chambers had heavy shelves that held enormous trunks. Taggie walked straight past them to a smaller room at the back. Her waving hands cast small enchantments into the lightstones on the wall as she went, reviving them. Soon the whole archive was illuminated with mellow blue-white light.

'Here we go,' she said as they looked round a small library of ledgers. Then she caught the way Dad was looking at her, with that kind of pride only he could conjure up. 'What?' she asked.

He smiled. 'Nothing.'

'This is the section,' an excited Mr Blake said, peering up at a tall bookcase. 'All of Queen Layawhan's private papers and letters.'

The ledgers and parchment rolls of Queen Layawhan's reign were taken down carefully. Mr Blake spread them out over the vault's three tables, and they all got to work.

Taggie scanned through the ledgers, checking the contents. The ink was old and fading, the writing thin and elaborate, which made it hard to read. She forced herself to go slowly, fearful she might miss something.

'I believe this is what we're looking for,' Lord Colgath's deep voice boomed over an hour after they'd started. He pushed a thick leather satchel across the table to Taggie. It contained letters, thin pages of parchment, each with the shell and feather seal of the prince regent.

With everyone watching her, she started to leaf through them. The breath caught in her throat as she read the dates of the final batch. 'The time of Rothgarnal.'

'Where's the last one?' Sophie asked.

'Here.' Taggie pulled the letter out of the satchel, and carefully unfolded it. The parchment was in poor shape, with ragged edges and peculiar stains. There was a cut through every page, which looked suspiciously as if a dagger had been stabbed through it.

With everyone gathering round, she flattened it out on the table and began to read.

My Queen, my greatest, my only, love.

I have survived Rothgarnal. Alas, this is not the triumph I expect you believe it to be. The fighting has raged for nine full days now. So many are dead, my friends, my comrades in arms, those I knew but briefly, those in the Grand Lord's army, those whose bodies I walked upon across the battlefield, so many more whose blood now stains the soil of this cursed place for all eternity. I know now there is no Hell Realm, for such a place is here and now.

We fought and fought, all of us, with valour and horror, with magic and with brute steel. Now, at the end of it all I love my enemy. Forgive what may sound as treason to your sweet ears, my love, but their suffering is equal to ours. In that unity, the War Emperor and the Grand Lord have called truce, and continue to parley while I write.

Neither side is the victor. Too many are dead for that to be called. Instead, we will begin to respect each other. This is the hope of both our leaders, and if needs be I will fight yet again to uphold that hope, for some good must surely come from this immense suffering and sacrifice. Somewhere at some time the folk of the Realms and the people of the Dark Universe must sit at the same table and learn how to live in harmony.

But this future is naught but a dream unless we can end the threat of the Dark Universe. On the other side, another battle is also being waged to control Mirlyn's accursed Gate. Nearly all of Rothgarnal's Great Gateways have been destroyed by the dark wizardry of the Karrak Lords, yet by bitter fate Mirlyn's Gate remains unscathed by the strongest magic the War Emperor and Grand Lord can summon. Instead they have bound it shut. But this cannot be enough. All are agreed, this most evil of all temptations must be taken away and hidden beyond any chance of discovery.

It falls upon me now to tell you with a heavy heart that I will not be returning straight away. I am a loyal officer of the Light Guards, as such it is my duty to accompany my War Emperor on this, his final task. We are due to leave Rothgarnal with the Grand Lord before daybreak, and take Mirlyn's Gate I know not where. Forgive me, my love, I do this in the belief that all Peoples will live longer and happier lives because of it.

I pledge to you that I will come back to you and our dearest Canarie as soon as I can. Keep a light burning for me, my love, so I might find you no matter what darkness falls across me on this last endeavour.

You are my love forever.

Your Prince Salaro

I entrust this letter to my squire Dyllian, who is a lad of sound heart, and will see you receive it.

Taggie stared at the parchment after she'd finished reading, even though she couldn't quite focus on the writing any more. She sniffed loudly, hoping she didn't cry because her tears would fall on the beautiful letter and spoil the ancient parchment.

'Prince Salaro really loved her,' Sophie managed to croak.

'Yes,' Taggie agreed. She slid the parchment across to Jemima, who was as silent and subdued as everyone else. 'Sight whatever you can,' Taggie said kindly.

With everyone watching her, Jemima took her runes out of their little leather pouch. Closing her eyes, she shook them in one hand while her other hand stroked the side of the letter. For once she didn't question her talent and how erratic it could be. She wasn't going to let her ancestors down, not today. She *would* read the runes and be granted the sight of Prince Salaro's resting place.

Jemima opened her fingers to drop the runes on to the venerable square of parchment.

There were several gasps around the table.

Jemima stared at the little black stones. They floated a few centimetres above the parchment, tumbling slowly so no one set of runes remained fixed.

'Air,' Jemima said in astonishment. 'He died in the Realm of Air.'

4

PREPARING FOR WAR

Bright midday sunlight shone down on the city of Shatha'hal. The capital of the Second Realm was made up of seven enormous buildings in the middle of an irrigated parkland that shimmered a lush emerald in the heat, a soft jewel set amid the barren sand of the vast desert surrounding it.

The War Emperor walked through the garden that formed the roof of the gigantic upside-down pyramid at the very centre of the city. Around him were the other royals who attended the Gathering of Kings, who in turn had their entourage of councillors and courtiers trailing behind them like ducklings behind their mother. Between them the royals represented all of the Realms, except for the poor unfortunate Fourth Realm, which was under the rule of the Karrak Lords and Ladies. Out of courtesy, the King in Exile from that realm had been given a seat at the table. Like everyone else (apart from the Queen of Dreams) he had agreed to the anointment of Manokol as War Emperor, a position that had not been filled for over a thousand years. Armies had been summoned from every Realm under his command. Once they were ready, the War Emperor himself would lead them in an invasion of the Fourth Realm, and destroy the Karrak invaders for good.

When he reached the edge of the roof, the newly appointed War Emperor stared down at the rows and rows of tents which had sprung up across the parkland far below. Already there were over fifteen thousand soldiers encamped, with more columns arriving as he watched. The river Zhila, which ran through the desert, was thick with long boats full of soldiers and their equipment. Many were having to wait outside the city's docks while regiments disembarked from boats already berthed.

Even from his distant vantage point, the War Emperor could see the different types of folk who had answered his call. The giants of the Ninth Realm, the elves from the Sixth, trolls from the Eighth; and humans with their more subtle variations; the four-armed Holvans from the Seventh, and the tall, red-skinned Shadarain of the Fifth Realm. To his delight, the air between Shatha'hal's mighty buildings was a-glitter from the multiple contrails of skyfolk from the Realm of Air, who had even brought some Olri-gi with them, imposing flying creatures who could easily challenge the rathwai which the Karraks rode through the air. Down on the ground, huge rinosaurs of the giants' cavalry were snorting impatiently in their hurriedly built pens.

'Where are our regiments?' the War Emperor asked.

'There, sire,' replied Welch, the senior general. He

pointed at a swathe of tents, each one as big as a house. 'Another seven regiments will be here before the end of next week.'

The War Emperor was pleased to see his regiments were pitched next to the smaller, but far more elaborate, bell-tents that had bloomed like colourful mushrooms the previous evening. Each one flew the heraldic pennant of a Third Realm sorceress house. He was relying on the power of the sorceresses to counter the wizardries of the Karraks when they invaded.

'Side by side,' Queen Judith of the Third Realm murmured to him.

The War Emperor smiled. 'Indeed, dear Queen.'

'At least some of us still honour our ancient alliances,' Queen Judith said, with a sideways glance directed at the woman standing beside her. It was obvious they were sisters, both of them tall with narrow faces and brown eyes. Both of them wearing the long bejewelled cloaks with high collars favoured by Third Realm sorceresses.

Nicola, the elder of the two sisters and Taggie's mother, showed no awareness of the barb.

The War Emperor was uncomfortable having her as part of the royal retinue, but there was little he could do about it. Since the Queen of Dreams had left the Second Realm, her mother was the official representative of the First Realm's royal family. 'Is there any word of your daughter?' he asked.

'Should there be?' Nicola asked lightly.

'She was last seen in the presence of a Karrak Lord,' Queen Judith said. 'Apparently they were very friendly. Some kind of alliance had been formed.'

The War Emperor turned to General Welch. 'What? Is this true? Why was I not told?'

General Welch gave an awkward shrug. 'We were waiting for confirmation, sire. Certain events that occurred in London yesterday were confusing. Captain Feandez hasn't reported back yet.'

The War Emperor gave the general an annoyed glance. 'Have Captain Feandez report to me as soon as he arrives.'

'Yes, sire.'

'And if he does not vouch for the Queen of Dreams?' Queen Judith asked. 'Rumour of how she defies your authority is already gossiped in the markets and halls of many realms. That cannot be allowed, nothing must weaken your glorious war effort. You must be firm with the wayward child.'

'As I recall, even the Third Realm follows the principle of innocent until proven guilty,' Nicola retorted.

The haughty smile on Queen Judith's face could have frozen a summer's day. 'She is allied with a Karrak Lord.'

Nicola faced her sister with an equally frigid expression. 'Yes. Why is she allied?'

A flicker of uncertainty crossed Queen Judith's face. 'Who knows?'

'Certainly not you, yet you throw these allegations around without a shred of evidence. Are you that insecure?'

The courtiers and advisers of the Gathering were slowly inching back from the two sorceresses. The air between the sisters seemed to haze with a faint blue light which drained the sun's warmth from the pyramid's roof.

'It is not my position which is fragile, sister,' Queen Judith replied.

'Then as true royalty, I'm sure you will ignore simple tavern gossip and wait for the facts to be presented,' Nicola snapped.

'Very well,' the War Emperor said, uncomfortable at the antagonism of the sisters. 'I will summon both of you as soon as Captain Feandez arrives. We will hear the truth together.'

At the same time as the War Emperor reviewed his troops in the Second Realm, Grand Lord Amenamon was standing in the courtyard of his castle in the Fourth Realm awaiting a display of his newest weapon. The castle was made from blocks of black granite, each one taller than a man. It had been twenty years in the building, using over five thousand slaves the Karraks had rounded up from across the Fourth Realm after Rothgarnal. They had cursed and spat on every hated stone as they laboured under their new masters to build walls and battlements the like of which had never been seen in the realms before. All their invocations and tears had come to naught. The new Grand Lord's impregnable citadel rose from the ruins of the old king's elaborate palace in Hothrielle, the ancient eastern capital of the Fourth Realm. It could be seen for miles in every direction, a brooding presence which seemed to drain the light from the land, as well as all hope. Smoky shadows drifted from its tall brutal turrets, winding their way up into the broken grey sky, the roots of the Fourth Realm's winter.

In the gloom of the central courtyard, formed by walls like cliffs, Grand Lord Amenamon strode along the front rank of his newest and strangest army. The soldier gols he inspected were as tall as he was, and he was the tallest of all Karrak Lords and Ladies. They'd been fashioned from clay in a roughly human shape, with a featureless cylinder for a head, and animated by a magic adapted from the art of the Second Realm's anamages. Over a thousand of the contraptions were lined up in front of him in neat ranks. Set deep in a head that was practically skeletal, his skin was stretched so thin over it, Grand Lord Amenamon's featureless black eyes examined the gol at the end of the front rank. Like all its kind in the courtyard, the contraption had no right hand. Instead, the wrists had been replaced by a peculiar metal socket.

'Show me,' Grand Lord Amenamon ordered.

Lady Lanatoth stepped forward, her smoke robe swirling as she lifted up the heavy Outer Realm machine gun. The modified gun's stock clicked neatly into the gol's socket.

'Kill,' Lady Lanatoth commanded the gol.

The solder gol swung round to face the Rannalal knight

44

who had been in charge
of the detachment
guarding Red Loch
Castle when the
Queen of Dreams
arrived to break
Lord Colgath out
of his prison. The
Rannalal was tied to
a post just in front of
the high stone wall,
his four legs chained
together. He was
still wearing
his scarlet
armour, with his

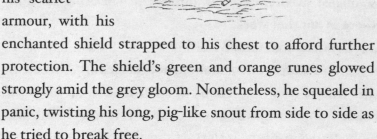

enchanted shield strapped to his chest to afford further
protection. The shield's green and orange runes glowed
strongly amid the grey gloom. Nonetheless, he squealed in
panic, twisting his long, pig-like snout from side to side as
he tried to break free.

The machine gun fired. Long pale flames flickered
around its muzzle as its roar reverberated deafeningly
round the courtyard.

Even Lord Amenamon swayed back slightly from the
brutal violence of the weapon. The gol stopped firing.
All that remained of the wooden post was a stump of
splintered wood jutting up from the frosted flagstones.

The wall of black granite behind was deeply cratered from the impact of the bullets with their bad-magic tips. Of the luckless Rannalal commander there was no sign.

Up on the ramparts, rathwai were crying in shock, their leathery wings extended unsteadily.

'That is good,' Lord Amenamon pronounced. The blue flames that were his teeth burned a little brighter in approval. He turned his skeletal head to Lady Lanatoth, the thin white skin paler than the flecks of snow that fell from the Fourth Realm's blanket of grey cloud. 'Fit all of them with the weapon. Then march them to Rothgarnal.'

'Rothgarnal, my lord?' Lady Lanatoth asked.

'Yes. That is where this began. That is where this will end. Have the gols dug in and camouflaged with your strongest magic, ready for ambush. I will bring my army there in another week.'

'I understand, Grand Lord.'

Grand Lord Amenamon strode back into the castle. His throne room was empty apart from the throne itself, made from the broken bones of the most ferocious beasts to be found in all the realms. He settled into it, and stared at the wall directly ahead. There were several small fires burning in alcoves, each of them with different-coloured flames that drew the heat out of the air. His gaze settled on the one with mauve flames, and his hand gestured at it. The flames grew wider.

'Where are you, brother?' he asked. The flames danced and spun, but they provided no vision.

The Grand Lord grunted in disappointment. The effort of the spell wearied him. He closed his eyes for a moment . . .

'You know where he is, my lord,' a smooth female voice said.

The Grand Lord opened his eyes and saw the chilly blue flames reaching the top of their alcove, and slowly a ghostly figure became clear. 'He is allied with the Abomination,' he whispered in fury.

The apparition spoke again. 'I understand your dismay, my lord. Truly I do. As I know you will do what honour requires, just as you have been doing all these long centuries. Do not falter now.'

The Grand Lord finally turned to face the wavering figure of Queen Judith. 'I know what has to be done. I simply don't trust you.'

Queen Judith smiled gently, as if the insult had never been spoken. 'I have delivered the War Emperor's armies to you, as our bloodbound agreement promised.'

'They're not at Rothgarnal yet, Queen. And the Abomination herself challenges the War Emperor. She knows of our preparations.'

'Ah,' Queen Judith said sympathetically as she glided closer. 'Is that the cause of your distress? Then I have some news that may please you.'

'What?'

The cold blue flames flared once more, licking up out of their alcove. On the opposite side of the throne room the spectre of an elegant seventeen-year-old girl materialized, her soft brown hair arranged stylishly around a pretty face with brown eyes that could produce an unnervingly sharp stare. 'Good day to you, Grand Lord,' Katrabeth said.

Grand Lord Amenamon's teeth flames stabbed out hot and bright as he snarled at the young sorceress he found so revolting. The one person he despised more than Queen Judith was her daughter. Now here her apparition came, defiling his throne room by shimmering sedately above the dark flagstone floor. 'You failed to kill the Abomination,' he spat. 'And because of that, Captain Feandez is on his way to the War Emperor. He could ruin everything.'

Katrabeth's answering smile was malicious as she held up a bullet whose tip glowed violet with bad magic. 'Behold: the only proof the Queen of Dreams possessed that you have armed your stolen gol army with Outer Realm guns. And I have it. Me. Not the War Emperor for whom it was intended.' As she held it, the brass case started to crumble into dust, fine grains slithering like liquid over her hand to fall away. With a flourish, she crushed the lead tip with its glimmer, and like a conjuring trick it was gone. 'Oops. No more.'

Grand Lord Amenamon nodded with some satisfaction. 'And what of those who were taking it to him?'

'Sunk without trace. It was all very sad.' She laughed grimly. 'So now there is little the Queen of Dreams can do to stop the War Emperor from invading the Fourth Realm.'

'The Abomination will cast as much doubt as she can,' Amenamon said.

'Most likely,' Queen Judith said. 'But hopefully now she has Colgath she'll embark on her ridiculous quest to find Mirlyn's Gate.'

'My father died to keep it hidden. It must never be found. I must not have anyone . . . *questioning* the path I have chosen for us. There can be no alternative shown to tempt them. My victory is close.'

'Quite right. But their quest plays to our advantage.'

'How so?' Grand Lord Amenamon asked.

'I suggested the War Emperor appoint Katrabeth as his special envoy, with his full authority to detain the Queen of Dreams and bring her to the Gathering,' Queen Judith said.

'I will know when they begin their journey,' Katrabeth continued. 'Wherever Mirlyn's Gate is hidden, it will be a long and lonely route to it. That is where I will strike.'

'No more mistakes, Katrabeth,' Grand Lord Amenamon growled. 'The Abomination must not return.'

'She won't.'

'Your victory will come swiftly, Grand Lord,' Queen Judith said. 'And then mine.'

'You think it will be a victory?' Grand Lord Amenamon asked scornfully. 'Don't be so sure. It has not brought me contentment.'

'I will not waste it as you have,' Queen Judith replied loftily.

The blue flames leaped out of the alcove, growing painfully bright – and Grand Lord Amenamon closed his smooth black eyes. When he opened them again, the throne room was empty. He directed a hateful hiss at the alcove where the icy blue flames now burned normally, then beckoned to one of his Ethanu servants. The creature walked over slowly and surely, wearing its leather coat and a hat with a wide brim, under which were a pair of circular mirrored glasses. 'Summon Lord Drakouth.'

The Ethanu bowed as far as it could. 'Yes, my lord.'

It didn't take long until Lord Drakouth strode across the throne room to kneel before the Grand Lord. 'My lord.'

'I have an important task for you,' Grand Lord Amenamon announced.

'I am honoured to be chosen,' Lord Drakouth rumbled smoothly.

'My brother has been bewitched by the Abomination. They will soon be travelling together. It will be a long and difficult journey. They will suffer many perils, not least the sorceress Katrabeth. Her strongest desire is to kill the Abomination, but she will also try to eliminate my brother. This must not happen.'

'I will ensure it does not, Grand Lord.'

'Yes. You will. I have chosen you because you have the last remaining private gate.'

Lord Drakouth remained kneeling, but his smoke cloak betrayed his concern by shifting in fast ripples. 'My lord?'

'I know it is near its end, but you will never need it again once we destroy the War Emperor's armies and extend our rule across every realm. So when you find my brother, you are to bring him directly back to me. Do you understand? Directly.'

'Yes, my lord.'

'If you have the chance you may also strike at the Abomination and her companions. And should Katrabeth perish during this endeavour I would not be displeased.'

'It will be my pleasure to serve you thus, Grand Lord.'

'Of course. And to demonstrate my gratitude in this matter, I will make a gift of the First Realm to you as your personal fiefdom after we have retaken it.'

'My lord is most generous.'

5

VISITORS

The large and elegant snow eagle swooped out of the sky and alighted on the narrow grassy path in front of a wooden doorway set into the hillside. A magical, dark grey haze boiled around the white bird, twisting and altering its shape. It fizzled away to reveal Taggie.

Sophie streaked down through the air in a red shimmer. Her wide, feathered feet folded up, and she landed to stand beside her friend. 'You're really getting the hang of flying,' she said with a grin.

'I'll never be as fast as you.' Taggie sighed.

Sophie pursed her lips contentedly. 'No. Shall we go?'

The door had no handle. It swung open as the two girls approached, revealing a curving tunnel, lined with dark-red brick. They walked along until they came to another handle-less door identical to the first. This one was shut.

'I am the Queen of Dreams,' Taggie told the Great Gateway. 'And I have a question for you, Arasath.'

'It seems as though I do nothing else but answer your questions these days, dear Queen.' Arasath's mild voice spoke from behind her. 'Perhaps someday I will once again perform the act I exist for, and grant passage to the Outer Realm.'

Taggie smiled and continued: 'You once told me that you believe Mirlyn's Gate is still intact.'

'He is the unheard, yes.'

'But not diminished? Not dead?'

'He was concealed after Rothgarnal. That is all we know.'

'I'm not sure that's quite right, is it?' she said sceptically. 'You see, we know he was taken to the Realm of Air.'

There was a slight pause. 'Indeed.'

Taggie gave the Great Gateway a sharp stare, knowing just how tricky it could be. 'Indeed, "yes"? Or indeed, "that's interesting"?'

'It is interesting that you believe that.'

'Really? You see here's the thing: if he was taken from the Fourth Realm, it had to be through a Great Gateway.' Her jaw muscles tightened. 'Isn't that right?'

'Undoubtedly.'

'Here's something else we found out: not every Great Gateway at Rothgarnal was destroyed at the time the truce was called. How many were left? And did one of them open into the Realm of Air?'

'Two of us survived the battle, Harrajan and Forilux; though they perished soon afterwards. Forilux opened to the Realm of Air.'

Taggie gave Sophie a knowing look. 'I see. And was Mirlyn's Gate taken through Forilux? Don't tell me a Great Gateway wouldn't know if Mirlyn passed through.'

The air blowing down the brick tunnel produced a sudden gust. 'You are correct. Mirlyn's Gate was taken through Forilux.'

Sophie stomped her foot. 'And you never told anybody?' she stormed. 'Folk have been searching for a thousand years!'

'There are aspects of Rothgarnal that your new Karrak friend has still to reveal to you,' the voice of Arasath said.

'Such as?' Taggie asked, suddenly uncertain. She had come to believe Lord Colgath was genuine, and that he'd been at Rothgarnal. If there was anything else to tell, he would have done so. *Wouldn't he?*

'In the days before the battle, the Karrak people crafted a terrible weapon, the Trakal. It had but one purpose: to destroy Great Gateways. That is how all those of us at Rothgarnal perished.'

'I didn't know about that,' Taggie said, refusing to be distracted. 'But why have you never told anyone where Mirlyn's Gate was taken?'

'As I believe you have already worked out, the Grand Lord destroyed Forilux from the other side,' Arasath said. 'So the Trakal was with him in the Realm of Air.'

'Ah,' Taggie murmured. 'I think I get it now. So Mirlyn's Gate is definitely somewhere in the Realm of Air,' she said with rising excitement.

'And so is the Trakal,' Sophie concluded.

'Precisely,' Arasath said. 'The one thing which can kill us of the Fellowship.'

'So whoever finds Mirlyn's Gate also finds the Trakal?'

'That is correct, Queen of Dreams,' Arasath said.

Taggie regarded the iron-bound doorway coldly, feeling she was being judged. 'I, the Queen of Dreams, give my heart's pledge to you, Arasath, that if we find Mirlyn's Gate I will bring the Trakal to you.'

'Thank you, Queen of Dreams. We of the Fellowship acknowledge your honour. None of us will stand in your way.'

A gust of warm air blew against Taggie, stirring her hair. 'You mean you were going to?' she asked suspiciously. Perhaps that explained why no expedition had ever succeeded in finding Mirlyn's Gate. Without the Great Gateways helping, such an endeavour would be fruitless.

The Great Gateway Arasath remained silent.

'If they went into the Realm of Air, they were supposedly going to sail into the sun,' Sophie said impatiently. 'Though I don't think that's actually possible.'

'Mirlyn has not diminished,' Arasath said. 'We of the Fellowship are certain of that.'

Taggie drew down a breath. She'd come here to confront Arasath, but now she felt a rush of confidence about her quest she'd never expected. 'Forgive my lack of history,' she said. 'But where did Forilux open in the Realm of Air?'

'The Isle of Banmula,' Arasath said.

'I've heard of it,' Sophie claimed. 'The old capital isle.'

'Then that's where we'll start.'

Again a gust of air swept along the tunnel. 'It is a cold, cold trail you follow, Queen of Dreams.'

'But now we know where it begins,' Taggie countered. 'That's one big advantage we have over everyone else who has looked in the last thousand years.'

Taggie and Sophie landed together on the top of Queen Layawhan's tower, and Taggie cancelled the shapeshift spell, transforming back to her real self. She couldn't believe how hungry she was after all that flying.

'Who's that?' Sophie asked, leaning over the thick parapet.

Taggie risked a quick look. Now that she had abandoned her eagle form, she felt a sensation of vertigo at being so high. A small procession of carriages was driving along the greenway towards the palace. 'Isn't that the pendant of the Second Realm?' she murmured.

'The War Emperor has come to you,' Sophie said in excitement. 'Captain Feandez succeeded!'

'I'm not so sure,' Taggie retorted dubiously.

Sophie leaped up to stand on the edge of the parapet. 'Race you to the bottom,' she said with a gleam in her eye, and dived off.

Taggie's heart did a flip as her friend plummeted down. Sophie's shimmering red contrail stretched out behind her. 'No way,' Taggie grunted, and opened the door to the spiral stairs that wound down the tower. There were an awful lot of them.

Taggie was seriously out of breath when she finally emerged into the hexagonal library annexe through a door disguised as bookshelves. The first person she saw was Queen Danise, a stately woman, who was embracing her son. Prince Lantic looked half embarrassed, half overjoyed, at his mother's affections. Then Taggie grinned in relief. Standing behind the Queen was Mr Anatole, an old Shadarain whose skin was a rich shade of terracotta. He disentangled himself from Jemima's hug and swished his formal robes aside to give her a formal bow. 'Majesty,' he said with a note of pride. Mr Anatole was Taggie's equerry, and provided advice she valued the most.

Taggie acknowledged him with a smile and a not-terribly-regal wave of her hand. She sat down heavily in a chair at the head of the table which was now covered with even more parchments and ledgers.

'Queen of Dreams,' Queen Danise said solemnly with a bow.

'Welcome to the First Realm, Queen Danise,' Taggie replied. 'Did the War Emperor send you?' she asked hopefully.

'No, I am here purely as a mother.'

Lantic turned a deeper shade of red.

'Then please, let's keep this informal,' Taggie said.

The others all found themselves seats. Taggie was pleased to see Earl Maril'bo sitting next to Lord Colgath. 'Can I ask you, how does the War Emperor respond to the items and news I sent with Captain Feandez?'

Queen Danise gave her a puzzled look. 'Captain Feandez has not yet returned to Shatha'hal. We know he left London with you. Everyone assumed you had imprisoned him here. The War Emperor was outraged.'

'No, he left for Shatha'hal two days ago . . .' Taggie gave Dad a desperate look.

'On our way here, we saw some wreckage floating on the sea just outside the fjord that leads to Harrolas,' Mr Anatole said. 'The pieces looked to be from a First Realm schooner.'

Taggie let out a cry of dismay. 'Oh no! Feandez had to reach the War Emperor, he simply had to. That was the only bullet we had as proof.' She bunched her hands into fists, and pressed them against her forehead. 'Why did I send him? I should have gone myself.'

'You know why you didn't go,' Lantic said softly. 'The

Gathering would have found a way to prevent you from going after Mirlyn's Gate. My father wants revenge for my brother's murder. I don't think he cares about the price.' He glanced at his mother. 'His grief is . . . powerful.'

Taggie drew herself up. 'I'll go and confront the Gathering. They'll have to believe me when I tell them about the bullets. I am still a Queen, their equal.'

'But that might be exactly what your opponents want,' Lantic said, looking pensive. 'Katrabeth and Queen Judith are playing some strange game of their own, I'm sure of it.'

'Prince Lantic is right, darling,' Dad said. 'Everything your aunt does helps to bring the invasion a step closer.'

'What are you saying?' Queen Danise demanded. 'Why was the captain so important to you?'

'I'll explain,' Prince Lantic said. 'In fact, you'd better know everything.'

When he finished telling his story, Queen Danise reached over and took his hand. 'You have visited the Fourth Realm?' she asked. 'How delighted Rogreth would be at such an exploit. Out of all of us, he never doubted you would ultimately fulfil into your role as prince.'

'And you, Mother?' Prince Lantic asked in a nervous voice. 'What do you think of me?'

'I am as proud now as I have always been,' she said with a sweet smile. Then her expression hardened. 'But I am also appalled that all of you would be so foolhardy. The Fourth Realm, indeed!'

'Hear, hear,' Dad muttered.

'Well, I'm going to the Realm of Air next, Mother,' Lantic said defiantly. 'I'm going to play my part in stopping the war. What father is doing . . . Rogreth would never have wanted it.'

'I know,' she said, and kissed him lightly. 'Did you really animate a bronze statue?'

'He animated two,' Lord Colgath rumbled. 'It was impressive.'

Queen Danise couldn't quite bring herself to look at the Dark Lord. Instead she turned to Taggie. 'So you have no proof left, you say?'

'Nothing physical we can show to the Gathering,' Taggie agreed. 'Just my word.'

'And my son's word,' Queen Danise said. 'Which is much more important than any physical evidence.'

'Not to the Gathering,' Taggie replied forlornly. 'And certainly not to my aunt.'

'I have been uncomfortable with Queen Judith for some time,' Queen Danise confided. 'My husband relies too much on her council.'

'Something must be done to convince the War Emperor,' Dad said. 'Perhaps it's best if I go to Shatha'hal and confront him.'

'No,' Queen Danise said firmly. 'I will return to the Second Realm with this news. Queen Judith might hold my husband's attention in the Gathering, but at home he listens to me.'

'Thank you,' Taggie said.

'Not everyone is in favour of war,' Queen Danise told her. 'You have more supporters than you might think, Queen of Dreams, in places you would not expect. The recklessness of the Kings must be held to account. There are too few voices in the Gathering that dare question what is happening.'

Taggie managed a weak grin. 'Yes, how is my mother?'

'She refused my offer to accompany me here,' Queen Danise said.

'The Queen Mother thought it best to remain with the Gathering of Kings, and Queens, as the First Realm's official representative,' Mr Anatole said.

'She makes them most uncomfortable,' Queen Danise said demurely.

Taggie smiled. *Good old Mum.*

'However, the Queen Mother did require me to pass a message to you, Majesty,' Mr Anatole said. 'She said you are always to do as your heart tells you to. And under no circumstances are you to worry about her.' He slid a finger round his collar as if he'd suddenly become too warm. 'She was most insistent about that. And your mother . . .'

'Can make her feelings known,' Taggie concluded. 'Yes, thank you.'

'With your permission, Majesty,' Mr Anatole said. 'I will return with Queen Danise to your mother, and tell her what has happened here.'

'Of course,' Taggie said. 'But please, be careful. I'll assign some of the palace guards to escort you.'

'Don't worry,' Queen Danise said. 'I am not Queen of the Second Realm just because of my looks.' Her lips twitched. 'And I did look quite something in my youth.'

Prince Lantic cleared his throat. 'Mother,' he moaned.

'If anybody tries to attack my ship they will be unpleasantly surprised,' Queen Danise said, ignoring him.

6

DAWN DEPARTURE

The moonclouds were still casting a deep nightshadow over the palace when Taggie rose and dressed in jeans and a dark purple sweater. She liked to think that slipping away under cover of darkness was a tiny connection to her ancestor, Prince Salaro. This was how he had departed Rothgarnal on his quest to help hide Mirlyn's Gate. Now here she was over a thousand years later, sneaking off on a quest to find that very same devilsome Gate.

She shouldered a small backpack as she gave the huge ornate bedroom a last wistful glance, then walked out into the broad corridor. Jemima's bedroom was three doors down. She waited outside until her sister emerged. Jemima was pulling a long blue dress over her *athrodene* armour, which had taken on the gloomy colouration of the corridor. 'It's practically the middle of the night,' she complained as she yawned.

'We're on a quest, Jem,' Taggie told her, and knelt down to tie Jemima's bootlaces properly. 'Getting up early is the least of it.'

'Huh. We won't be camping, will we?' Jemima said, frowning at her own backpack. 'I hate sleeping in tents.'

'I've no idea.'

'I brought some money,' Jemima said helpfully, holding up a bulging leather purse that clinked loudly. 'I told the master of the treasury that I was going on an official state trip, and he gave me tons of gold coins – look. We can easily afford to stay in some nice taverns and hotels on the way. So we don't need to take tents, see?'

'Jem!' Taggie began in exasperation. Her hands went to her hips, and she took a deep breath.

'I didn't tell him *where* we were going.' Jemima looked up at her older sister with the full lost-puppy expression. 'I'm not stupid, you know.'

Taggie gave up. 'I know. Did you at least remember to bring your rune stones?

'Yes!' She patted the backpack. 'And Prince Salaro's letter.'

'Come on, then.'

Sophie emerged from the guest suite, her blue-grey eyes wide with excitement. Her repeat-fire crossbow (a contraption she'd bought in the Second Realm) was slung down her left side, and a long enchanted dagger was hanging from the belt of her green and grey tunic. She carried a small pack, which seemed to be mostly full of spare crossbow bolts, whose violet tips teemed with bad magic. Sophie caught Taggie eyeing the pack, and shrugged. 'You can never have too many bolts,' she said.

Lantic was waiting at the top of the great stairs.

'Wow, Lantic,' Sophie said, mostly in surprise,

but with some appreciation, too.

He wore the flamboyant red and black tunic of the Second Realm's Blue Feather regiment. It was a little baggy on him, and the legs and sleeves had been rolled up. Despite that, he did look quite dashing. 'Captain Feandez gave it to me before he left,' he said self-consciously, and flicked some of the hair out of his eyes. 'It's enchanted, so it becomes armour if I have to go into battle. He said . . . he said he had promised Father he'd protect me, and this was the best way he could do it while he was away.'

'It looks good on you,' Taggie said approvingly.

He slung his worn satchel over his shoulder, which slightly spoilt the tunic's glamorous appearance.

Felix bounded along the corridor, his impressively fluffy snow-white tail held out horizontal as he ran. This morning he was quite large, standing higher than Jemima's knees. His shining black eyes glanced round the companions. 'Together again,' he said. 'Let us ask the Heavens that we are as successful as we were on our last endeavour.'

They all smiled at that, and started off down the stairs. Sophie was so excited to be going to the Realm of Air that her wings were flapping about uncontrollably.

Three figures waited for them in the poorly lit hall at the bottom: Dad, Lord Colgath and Earl Maril'bo. The elf stood at the head of the trio, nodding in approval as Taggie walked towards him. 'Little Queen. Are you sure this is what you want to do?'

'Absolutely.'

'Cool. Then let's go find us that Gate.' He raised his arm in salute. 'No matter where we are, no matter what we face, we will not leave you.'

'No matter where,' everyone echoed. 'No matter what.'

Taggie felt a lump in her throat. Even Lord Colgath had pledged himself along with the others. She turned to say goodbye to Dad, which was when she realized he was wearing his old olive-green greatcoat over a sweater and frayed jeans, and he had his waxed hiking boots on his feet. A full backpack rested on the floor beside him.

'Dad?' she blurted in alarm. 'Where are you going?'

'With you, of course,' he said, with a knowing smile.

'But . . . !' Taggie hadn't reckoned on that at all.

Dad looked a little smug. 'What? You thought I'd let you and Jemima to go gallivanting into the unknown by yourselves? I might not have the kind of Third Realm magic you and your mother possess –' he patted the hilt of the short sword hanging from his belt – 'but I'll have you know I used to be a mean swordsman.'

'You did?'

'I practised every week with the palace guard till the day I left on my own quest.'

'Dad, that was well over fifty years ago,' she chided.

'It's just like riding a bike – you never forget how. Besides,' he finished, 'you're only thirteen, so you don't get to go without me: that's final.'

Taggie narrowed her eyes. 'Why didn't you say you were coming before, when we were arranging this trip?'

'So you could sneak out of the palace without me? Do I look stupid?' He lifted his backpack and settled it on his shoulders.

Taggie couldn't help grinning. 'No, Dad. None of our family does.'

Jemima cast a wardveil around them, and with the rest of the palace asleep, the eight travellers crossed the gardens to the treehouse which was the Great Gateway Taslaf. This Gateway opened into the top of the old Kingsway tram tunnel in the heart of London, in the Outer Realm.

The Realms never seemed to share the same days and nights. It was dusk, which had begun to reach out for the city when they emerged. Prince Harry had arranged for three big Range Rovers to pick them up, driven by Knights of the Black Garter. The cars took them to Buckingham Palace where an RAF helicopter was waiting in the garden.

'Really?' Lantic asked, his eyes shining. 'We're going to fly in a machine?'

'Yes,' Taggie told him with a grin. He was always so endearing when he was happy like this. 'We're going to fly in a machine.'

'That's if you call this flying,' Sophie muttered sourly as she clambered up into the helicopter's fuselage.

'It would take hours to drive to Toramus, the Great Gateway to the Realm of Air,' Taggie explained. 'I didn't want to risk us being seen. We are travelling with an elf and a Karrak Lord, after all.'

'Good thinking,' Lantic said.

'How long is this going to take?' Jemima asked as she sat on a bucket seat in the cabin. One of the crew handed her a set of bulky headphones and checked her seatbelt.

'About an hour, miss,' the co-pilot said over the headset. 'The wind is in our favour this evening.'

Dad sat beside her. 'Are you OK?' he asked Jemima.

'Fine. Yes.'

'You look nervous.'

'No, I'm not,' Jemima said hotly. 'I've flown loads of times before.'

Taggie grinned at Jem's indignation, even though she could tell her sister was scared.

'Seatbelt,' Dad told Taggie.

She rolled her eyes, and fastened the metal buckle. *If he's going to babysit us like this the whole time, we really will have to sneak off without him*, she thought.

They lifted off, and flew high across the city. It wasn't long before London's massive grid of bright orange streetlights fell away, and they were over the dark countryside. The crewman handed out bacon sandwiches wrapped in foil. Taggie chewed happily on hers as she watched Lantic, who had his face pressed up against the window.

'We need to decide what we're going to tell people that we meet,' Dad said after they'd passed over the M25 motorway.

'What do you mean?' Lantic asked.

'Who we are, and why we're travelling. A group like this – even in the Realms, folk are going to ask what we're about.'

'We just tell them we're travellers,' Sophie said. 'It's none of their business what we're doing.'

'It might not be,' Felix said. 'But tell them that to their face and they'll become even more curious. We cannot risk attracting attention.'

'A good point,' Earl Maril'bo said. 'We are an odd group, and these are anxious times. I can avoid the sight of most people, but we'll need to take a ship to Banmula. That will put us in close proximity to the crew for many days.'

'So we want new identities, like we're secret agents,' Jemima exclaimed joyfully.

'Not that sort of cover!' Dad said wearily. 'Just a plausible reason why we're travelling.'

'All right then, we're a family,' Jemima said. 'On a holiday visiting relatives.'

'Odd family,' Sophie snarked. 'You and I might be friends, but we can hardly be related. And who's Lord Colgath? Your long-lost uncle?'

'I think we all appreciate I will be wardveiled and spending a lot of the time in my cabin during the trip,' Lord Colgath said. 'But we do need to concoct a reason for travelling, else we will never gain a cabin for me to lock myself away in.'

'I know,' Taggie said, suddenly enthusiastic. 'The three of us could be a girl group,' she pointed at Sophie and

Jemima. 'We sing at taverns and halls all across the realms, which is why we're travelling. Dad, you're our manager; and everyone else is our road crew.'

'Hmm, you know I have been told I've got a good voice,' Sophie said thoughtfully. 'What are we going to sing?'

'Why do I have to be your road crew?' Lantic asked peevishly. 'Why can't I be in the group as well?'

Felix groaned and lowered his head into his forepaws. 'This isn't happening.'

'Ooh! Ooh!' Jemima was bouncing around in her bucket seat. 'What are we going to call ourselves? How about *The Sugar Angels*?'

'Nah,' Taggie said, unconvinced. '*The Taggerettes* has a good ring to it, don't you think? We could do soul numbers.'

'*What?*' Sophie exclaimed. 'OK, first, I would never join any group called *The Taggerettes*. And second, I've heard your Outer Realm soul music. It's boring.'

'Tell me you didn't just say that! Soul music is fabulous.'

'Enough!' Dad said loudly. 'Everyone is to be told I am a scholar from Lorothain University, and all of you are my assistants and apprentices. We are visiting libraries and academies, searching out and copying scrolls of historical importance. And that's an end to it.'

After an hour in the air, the helicopter was flying low over St Ives in Cornwall. The little town was spread across a peninsula with a grassy hill rising out of the northern tip.

Tiny streets of ancient granite cottages formed a chaotic maze that covered the steepish slopes.

'The tide's out far enough for us to land right on Porthmeor beach,' the co-pilot announced. 'Down in one minute.'

Sophie grimaced and started to pull on a baggy plastic raincoat so no one would see her wings. Opposite her, Lord Colgath swirled an ordinary velvet-lined black cloak around his phosphorescent smoke cloak, and put on a hat similar to those worn by the Ethanu. With his white skeletal face and mirror eyes, Taggie thought he looked like a particularly odd Phantom of the Opera.

Lantic muttered an enchantment. The black embroidery on his extravagant Blue Feather tunic swelled out, spreading across the scarlet fabric, toning down his appearance. Earl Maril'bo watched them all preparing, and shook his head in bemusement.

Taggie peered out of her window again, to see the helicopter descending on a long, curving beach with pale sand that was glowing silver in the moonlight. They touched down with a rocking bump. The crewman shoved the door open, and gave them a thumbs-up.

'Wardveil,' Taggie shouted at Jemima over the roar of the turbines and thrumming rotors.

Jemima nodded. The quest had been so exciting and important, it had just carried her along, allowing her to completely forget Mum's messenger. She cast a wardveil around the group, just as she had done when they left the palace. But with one small alteration that would allow the old woman in black to sight them.

Taggie jumped down on to the beach, holding her hand over her face to protect her skin from the harsh blizzard of sand the rotors were churning up. Holding on to Lantic, she led him towards the town.

The back of the beach was a high wall of granite stones, made up from cottages with glass-fronted balconies, artist studios that boasted tall windows to let in the clear Atlantic light, and a couple of long holiday-flat blocks. Looming up behind them was the Tate gallery, occupying an old converted gasworks.

Dad pointed at a set of stone steps that led up to the road running in front of the gallery. The helicopter lifted off behind them, quickly shrinking away into the night sky. Lord Colgath's cloaks billowed dramatically around him as he glided smoothly across the clean Cornish sands. Dogs being taken for their evening walk scampered away fearfully, their confused owners running after them. Earl Maril'bo walked beside the Dark Lord, unseen by any humans as he blended eerily into the undulating shape of the beach, then the rigid granite blocks.

Taggie followed Dad up the steps. On her right, the customers of the chic Porthmeor Café gawped at the strange travellers from behind the safety of their glass-and-aluminium balustrade, where they sat enjoying their gourmet suppers. One of the customers right at the back of the café was an old woman in a heavy black dress, wearing a veil. Jemima saw her and smiled secretively. 'Is the cure here yet?' she asked silently.

The unseen head behind the veil turned to face Jemima. Curiously, none of the other customers in the café seemed to notice her. 'The sorceress mistress is only a day from the Great Gateway to the Second Realm.'

'So Mum'll have the cure in a day?'

'I hope so, yes.'

Jemima raised her hand in a sneaky wave, then she was at the top of the stairs, hurrying after the others.

The road curved round into the Digey area of town, with elegant, slightly crooked, stone cottages on both sides. Dad led them round the corner. Then he turned sharply into a tiny alley called The Meadow. There was another turn after a few paces, followed by some granite steps. High white-painted yard walls were on both sides, with old net float bottles strung along them in decoration. Wheelie bins made the alley even narrower. Another turn. More steps. A junction. The alley rose steeply. At the next corner there was a black-painted door that looked like it led into a cottage. By now Taggie had no idea where they were, they'd turned so many times, but she did sense a powerful (and familiar) magic close by.

She stood in front of the door. 'Toramus, I am Taggie Paganuzzi, the Queen of Dreams. I ask that myself and my companions may pass into the Realm of Air.'

The glass net floats rattled against the walls. 'Greetings, Queen of Dreams,' Toramus said in a light voice. 'Arasath said you would be travelling this way. May your visit bring peace to all the Realms.'

The black door swung open, showing a low, unfurnished room beyond. Sophie dashed past Taggie. 'Come on!' she implored, tugging her raincoat off.

Taggie caught hold of Jemima's arm as her sister hurried past. 'Just remember, we don't want to draw attention to ourselves, OK? That means you keep it quiet.'

'Taggie! I'm a seer, I know what we're facing. Stop treating me like I'm ten.' She shook off Taggie's hand and stomped into the little room.

Taggie waited until everyone was inside. 'I would also ask that you remain closed to anyone else for several days,' she said to Toramus.

'Of course,' the Great Gateway replied.

Taggie gave the heavy black door a suspicious glance. Was that *Of course I will* – or *Of course you want me to*? The Great Gateways did so enjoy being tricky.

The room was completely bare inside, with wooden floorboards and granite walls and a single oil lamp flickering on the wall. There was only the one door. It swung shut behind her.

Taggie could just make out the door's brass handle in the gloom. With everyone standing behind her, she turned it, and pushed.

Brilliant sunlight flooded into the room, making her blink against the glare.

Sophie was the first out, her hair bustling about as if

she'd emerged into a gale. Taggie followed eagerly. The Great Gateway opened into a small square surrounded by cottages similar to the ones they'd just left behind in St Ives. Here, though, they were all four or five storeys high, and covered in vines heavy with grapes. Taggie peered straight upwards, but the cottage walls were so high, all she could see was a square of bright sapphire sky. She noticed that the windows on every top floor were actually glazed doors, even though none of them had balconies. It took a moment to realize that would be for skyfolk to come and go.

Sophie launched herself upwards, arms out wide, turning as she went. They all heard a long whoop of rapture as she soared above them. Then, once she was clear of the cottage roofs, she began to accelerate hard, streaking away, with her sparkling red contrail almost lost in the bright sunlight.

'Sophie!' Taggie called in annoyance – but not very loud: she didn't want to draw attention to them. Sophie had completely vanished from view now.

'I don't understand,' Lantic said. 'This looks just the same as any other Realm.'

'Just you wait,' Earl Maril'bo said. 'This is Tarimbi, one of the medium-sized isles. We need to grab ourselves a proper view. This way.'

'What about Sophie?' Jemima protested as the elf chose one of the narrow roads leading out of the square.

'She'll come back soon enough,' Taggie said. 'If not,

you'll have to find her with your runes.'

Lord Colgath kept his velvet-lined cloak and dark hat on. Taggie suspected he was also using a mild shadecast. Nobody seemed to notice him as they followed Earl Maril'bo down the uneven road. The residents of Tarimbi seemed normal enough – not that there were many of them walking about. They were mostly humans, with a few four-armed Holvans, and even a green-haired giant or two lumbering along.

After a couple of minutes, they came to a much larger square, where the surrounding buildings were grander than the cottages behind. The ground sloped away steeply, and they were given their first true glimpse of Tarimbi.

The isle resembled a mountain torn out of the ground by its roots. It looked as if it was about five miles from tip to tip, with a diameter of about two miles. The middle section was covered in thick emerald vegetation, with citrus trees packed close together amid banana trees and palms and breadfruit and pineapple.

Above them, the sky was a brilliant, clear azure, with the sun burning a hot blue-white just above the isle's far tip. As Taggie shifted her gaze round, the sky began to shade darker until opposite the sun it became the hazy indigo of dusk scattered with twinkling stars. Tiny green specks glimmered in every part of the blue firmament through which the isle drifted. Taggie drew a sharp breath of realization when she saw them. *Other isles!* There must have been hundreds in view, stretching away for hundreds, thousands of miles, into the unbound expanse of Air. The isles spread throughout the entire Realm, an archipelago that never ended. Her jaw dropped as the size of the Realm finally hit her. *You could fit a thousand First Realms into the Realm of Air*, she thought. *A million. And still you'd hardly notice them.*

Jemima was laughing giddily, while Dad had his arm round her shoulder, smiling in delight.

'No wonder they brought Mirlyn's Gate here,' she murmured. 'How would you ever find anything? It's the greatest hiding place in the universe.'

Beyond the palm-thatch rooftops that stretched away down the slope was a flat section of land where Tarimbi's port park was situated. Five huge wooden towers rose from the ground, shapes similar to the Eiffel Tower in Paris, but twice the height, and with branches sticking out horizontally all the way up the top half, forming wharfs where big cylindrical ships were docked. Skyfolk buzzed around them like bees round a nest.

'Look at the ships!' an awed Jemima blurted. 'Aren't they amazing?'

'Yes,' Taggie agreed. 'They are.'

Sophie reappeared, sinking down into the square in front of Taggie. 'The sky just goes on forever,' she said with tears of joy in her eyes. 'I could fly for my entire life and it would never end.'

Taggie embraced her friend, unsurprised to find Sophie

was trembling with happiness. 'I know,' she said. 'It's wonderful here.'

'We need to find some rooms,' Dad said. 'And get Lord Colgath out of sight. Then we'll see about chartering a ship.'

'The taverns around the port park would be best for that,' Earl Maril'bo said. 'That's where the crews spend most of their time and their pay.' They all set off down the slope.

Taggie watched the shadows cast by the buildings slowly moving across the ground.

'The isles all rotate,' Sophie told her when she

mentioned it. 'So the town will eventually turn round to face darkwards.' She pointed to the dusky side of the sky. 'It gives the isles a kind of night, but nothing like as dark as those in the other realms.'

'How long do they take to turn?' Jemima asked.

'Depends on the size of the isle. Some are no bigger than boulders; they turn fast, in a couple of hours or so. One this size will take about a day to rotate completely.'

Taggie scanned the brighter section of sky again. In the far distance, right on the edge of her sight, she could see layer upon layer of thin cloud. Some were white like gauze, while others were a deeper blue, which made them no more than phantoms against the immensity of the sapphire void.

There was so much strangeness to take in, but she held off peppering Sophie and Earl Maril'bo with questions. She would find out all about it soon enough.

7

THE *ANGELHAWK*

They paid for lodging at the Harpooned Paxia, a four-storey inn on the perimeter of the port park, nestled between a warehouse and a ship's carpentry shop. Lord Colgath stayed in his room as the isle's rotation slowly turned the town into shadow. The rest of them went back outside and followed Earl Maril'bo, who led them round the edge of the port park to a smaller tavern called the Dark Phoenix. 'This is where the captains and senior crews drink,' he explained.

The inside was lit with green and blue lightstones. It was filling up already as the town turned to face darkwards. Humans and skyfolk drank at the same tables. Giants had their own much larger booths at one end where the roof was higher. Earl Maril'bo went off to talk to a couple of elves at the bar while Dad claimed a table in the corner. He ordered some bread, cheese and fruit from one of the serving lads. 'Now remember,' he warned his daughters. 'I'm a scholar, and you're my apprentices. Taggie, we'll use your proper name. A girl your age called Taggie is just going to raise suspicion.'

'Yes, Dad,' Taggie scowled. She really didn't like 'Agatha'.

It wasn't long before Earl Maril'bo came back to join them. 'OK then, I have good and bad news,' he said. 'This whole realm is like totally buzzing right now. The guild of watchers has seen a comet falling sunwards. All the captains are getting their ships ready to chase it, and not just on this isle.'

'Why?' Lantic asked.

'Comets are the bodies of angels on their final flight into the sun,' Sophie said. 'They fall through Air in fire and thunder to add their glory to the sun.'

'That doesn't sound very safe,' Lantic said. 'Why would the captains want to chase something like that?'

'As the angels fall, their blood boils into the sky,' Sophie said. 'Sometimes their heart bursts open as well.'

'*Athrodene*,' Taggie said as realization struck her. 'The heart of an angel.'

'Yeah, you got it, little Queen,' Earl Maril'bo agreed. 'It's incredibly difficult and dangerous stuff to catch, ships are always getting smashed by fragments and flame that the comet shoots out. Captains have gotta be major league to manoeuvre close enough and avoid damage. You have to zigzag through the tail just after the comet's flashed past you. If you're too eager, and get too close, the slipstream will suck you in and drag you along – all the way into the sun.'

'It's worth it, though,' Sophie said. 'A chunk of *athrodene* the size of your fist can pay a ship's crew for a year. By the time it reaches another Realm it commands triple that price, or more.'

Jemima started pinching the armour she was wearing under her blue dress, making sure she hadn't lost it somehow.

'Such events are seriously rare,' Earl Maril'bo said. 'That you've got a comet falling at the time when the War Emperor is preparing to invade the Fourth Realm is seen by many here as an omen. Not that anyone is like sticking their neck out and saying if it's a good or a bad one . . .'

The serving boy arrived with a tray. Platters were handed round. Dad and Earl Maril'bo poured wine into their glasses. A bowl of nuts was provided for Felix.

'Thank you,' he said to the serving boy, who gave him a surprised grin.

'So if all the ships are going off to chase this comet, we won't be able to buy passage to Banmula, then,' Taggie said glumly as she slowly peeled a banana.

'Not quite,' the elf said with a knowing grin. 'There is one ship in port which has suffered a misfortune. The *Angelhawk*. It lost several sails and snapped two masts when it was caught in a violent storm. They had to jettison most of their cargo just to make it back here. The captain has no money to pay for a refit or compensate the merchant who chartered her. If you listen to rumour, she can't even pay her crew.'

'Ah,' said Dad, brightening. 'Where is she?'

Earl Maril'bo turned round and pointed discreetly at a table close to the bar, where a miserable-looking man and a skywoman sat drinking from a single bottle of cheap wine set between them. 'There. Captain Rebecca, and her shipsmage, Maklepine.'

Dad beckoned the serving boy back over. He was quickly dispatched with some coin to take a bottle of good wine over to the captain's table.

'If she got caught by a storm, should we be hiring her?' Taggie asked in concern. 'She can't be much good.'

'Storms here can be very big,' Sophie said. 'The winds from sunwards can carry storms hundreds of miles across. While the freezing winds that blow in from darkwards bring blizzards with them, they have hailstones the size of your fist that travel so fast they can break your bones or a ship's decking timber.'

'Really?' Jemima said eagerly. 'Cool!'

Taggie sighed, rolling her eyes.

Captain Rebecca made her way over to Taggie's table, carrying the new bottle of wine that the serving boy had given her. Taggie was used to skyfolk being almost delicate in appearance, but the captain was very different. For a start she was large, probably a couple of inches higher than Dad, though not as tall as Earl Maril'bo. While Sophie's skin was pale and almost translucent, the captain was tanned a dark brown, with dozens of tiny pale scars on her cheeks as if she'd been scratched by some animal with a dozen slender talons on each paw. 'So who is it that has

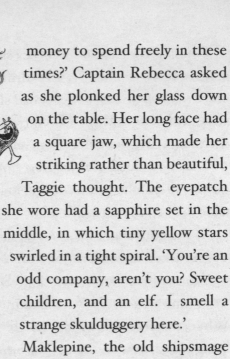

money to spend freely in these times?' Captain Rebecca asked as she plonked her glass down on the table. Her long face had a square jaw, which made her striking rather than beautiful, Taggie thought. The eyepatch she wore had a sapphire set in the middle, in which tiny yellow stars swirled in a tight spiral. 'You're an odd company, aren't you? Sweet children, and an elf. I smell a strange skulduggery here.'

Maklepine, the old shipsmage who followed her over, placed a restraining hand on the captain's arm. 'Now, Captain, these kind people have travelled far to talk to us. Let us thank them for their fine wine and listen to what they have to say. Hmm?' He was a less impressive figure than his captain, wearing the emerald and sapphire tunic of his profession, with a yellow bandana round his head, holding what was left of his greasy hair. Every finger had a ring that glowed with a soft magical light, and his tiny ruby nose stud twinkled like a livid pimple. His thick beard was trimmed in an elaborate spiral on his cheeks, showing tattoo runes that slowly changed shape.

'I apologize,' Captain Rebecca said. A thick curly mane of hair blacker than an elf's drifted slowly around her head, the tips licking at her broad shoulders. She sat down heavily on a stool while Dad introduced everyone. Taggie tried not to grimace as she was announced as Agatha.

'A scholar on a trip to scribble down even older scribblings, eh?' Captain Rebecca said scornfully when he finished. 'And your boy here . . .' She smirked at Lantic. 'How long have you been an officer of the Blue Feather regiment then?'

Lantic glared at her as he started coughing.

'Lantic is not of the regiment,' Felix said. 'He simply wears an old friend's tunic.'

Captain Rebecca peered at the white squirrel. She blinked, and pushed her face closer. 'Either this is *very* good wine, or you talked.'

Taggie realized the captain was quite drunk.

'I do many things,' Felix retorted.

'Yes, a very strange scholarly company,' Captain Rebecca said, as if saddened by the fact. 'What can I do for you?'

'We would like to charter your ship,' Dad said.

'Ha! You. I know you. You come to me because you've heard the *Angelhawk* has fallen on hard times. You think I will be cheap and grateful. You are wrong.' She picked up her glass and defiantly swigged some wine.

'I know you won't be cheap,' Dad said in a steely tone. 'You have repairs to make.'

'What of it?' Captain Rebecca said, suddenly defensive. 'We hit a continent storm. Any lesser ship would have been torn apart.'

'What's a continent storm?' Jemima asked.

Captain Rebecca gave her a hard look. 'You, young thing, are from the Outer Realm, I see that from your clothes. Yet, what is this . . .' She sniffed the air, still looking at Jemima. '*Athrodene*, and worked with true skill, too. That must have cost you a pretty penny. Are you some kind of warrior maid?'

'A storm the size of a continent, to answer your question,' Maklepine said before Jemima could fire off a cheeky answer. 'Few captains have the skill to ride such a calamity and escape with their ship intact. Fortunately, Captain Rebecca is one of them. That is why the crew stay with her.'

'How long will it take to repair the *Angelhawk*?' Taggie asked.

'You'd have to pay for that.' Captain Rebecca gave Dad an uncertain glance.

'I will pay for it, providing you agree to my charter,' Dad said.

'What is your cargo?'

'Just those of us sitting here, and one other.'

'Where do you want to go?' Maklepine asked.

'The Isle of Banmula,' Earl Maril'bo said. 'To start with.'

'Interesting choice. Why there?'

'The old university has a wealth of books,' Lantic said.

Maklepine's deep blue eyes turned to scrutinize Jemima. 'And you would see how valuable those books are, wouldn't you?'

Taggie was growing uneasy with the old shipsmage. He could obviously sense they had magical ability.

'Look, we just need to know if you'll accept the charter,' Dad said. 'The terms are simple enough.'

'Repair and passage?' Captain Rebecca said.

'And you take us onward after Banmula.'

'Where to?'

'I'll tell you that when we leave Banmula.'

Captain Rebecca turned to Maklepine. 'What do you think, shipsmage?'

'I think, Captain, we won't get a better offer this day, nor this month.'

'Are they trustworthy?'

'Hey!' Jemima cried. 'We can hear you, you know.'

Maklepine gave Taggie a troubled look, and bowed his head. 'I have never met anyone more trustworthy, Captain.'

'Don't go soppy on me now, shipsmage.' Captain Rebecca grinned, revealing three gold teeth, and stuck out a hand. 'Deal then,' she said heartily.

'Deal!' Dad shook hands.

The isle of Tarimbi turned slowly, bringing its town round to face lightward again. After a sleepless few hours, Taggie's company had an early breakfast at the Harpooned Paxia, then walked down to the port park to inspect the

Angelhawk. As they left, Taggie looked round to see Lord Colgath watching them from his window. He'd agreed to stay inside and out of sight until the ship was ready to depart, a forfeit she felt obscurely guilty about.

The *Angelhawk* was berthed at the second tower. Taggie stood at the foot of the main stairs which protruded from one of the four huge buttress legs, and tilted her head right back to look up at their ship. Squinting against the sun, she could finally appreciate how immensely tall the towers were.

High above them, the *Angelhawk* was tethered to the tower's third wharf. A couple of skyfolk were flying round it, and she could see more crew on deck.

'There's no lift?' Taggie said in dismay. 'That's a lot of stairs.' She was seriously considering shapeshifting to her eagle form and flying up there.

'This is when you really need an olobike,' Lantic told her with a wide grin.

Sophie laughed. 'The pair of you! You only have to walk up the first buttress. Gravity fades away after that. See you at the ship.' She launched herself into the air, flying up parallel to the tower.

Dad shrugged and smiled. 'Come on.' He held out his hand to Jemima, who had a suspicious expression on her face. She took his hand, and they started up the stairs.

Taggie followed them up. She soon found Sophie had been quite right: her weight dropped away, the higher she was above the isle. The stairs began to get broader and further apart to accommodate the way each step became easier. The ordinary push her legs applied carried her higher and higher each time, until the slightest tap with her toes sent her gliding along. At the top of the buttress there was no gravity any more. She floated gently about in the air, just like the astronauts she'd seen on television. It was scary for the first few moments, until she became accustomed to it. Then she gave a tentative smile.

'This is so cool!' Jemima yelped as she sailed past Taggie, turning the slowest somersault as she went.

Taggie grinned and tried her own somersault. The spinning motion made her feel queasy, and she grabbed one of the crossbeams to steady herself.

There were several wide tubes made from a lattice of bamboo canes leading up the centre of the tower. Now there was no gravity, they were the way people scrambled up and down. Taggie pushed off, and glided along one. She drifted about as she slid up, so every now and then she'd reach out and push herself off the bamboo lattice with a tiny slap of her palm. When she was halfway along, Felix came flashing past her, his paws flicking at incredible speed against the bamboo, tail wiggling wildly from side to side. 'Yayeeee!' he yelled gleefully as he went.

It took very little effort to reach the third wharf that stuck out at right angles to the main tower. Another bamboo tube ran along it to where the *Angelhawk* was docked.

Captain Rebecca's ship was made from three cylinders

of dark hardwood planks stacked one on top of the other. *Like a giant wedding cake*, Taggie thought. The largest cylinder was the lower deck, which was mostly the cargo hold and stores. It also housed the harpoon-launcher compartment, ringed by hatches through which the big weapons could be deployed. At the stern, five fan-like sail tails were folded up against the hull, ready to open out and steer the ship when she was underway.

The mid-deck was a smaller cylinder, divided up into crew cabins, the galley, a small carpentry shop, and the wardroom. Above that was the topdeck, the smallest of the three cylinders. Captain Rebecca's cabin took up most of it, though there was also the glass-domed duty officer's watch chamber, with the remaining space taken by two harpoon-launcher positions.

Three long masts normally stuck out from the top of the lower deck like spokes from a wheel hub, each with three levels of sails to catch the winds that would carry the *Angelhawk* between isles. As Taggie drew near the lower deck, she could see only one mast and two jagged stumps where there should have been three. *It must have been a really fierce storm to break the masts off like that*, she realized. They looked like solid oak. *Maybe the captain is as skilful as Maklepine claims, after all?*

Captain Rebecca was waiting for them by the large helm wheel, which was on the walkway circling the mid-deck. Maklepine was with her, along with the bosun – a skyman by the name of Jualius. They hung on the netting which caged the outside of this level to prevent the non-skyfolk crew from drifting away into Air when the *Angelhawk* came to rest. While it was docked there was little danger, Jualius explained, but between the isles an ordinary human tumbling overboard could soon be lost.

Jualius was big for a skyman, though not as large as his captain. Pale, beaded dreadlocks meandered round his head as if they were sleepy serpents. Like the captain and Maklepine, he had hundreds of tiny scars on his lucid skin. 'Ice cuts,' he told Sophie when she stared in puzzlement. 'I've been caught outside in my fair share of storms sweeping in from darkwards.'

They were soon joined by two of Tarimbi's port park shipwrights, who started to assess the damage with Dad, Earl Maril'bo and the captain. Jualius showed Taggie, Jemima, Felix, Sophie, and Lantic round the *Angelhawk* while that was going on. They floated down corridors and drifted like a shoal of clumsy fish through cabins, chattering excitedly, asking dozens of questions about the helm and the chart room, and the storm that broke the masts, and the odd crockery every ship used for holding food while they were floating at rest. They also met the remaining crew: Ormanda, a Holvan who served as the sailmistress, eight more humans and five skyfolk, along with Mr Marcus, a Jannermol who was the ship's cook. Even the egg-like shell that protected his body was covered in tiny healed-up cracks, Taggie noticed – more ice strikes. She was starting to get concerned about the storms they might pass through, and reviewed the shield enchantments in her charmsward.

After an hour, a price was agreed and Dad handed over a deposit of several gold coins to both shipwrights. 'Two days,' he announced happily to Taggie. 'They have the timber in store to make new masts, and the damaged hull planks are simple enough to replace. Captain Rebecca says she can launch as soon as the work is complete.'

'Almost,' the captain said in a voice that was a lot louder and more cheerful than it had been in the *Dark Phoenix* the previous night.

'What do you mean, almost?' Dad asked sharply.

'We need new sails for the new masts, of course, and our stores are almost empty. It's a long way to Banmula, you know.'

'Right,' Dad said wearily. 'Where do we buy supplies?'

8

THE ENCHANTMENTS OF DECEIT

Queen Danise arrived back in Shatha'hal to find the armies encamped around the capital had tripled in size in the few days she'd been away. As she walked along one of the palace's broad, airy cloisters she stopped and looked down on the rows and rows of tents with a growing sense of dismay. There were tens of thousands of young soldiers down there, eager for war. They would obediently follow their King and the War Emperor wherever they were told to go. And now she knew what horrors that would mean.

She found her husband in the small ornate chamber behind the throne room where he took council in private. It had become his war room, with maps on every table, and a constant flow of generals in and out discussing plans and strategy. She looked at him silently for a long moment, seeing the man she loved hunched over a chart on his desk. Blue and red lines wiggled across the parchment. He was obsessed with them, she could see. His grief had blinded him to anything other than vengeance for Rogreth's death – exactly as Grand Lord Amenamon intended. It was a grief so strong it prevented him from mourning as every man should. It stopped him from looking to the future with hope. And if it was allowed to continue it would condemn thousands to their death and endanger the very Realms themselves.

Manokol looked up, and gave her a weak smile. 'There you are, my dear. Where have you been?'

Queen Danise walked over to him, and took his hands. 'I have been to see our son.'

Manokol's expression was blank for a moment, then he started to colour. 'The First Realm? You have been to the First Realm, and visited with that stupid girl?'

'I have spoken to the Queen of Dreams, the compassionate and lovely young woman who rules the First Realm, yes.'

'She may rule there, but she is causing havoc here. Everyone knows she is opposed to the war.'

'With good reason.'

'*WHAT?*' Manokol roared. 'What say you?'

Queen Danise faced his rage completely unperturbed. 'I spoke with our son.'

'Ha!' Manokol barked contemptuously. 'That fool? She bewitched him, you know. She's led him astray. He knows no better. He needs to be brought back here and reminded of his true responsibilities.'

'Our son. The son you mock, and sneer, and scorn at every opportunity. So much so, you have driven him away, and almost killed him.'

'I did no such thing. I show him how to conduct himself as every father should, especially a royal father. The boy has to learn how to be a true prince.'

'That boy has travelled into the heart of the Fourth Realm. He has shown a courage you and I will never possess. He has faced an army of dark creatures and escaped. Barely. You drove him to that. He thinks he has to prove himself to you.'

'What nonsense is this?' the War Emperor asked with growing irritation. 'The Fourth Realm? Nobody can travel there without me knowing. Every Great Gateway to that bedamned Realm is watched and guarded.'

'I'm sorry, Manokol, you know very little of what you face. If only Captain Feandez had survived, your words would be so different.'

'Feandez? What of him? The Queen of Dreams keeps him captive in her Realm.'

'No. She does not. Nor does your son lack for any quality.'

The old King sighed, and looked at her with heavy, tired eyes. 'I'm sorry about Lantic, really I am. But the terrible threat we face has to be dealt with. Fate and the Heavens have chosen me to lead this campaign against the Karrak invaders.'

Queen Danise gave him a sympathetic look. 'No, my love. It was neither the Heavens nor fate, it was the Grand Lord himself who chose you.'

'This is—' he began to protest.

'Enough.' Queen Danise drew herself up, a haze of purple magic shimmering along her fingers. 'I am your wife, and you will listen to the truth I speak. You are walking into a trap, you and every soldier you command. And this is how it will be sprung . . .'

The War Emperor listened with growing dismay to the story his wife told him: of Amenamon's plan to goad the royals of every Realm into invading; of the Outer Realm guns that fired bullets tipped with bad magic, which no one in the Realms could defend themselves against; of the suspicions surrounding Queen Judith; of his son's valour; of Taggie's hope to recover Mirlyn's Gate; of Feandez's unexplained death.

'This cannot be,' he whispered in dread.

'It is so,' Queen Danise said. 'You can believe the words I speak, the acts of your own son, or you can destroy the Realms in this calamitous war. That is how history will judge you — if there is to be any future where such things are judged.'

He gripped her hand again. 'Your compassion and understanding, as always they dazzle me.'

'What will you do?' she asked, studying his features for any sign of remorse.

'What needs to be done.' He smiled bitterly. 'I am not so vain, so lost in my selfishness, that I will not heed my own wife. All will be well, my love. I promise.'

'Thank you.' She embraced him. 'You are a true King.'

'I will speak with the Kings and Queens of the Gathering,' he said resolutely. 'We will draw back from conflict. Another way will be found to punish the Karrak

Lords and Ladies for the atrocity they committed against us. They must be made to obey the bloodbond pact the last War Emperor made with their own Grand Lord. They must never again venture from the Fourth Realm.'

After Queen Danise left, the War Emperor sank down into the curving chair behind his desk. His head fell forward, and before long he started to weep.

He was still weeping when Queen Judith appeared in front of the desk with a goblet in her hand. 'Dear friend,' she said softly. 'What has brought you to this?'

The War Emperor used his knuckles to clear the moisture from his eyes before raising his head to regard his strongest ally in the Gathering. 'How are you here?' he asked in confusion.

'I heard your poor soul in torment. I came to soothe you.'

'My wife was here,' he said, frowning. 'I think she was. My head is so cluttered. I have so much to do.'

'Of course you do. You are our War Emperor, our leader. We depend on you to bring us victory.'

'I will. But . . . there are doubts now. The Karraks have new weapons. My wife . . . she told me they lie in ambush.'

'An ambush unmasked is an ambush turned,' Queen Judith assured him.

'Is it? Oh, my head. I cannot think. I am so tired.'

'Would you like me to help, dear friend?'

'Can you? That draught you have. Is there more of it?'

'There is always more for you.' Queen Judith produced

a small phial from inside her imposing robe with its glittering jewels. She tipped it into the goblet of wine she was holding and handed it to the War Emperor. 'Drink this. It will cool you. Your thoughts will soon be clear.'

The War Emperor took a sip. 'My wife said something about you, too.'

'Did she?' Queen Judith's eyebrow was raised in surprise. She stood behind him, and began to massage his head with her long fingers. Subtle enchantments slithered out from her hands and eased themselves into his scalp. 'You are the War Emperor,' she said in a dreamy voice. 'All the peoples of every Realm believe in you. We place our trust for victory in you. That is what matters. Victory.'

The War Emperor's eyes began to droop as a welcome sleep rose to claim him. 'The Queen of Dreams doubts me,' he murmured. 'She has

98

turned my remaining son against me.'

A flicker of annoyance crossed Queen Judith's face. 'Katrabeth will deal with the Queen of Dreams, have no worries on that score. But your dear son Lantic should come back to you, as is only right. He is a good boy, if hotheaded, as all that age are. Might it be that he listens to his mother?'

'Yes. Yes, he does.'

'Then send her to the First Relam to fetch him back here to your loving home. He will listen to her, he will come at her bidding. She can tell him that you wish to hear everything he has to say, that will convince him. Your son will come back to you.'

'Yes. That is an excellent idea. I will do that.'

'And in the meantime you can lead your armies without this trifling distraction. Do not doubt yourself. Do not fail yourself. Do not fail Rogreth.'

A tear leaked out of the War Emperor's eye. 'My son.'

'Your *murdered* son is depending on you.' Queen Judith smiled down serenely at the sleeping War Emperor, and removed her hands from his head. 'Avenge him.'

9

THE VOYAGE BEGINS

The shipwrights of Tarimbi were true to their word. After two days of frantic activity, and a great deal of money changing hands, the *Angelhawk* was ready to depart.

As the isle turned, bringing the port park and its towers round to face lightward, Sophie launched herself from the ship's upper deck through a tough elastic opening in the net. She didn't really have to fly: not up here, so high above the isle's gravity. A few flicks from her wings set her going, then she swayed her feet gently to steer. Behind her, commands were shouted between the *Angelhawk*'s decks as the crew prepared to launch. Towerhands withdrew the wharf's bridge lattice from the ship's lower deck, and started to wind in the mooring cables as Captain Rebecca ordered them let loose.

Sophie manoeuvred herself to a position twenty metres out from one of the mast tips, and came to rest. From here she could easily see the entire ship. Taggie, Jemima, Felix and Lantic were all on the upper deck, clinging to the netting as they floated about. Prince Dino and Earl Maril'bo were on the larger lower deck, close to the helm. She couldn't see Lord Colgath; he'd come aboard quietly last night while most of the crew were having a last few hours in the taverns, and claimed the smallest cabin for himself.

'Make ready tail sails,' Captain Rebecca bellowed from her position on the upper deck, directly above the helm. On the deck below, crew started frantically cranking winch handles. Sophie watched the thick yellowish canvas of the five sail tails open like grubby petals reacting to the dawn light.

'Tipsails away,' came the next order.

On the top spar of each mast, a waiting crewman started to unfurl the highest sails.

'Cast off!'

The remaining mooring ropes were released, curling limply in mid-air before they were wound back on to the wharf. Sophie saw the tipsails starting to fill as a gentle breeze caught the startlingly white new canvas.

'Hey, Sophie!' Jualius called. He was flying out towards her. 'Get back inside the netting. Bad luck not to be on board when we launch.'

Sophie grinned and gave him a thumbs-up, before darting back to the bulk of the *Angelhawk*. The ship crews in the Realm of Air were even more superstitious than their nautical counterparts, she'd discovered over the last two days. She slithered through the opening in the net to join her friends floating round on the topdeck.

The masts were creaking as they started to feel the first push of the wind. Captain Rebecca was studying the two new masts closely, checking to see that the mountings held. Sophie watched the tower wharf begin to slide past as the big ship slowly started to back away from the tower. Right at the end of the wharf an old woman in a stiff black dress hung to the lattice. Sophie couldn't tell if she was watching them or not: her face was covered with a veil.

'North-lightwards-east, helm,' Captain Rebecca ordered. The big wheel was spun accordingly, turning the sailtails.

The *Angelhawk* began to angle upward from the isle, still moving cautiously.

'Full about,' came the order when the prow was well clear of the tower and its wharfs. Sophie and her friends laughed half nervously as the isle seemed to suddenly slip round. All of them gripped the net tighter. The tipsails suddenly became limp as the ship turned sideways to the breeze.

'Mainsails away,' Captain Rebecca ordered.

Huge sheets of canvas rippled out, stiffening quickly as the ship finished its turn and they captured the breeze. The *Angelhawk* began to pick up speed, heading forwards now, a course which sent them soaring over Tarimbi's town.

Everybody laughed nervously again as the acceleration pushed them down on to the decking. Their weight returned, allowing them to stand normally again. 'That just feels weird now,' Jemima said as she took a few experimental steps. 'I liked floating around.'

'Midsails,' the captain called, and crew members scampered along the yardarms to obey.

'Makes eating easier,' Lantic observed. 'I'm not surprised everyone's covered in little scars. I kept burning myself on tea drops. They get everywhere when you're drinking, even with those special squeeze cups.'

Jemima was pressing her face against the netting, trying to see Tarimbi, which was now almost directly behind them. 'We're really moving now,' she said.

Captain Rebecca patted Jemima firmly on her back, grinning broadly. 'That we are, warrior maid. Your father chose a good ship to carry you to safety.' She winked at

Taggie. 'So what was it, Agatha? Did some arrogant ugly old prince demand an arranged marriage?'

Sophie laughed at the indignation on her friend's face. Nor did she miss the way Lantic started to blush.

'We're not running away from anything,' Taggie said, a little too earnestly. 'We're here to study ancient scrolls.'

'Well, certainly nobody runs to Banmula, not these days,' Captain Rebecca snorted.

'Why not?' Lantic asked.

'A long time ago it used to be the capital of Air,' the captain said. 'The richest, grandest town, so large it was practically a city, as they have in other Realms. Twenty towers it had in its port park, and mansions and palaces almost as tall. It was the centre of trade, with fat merchants sitting on chairs of gold in their halls. *Athrodene* and volpas meat went through the Great Gateway to every Realm, and their coins flowed back to us.'

'What happened?' Jemima asked breathlessly.

'Rothgarnal,' Taggie said bluntly.

Captain Rebecca faced her, the minuscule stars in her eyepatch sapphire contracting to a dense swirl. 'Well done, my young sorceress. The Great Gateway that led to Rothgarnal was destroyed in the battle. Trade ended that day. Piaffelo, the Highlord of that time, moved his eyrie palace to the isle of Tonba, which has a Great Gateway to the Fifth Realm. All the merchants and captains followed him – what else could they do? Banmula slowly declined, as is the way of things.'

'That's sad,' Jemima said.

'For Banmula, but not for Tonba,' Captain Rebecca said cheerily. She leaned over the rail, pressing herself against the netting, and yelled down to the lower deck. 'Shipsmage, we're two isle-lengths out and have a sound hull. Kindly rouse yourself and bless this voyage. I don't waste my precious coins carrying deadweight.'

On the decking below, Maklepine gave a quick salute. He walked over to the rail beside the helm wheel, where two strange carved bulbs of wood stuck out, resembling giant acorns. Maklepine put his hands on them. The crew became quiet and watched him respectfully as the rings on his fingers started to glow brightly.

'We ask the ever-watching angels to smile upon us,' Maklepine said. 'And grant us clean winds to carry us onward without harm through this most glorious of Realms we are privileged to live in.' He closed his eyes, and began to incant. Slivers of light from his rings began to flow across his hands and seep into the wooden bulbs.

Sophie grinned in appreciation as Maklepine's magic started to illuminate the runes carved across every part of the hull. She hadn't noticed them before: the runes were little more than scratches. But now they filled with red and gold and green and violet light, spreading out from the wooden bulbs, flowing like liquid along the tiny lines until the entire ship was festooned by shimmering protective enchantments. Slowly the light began to sink away into the timbers, strengthening them against the dangers and surprises spread throughout the blue void they sailed in.

'Thank you, shipsmage,' Captain Rebecca shouted down at him, sounding completely unimpressed. Sophie reckoned that was all part of the act, and smiled over at the imposing captain.

'What's your problem, gnat?' Captain Rebecca barked.

Sophie giggled, shaking her head.

The captain gave a disgusted grunt. 'Patrina, take top watch, and no dozing – I see cloud ahead. Isairis and Favian you have lower deck watch. Jualius, take the con. Keep this heading for now.'

The crew hurried to their stations.

'And you lot –' Captain Rebecca rounded on Taggie and her friends. 'Stay out of the way. Don't ask foolish questions. Obey every order you're given. Don't touch any of the ship's equipment. If you annoy me I'll use you for volpas bait.'

'What's a volpas?' Jemima blurted.

'Its tentacles are the tastiest meat you'll ever eat,' Captain Rebecca said with a wicked smile. 'Trouble is, the tentacles are attached to the widest mouth with the sharpest teeth you'll ever see. And they're big, bigger than the *Angelhawk* – and that's just the babies. Their mums and dads, now they lurk in the middle of clouds where you can't see them until too late. Miles wide they are, their tentacles kill with lightning bolts, and slash isles in half, they're so strong. So you be a good little warrior maid for me or you'll be seeing one from the inside.' She flew a few inches off the deck, chortling all the way to her cabin.

A pale Jemima turned to Sophie. 'She's joking, isn't she?'

'Not about the volpas, no. They're very, very dangerous. But they normally live closer to the sun, I think.'

'Jem, she won't actually throw you to the volpas,' Taggie said.

'Humm,' Jemima said, giving the captain's closed door a suspicious look.

'She's curious about us,' Felix said. He was clinging upside down to the netting just above their heads. 'We'll have to be careful not to give anything away.'

'She already knows a lot about us,' Lantic said. 'She must have some kind of sight.'

'Air-sense,' Sophie told them.

'What?' Felix asked.

'They call it Air-sense in this Realm. That's what makes a real captain.' She was staring darkwards into the indigo sky they were sailing towards. 'Rebecca said there were clouds up ahead. I can barely see them.'

'How far away are they?' Felix asked, twisting round on the net.

'It's hard to tell,' Sophie admitted. 'Tiny and close, or else far away and big.'

'I bet I know which it is,' Felix said gloomily.

Jemima shared a cabin with Sophie and Taggie; though she thought 'cabin' was an exaggeration. 'Cupboard with three shelves' was more like it. Her bunk, the lower one – which she was still cross about – had straps across to hold the sleeper in place should the *Angelhawk* perform any sharp manoeuvre or stop sailing. It always surprised Jemima that she could fall asleep so easily in it.

That first night after they launched from Tarimbi she fell asleep quickly. In her dream she was standing outside Mum's house in the Outer Realm. It would have been comforting but for the sky, which was scarlet. The old woman in black walked slowly out of Mum's house, all stooped over as if she was carrying a heavy burden. The veil gave no hint to the face behind it.

'Has Mum got the cure?' Jemima asked.

'She talks to the sorceress mistress this very hour, my dear,' the old woman said.

'That's wonderful. Felix is going to be so happy. His family has suffered really badly, you know, for so long.'

'Oh I do, Blossom Princess, I do indeed. Now then, part of the cure is a potion young Felix must drink. Your mother has told me to bring it to you. I sighted you launching from Tarimbi: where are you going?'

Green snow began to fall from the red sky. Jemima shivered at the cold it brought, rubbing her arms. 'Banmula.'

'Thank you, my dear. I will buy the ingredients, and meet you there.'

'Then it'll only be a few more days until he's cured.' The dream-sky was darkening now, and the wind began to rise. All the trees and bushes in the garden began to lose their leaves, which fluttered down to a lawn which was shrivelling up. 'How will you get a ship?' Jemima asked curiously. 'We only just managed to charter the *Angelhawk*. The other captains are all going to chase the comet.'

'I'll be there.' An unpleasant chuckle sounded from behind the veil. 'Don't you worry about that.'

Jemima's sudden unease sent a rush of cold down her veins, worse than anything the green dream-snow could inflict. 'Who are you?'

The chuckle grew louder until it was stronger than the pealing of church bells.

'Who are you?' Jemima shouted. 'Who are you really? Show me your face!'

The chuckling began to crack the glass in the windows. With a slow menace, the woman reached up, and began to lift the veil.

'No,' Jemima wailed, knowing she was going to see something utterly horrible. 'No, no, no!'

'Jem! Jem, wake up.'

Jemima woke with a start to see Taggie and Sophie peering down at her, their faces creased with worry.

'What's wrong?' Taggie asked.

Jemima glanced round the cabin, fearful that the shadows would melt and merge into the shape of a black dress. 'I . . . She's . . . ' Her heart was pounding inside her chest. 'A dream,' she said. 'I had a bad dream, that's all.'

Taggie hugged her. 'It's all right. I'm here. Nothing can hurt you.'

Jemima was grateful for the hug, but she didn't dare tell

Taggie about the old woman. After a couple of minutes, she agreed that she felt a lot better, and everyone lay back down and tried to get to sleep again.

Jemima couldn't even close her eyes for fear of what might lurk in her dreams. She thought about what she'd done, and realized that the old woman had never actually given her any proof that she was Mum's friend. A tear of dismay leaked down her cheek, unseen in the dark cabin. *I was so stupid*, she thought. *After all those warnings at school about 'stranger danger', I believed her because I wanted to, I wanted Felix to be cured, and she knew that. Now I might have ruined everything.* The tiniest whimper escaped from her lips. *But I have the sight*, she told herself. *Better than anyone. I'll keep special watch so no one creeps up on us. I won't let Taggie and my friends down again. I won't!*

10

GONE SURFING

With the sun shining constantly in the Realm of Air, day and night on a ship was marked only by a clock, not the coming of darkness – for there was none. Traditionally, a ship remained on the cycle of the isle it had just departed from, changing only when it moored at its destination port park.

That made it slightly easier for Taggie and her friends to adapt to life on board the *Angelhawk*. For the first few hours it was tremendously exciting: watching Tarimbi shrink rapidly aft until it was indistinguishable from any of the innumerable specks that drifted through the blue domain which surrounded them; jumping out of the way of the crew as they scurried about their duties, powered by a bellow and a curse from Captain Rebecca. Then there was the harpoon practice every day, with Maklepine supervising everyone rushing to their stations and cranking open the hatches.

But after a while the monotony of the shipboard routine started to bite. There were slight moments of activity every now and then, when one of the watches spotted a boulder floating close to their course, and the helm spun the wheel, angling the *Angelhawk* round the dangerous rock.

The only break came from meals. If Mr Marcus was surprised at how many volunteers he got to prepare the food, he never said. At mid-morning on the second day they all sat round the galley's long table, scraping and chopping vegetables for the lunchtime stew. Ship's food was always a pulp or mash of some kind, making it easier to hold and control if they weren't under way. The mash was served in cylindrical pots with a funnel at the top and a base that moved up like a syringe, forcing the thick paste out of the nozzle.

'*Sophie and the Outer-Realm Girls,*' Sophie suggested as she diced some parsnips.

'That's dreadful,' Jemima said. 'Worse than *The Taggerettes.*' She threw her rune stones again, studying them after they landed on the table amid the vegetable scrapings.

'At least we wouldn't have to sing soul music.'

'People like dancing to soul music,' Taggie insisted as she peeled potatoes.

Sophie's wings gave a dismissive flap.

'Well, what sort of songs do you think we should feature?' Taggie asked. She'd been watching Jemima quietly, for two days now. Jem had been casting the stones constantly, as if she was searching for something. So far, Taggie hadn't asked what, but it was starting to concern her.

'I don't mind songs we can dance to,' Sophie said. 'Just not soul.'

'And I still think I should be singing with you,' Lantic said from behind the broccoli he was chopping. 'Would you like to hear me sing? I have a fine voice.'

'Doesn't matter how good you are,' Sophie said, waving her slicing knife in his direction. 'A boy's voice wouldn't harmonize right. We want to be light and sparkly, a fun group that people will always want to book again.'

'Soul can be light and sparkly,' Taggie said.

'No it can't. You played me hours of it when I visited the Outer Realm. It's all sorrowful and broken hearts and lost loves. If we're going to do weddings and parties, people don't want misery.'

'*Jemima's Lightheart Band*,' Jemima said. 'It sounds quite classic.'

'No,' Taggie and Sophie said in unison.

'You'll need someone to accompany you,' Lantic said. 'A pianist, perhaps?'

Taggie gave him a surprised look. 'You play the piano?'

'The flute, actually.'

Her hand came down on top of his, and she patted encouragingly. 'I don't think a flute is quite right for us.' Then she realized where her hand was, and hurriedly withdrew it.

Sophie and Jemima exchanged a look, and grinned.

'No, no, no,' a very irritated Felix said. 'How can you turn down the offer of a flute – which *can* be light and cheerful – when you can't even think of a name for yourselves, let alone decide what music you're going to sing?'

'Well, why don't you think of a name for us, then, Mr Big-Shot Manager?' Jemima said.

Felix stopped shelling peas to jam both forepaws against his waist. 'I don't want to manage you! You'd be a nightmare. However, I can offer a great deal of practical advice on musical taste. You might actually get a booking if you have a decent selection for the host to choose from.'

'You?' Sophie exclaimed. 'Since when are you a music expert?'

'I know what I like,' Felix said, the fur on his tail fluffing up. 'And what I like is popular.'

'All right, how about this?' Jemima said. '*Moonlight Sisters.*'

'Sisters?' Lantic said curtly, and sniffed.

Felix tipped his head to one side, and sucked down a breath. 'I think I've heard that name before.'

'Could you play saxophone?' Sophie asked. 'It can't be much harder than playing a flute, surely?'

'Ah, no, you're thinking of "Moonlight Serenade",' Taggie said confidently to Felix.

'Isn't the saxophone a bit soul-ish?' Lantic queried.

'Oh, sweet Heavens save us,' Dad groaned.

Taggie looked round to see him standing in the galley's hatchway. She wasn't sure how long he'd been there. 'Oh, Daddy, you know all about old music, can you think of a name for our group?'

He shook his head in dismay and backed out of the hatchway as if the galley was full of wild tigers. As he walked away they all heard him saying: 'How long is this voyage going to last?'

On the third day out from Tarimbi the watch spotted a cloudstorm up ahead. It was a mild one, the crew kept saying. Taggie knew she didn't ever want to see a big one.

A huge haze stretched across the sky in front of the *Angelhawk*. Sunlight shone across it, producing a glimmering iridescent light that just permitted a glimpse of what lay behind. But that glimpse was enough.

Individual clouds were arranged in long ragged swirls, dark and thick, ten to twenty miles across, twisting like slow-motion hurricanes. In turn, they also churned through the sky in a vast, tattered river, hundreds of miles long, that was like a barrier placed directly in their path.

'Can we go around?' Lantic asked, as they stood on their usual place on the upper deck. The air had been growing colder for hours as the ship sailed resolutely towards the cloudswarm.

'We could,' Maklepine said. 'But that's a wide chunk of cloud to avoid. You'd add another couple of days to the voyage.'

'How safe is it?' Felix asked from what had become his customary perch halfway up the net.

'It's not the cloud you have to worry about,' the shipsmage said. 'It's what's hidden inside it that matters. Sea globes, rock isles, a paxia hoard, all sorts.'

'Nonsense!' Captain Rebecca said, flying steadily along the deck. 'Stop panicking the paying passengers. That cloudswarm is too loose to have a sea globe at the centre. Besides, we would have heard about it in Tarimbi's port park. Don't worry, my young friends, the only danger here is a few hidden rocks, some loxraptors and maybe some volpas.' She ruffled Jemima's hair as she swept by. 'Best go put that armour on, warrior maid. It'll snap those pesky fangs when they try to eat you.'

The captain slipped effortlessly down the ladder tube to the lower deck.

'Loxraptors?' Jemima asked.

'Big birds,' Maklepine explained. 'They eat a lot of little birds. But volpas eat them. So the good news is that if we see loxraptors there's probably no volpas around.'

Jemima waited until the shipsmage had gone round the upper deck. 'Can't you do your cloudbusting thing on them?' she asked Taggie in a quiet voice.

'I think this cloudswarm is too big for magic to shift,' Taggie told her.

Earl Maril'bo came up the stairs from the lower deck. 'Now that, my friends, is what I call one fizzy rainbow.'

'That?' Taggie asked in surprise, looking again at the shimmering veil of reflected sunlight. 'That's a rainbow?'

'What did you like think it was?' the elf asked.

'Bright fog?'

'Oh no. That's realler than the real thing.'

Jemima grinned. 'Take me surfing with you, please!'

116

Taggie wanted to stamp her foot. She'd been about to ask that!

'Sure thing, little Princess. But we'd, like, better be quick about it.'

'I'm ready!'

Which was why, five minutes later, Jemima was standing with wobbly legs on Earl Maril'bo's mirror board, with the huge elf directly behind her, one arm protectively round her tummy. They were balancing on the edge of the *Angelhawk*'s prow as the swirl of multi-coloured light grew closer and closer until she was looking up at what must surely be the glistening roof of the universe. All she could see in every direction was swirls of colour.

Somewhere on the lower deck she heard Dad calling: 'Jemima? Where are you? Jem?'

Now might not be the best time to tell Earl Maril'bo she hadn't bothered asking if Dad minded her surfing.

The *Angelhawk* sailed cleanly into the illuminated haze surrounding the cloudstorm. Jemima felt Earl Maril'bo tense up as the warm mist swept over her.

'Now,' he yelled. And they slid forward, over the edge of the prow. She whooped with joy and fear, every sense telling her they would plummet for weeks until they fell into the sun. But no, the mirror board cut clean through the rainbow, and they swept away at an angle from the *Angelhawk* at a giddy speed.

He bent his knees, pushing the mirror board into a

modest curve, and Jemima whooped again as they swooped round the *Angelhawk* in a wide, lazy spiral, climbing the flickering wet light with a speed and grace even the skyfolk couldn't match. The damp air sent her hair streaming out behind her. Earl Maril'bo twisted the other way, and they were climbing parallel to the ship, zooming ahead. Jemima laughed in delight. Weird ripples of twinkling light raced away from the edge of the mirror board on either side.

'Your turn,' Earl Maril'bo said, and straightened his own body. They seemed to slow, moving sedately forward. 'Use your ankles to lift your toes up so the weight's on your heels, and shift the board like you want to dig the back in.'

Jemima carefully did as she was told, the tip of her tongue jammed in the corner of her mouth as she concentrated, and grinned appreciatively as they picked up speed again.

'I'm doing it!' she yelled. 'I'm surfing a rainbow!'

With the elf guiding her, she shifted from side to side, pushing the board into gentle curves as they shot through the gleaming colours.

'Now throw back,' Earl Maril'bo instructed, and his arm pulled her gently, and both of them swayed on to their heels. The mirror board moved so fast the light became a smear on either side of her.

'Look up!' The elf laughed.

Jemima did, and squealed in outraged joy. Seemingly, directly fifty metres above her, the *Angelhawk* was powering towards them. They were looping right over the ship!

Earl Maril'bo shifted his position smoothly, and the mirror board twisted them into a complete roll, then plunged down to dive below the *Angelhawk*, splitting the rainbow into two jets of glittering light waves behind them. Jemima laughed and squealed the whole way down.

As they went under the ship she felt the elf stiffen, and the board slowed as he brought his weight forward. They drifted along, barely moving.

'Did you hear that?' he asked.

'What?' she asked, nervous now.

'Let's go.' He crouched down, and the mirror board leaped forward, curving sharply. Within seconds they were level with the ship, and angling in sharply.

They landed smoothly on the prow.

'Jemima!' Dad's furious shout filled the moist air.

She sighed, ready for the storm of anger. *Worth it, though!*

Earl Maril'bo leaned over the edge of the cabin roof, looking down to the upper deck. 'Captain,' he said urgently. 'I heard loxraptors circling.'

Jemima hurried down the spindly ladder from the prow.

'We will be discussing this on the other side of the cloudstorm,' Dad was saying angrily as he followed her. 'And at considerable length.'

'Yes, Daddy,' Jemima said meekly, and completely unrepentant.

'Where are you going?' Taggie asked as Jem walked past, her face set in determination.

'To put my armour on. What do you think?'

'We should get inside,' Lantic said. Isairis and another crew woman, Gracieia, hurried past him on their way up to the upper deck's two harpoon stations. Down in the lower deck, every launcher was being prepared to shoot the long metal barbs at any loxraptor that flew close. Captain Rebecca had promised a gold shilling to anyone who hit one of the predators.

'Furl the tipsails,' Captain Rebecca bawled. She'd taken position at the helm, both hands gripping the wheel tight, staring up past the topdeck towards the approaching cloudswarm.

'Yes,' Dad said. 'Come on, inside. And you're not to go out again until the captain says it's clear. Understand?'

'Yes, Dad,' they chorused.

The air was chilly now as Taggie made her way down

to the lower deck, and the cabin she shared with Jemima and Sophie. Raindrops started to patter on the wood. Far behind them on the other side of the rainbow, the sun was nothing more than a slightly brighter circle of light.

Taggie grinned regretfully at Earl Maril'bo as he headed for his cabin.

'Next time, little Queen,' he said softly.

Captain Rebecca spun the wheel hard, and the *Angelhawk* shifted direction, curving round the fringes of the first whirling clump of dark cloud. The wind was picking up and the rain turning to slush. Taggie went into the cabin and shut the door.

Rain lashed against the hull, smearing the cabin's small window. Taggie, Sophie and Jemima pressed their faces up against it nonetheless. The *Angelhawk*'s usual smooth ride had vanished. The ship was bucking about now as she rode through the turbulent winds generated by the cloudswarm. Then the sun vanished behind a dense grey bank of stormcloud. It was the first time since they'd launched that the sun was missing from the sky, and Taggie found it mildly perturbing. The *Angelhawk* lurched suddenly, her prow lifting so she soared past mountains of cloud. When Taggie glanced up, she saw a boulder tumbling wildly inside the grey vapour. It was close, missing the *Angelhawk* by less than a hundred metres. She winced. Lightning flared between the cloud tips.

Then they were past the first swirl, and into clearer air. It was still gloomy, with lightning flashes sizzling in the distance. Rain continued to pound the planks. A weird tapping noise began as something started striking the hull – coming from every direction.

'Hailstones,' Taggie said. 'So that's where they all get their ice scars from. We should have bought ourselves some of those leather hoods back in Tarimbi.'

'Favian, get that sail furled, curse you!' the voice of Captain Rebecca bellowed.

'More rocks – look!' Jemima said.

'Those aren't rocks,' Sophie told her.

'Oh sweet Heavens,' Jemima groaned nervously. 'That's what Earl Maril'bo heard.'

'Harpoons ready!'

The girls watched nervously as the flock of loxraptors arrowed in towards the *Angelhawk*. Flying reptile predators, with scaly, grey and green wings that were ten metres across fully extended, they opened their long, fang-lined beaks to screech their challenge at the lumbering intruder. Long, powerful fin-tipped tails lashed about frenziedly.

Then Taggie saw Favian still struggling with the tipsail, whose canvas had escaped the ropes to flap about wildly, beating at him as he desperately tried to haul it in. The loxraptors had also seen him. Three of them turned towards him and hurtled inward.

A pair of lower deck harpoons streaked out, followed seconds later by both upper-deck harpoons. Two loxraptors veered away sharply. A harpoon struck the third, its bad magic tip slicing clean through flesh and bone. The creature howled, and started to flail, slowing rapidly. Captain Rebecca sent the wheel spinning, pushing the sailtails over to their limit. The *Angelhawk* bucked as cold winds pummelled at it. And then Favian lost his grip. Taggie saw it happen. When the ship's abrupt lurch came, his hand slipped on the wet spar and he went cartwheeling away from the mast, making a desperate grab for the flapping sail as he went. Somehow he managed to catch the corner of the canvas, to be tugged along by the ship as the wind buffeted it through the cloudswarm.

'Harpoons!' Captain Rebecca hollered above the growl of the wind and rain.

But they took time to reload, Taggie knew. She'd watched the crew practise often enough. In the meantime, Favian was swinging roughly on the end of the sail, and several loxraptors were banking sharply to line up on him.

Taggie burst out of her cabin. On her wrist the charmsward bands slid round smoothly and efficiently, their tiny symbols emitting a sharp blue light as she prepared to cast her spell. Outside, the rain struck her like a solid sheet, drenching her instantly. Hailstones hit her unprotected skin – it was like getting stung by a swarm of wasps. She hurriedly cast a shield enchantment, feeling the spell spin protectively round her.

'Get back inside, girl!' Captain Rebecca roared at her, wings beating steadily. Taggie ignored her. The first loxraptor was speeding forward, its wings pumping slickly, rain streaming along its scaly flanks. Favian dangled enticingly, just ahead of it. Taggie lined her hand up on the loxraptor's powerful sinuous body, holding her forefinger rigid, pointing – '*Droiak!*'

The destruction spell ripped out of her fingertip like a bolt of sunlight, dazzling everybody. The loxraptor's corpse tumbled away into the rain.

The rest of the flock squawked in alarm, shooting off in all directions. Except for one, which remained intent on the precariously swaying crewman.

Taggie brought her arm round, utterly determined. '*Droiak!*' The second loxraptor disintegrated.

'Oh yes!' Captain Rebecca laughed uproariously, her sodden hair reduced to long worms that wiggled fast, shaking droplets from their tips. 'That's my sorceress girl! Send them all back to the Hell Realm where they belong.'

Lantic was at Taggie's side, gripping the deck rail. 'He's falling,' he yelled above the noise of the fierce squall. Hailstone strikes had produced several tiny cuts on his cheeks that were trickling blood down his skin.

'Don't you dare,' the captain warned. 'My charter is live passengers, not dead heroes.'

But Lantic was already running along the slippery deck towards the foot of the mast. Hailstones bounced off the deck and hull around him. The *Angelhawk* floundered in a wild gust of wind and the whole ship bucked, sending the prow swinging across the livid clouds. Taggie caught a glimpse of the loxraptors circling behind the stern. And Lantic had reached the mast.

'No!' Taggie yelled at Lantic.

He turned, the blood on his cheeks mingling with rainwater to drip off his chin. 'He'll fall. Nobody can hold on through this.'

'You'll slip off the mast and be lost. Please, Lantic! I can't lose you.'

Lantic let out a moan of frustration.

'I'll go,' Sophie said.

'No.' Felix came streaking nimbly along the net, his white fur slicked back flat from the rain, his tail a soggy spine. 'My job,' he said.

Lantic paused, then nodded. He rummaged through his satchel, and pulled out one of his little spider contraptions. 'Here!' He thrust it into Felix's forepaws. He was still incanting instructions to the contraption when Felix dashed out through the net and on to the mast.

Wind, rain and hail hammered against the mast as Felix raced along it. But the squirrel kept perfect balance. Even the erratic judders that ran through the ship didn't affect him. He reached the tip, and let go of the spider. The little metallic contraption whirled round the wood, spinning out a gossamer thread; then it was scampering down the sail, its pointed legs wiggling too fast to see. It arrived at Favian's desperately grasping hands, and darted along his arm, still spinning out its single gossamer strand. Once it had looped the strand under his shoulders, it began to pull itself back up, towing Favian with it.

'Come on,' Taggie urged the little anamage contraption.

She could see the loxraptors spiralling in closer to the stern as the spider gradually hoisted Favian level with the mast. The crewman wrapped his arms round the pole and began crawling back to the deck. Felix stayed with him.

'Yes!' Taggie exclaimed joyfully. Lantic was grinning wildly.

'Taggie!' Jemima screamed from the open cabin door.

Taggie was just turning when she heard the harpoon launcher on the deck above her firing. The slender metal barb flashed away, missing the loxraptor which was hurtling down vertically directly at Taggie, its beak open wide—

Just before it reached her, a blue-green death spell hit it smack between the eyes. From being a ravenous, lethal predator it was instantly transformed into a ton of dead meat whipping past the *Angelhawk*.

Everyone looked round. Lord Colgath stood on the decking, his smoke cloak a-glimmer in the icy rain. An arm was extended up, bony fingers covered in elaborate rings. The diminishing death-spell wizardry clung to them like a layer of phosphorescent mist. 'I thought you could do with some help,' he said simply.

'Oh sweet Heavens preserve us,' Captain Rebecca croaked in fear.

THE ISLE OF BANMULA

'You brought a *Karrak Lord* on to my ship,' Captain Rebecca thundered. Even trepidation didn't diminish her ire. Every strand of her black hair was sticking up stiffly, crowning her in ebony spikes.

After three hours toiling through rain and clouds, the *Angelhawk* had finally cleared the storm cluster, sailing out into clear skies; the warm sun drying the water from its decks and sails. Now the united crew confronted the passengers in the wardroom. Several of the crew carried enchanted daggers, though they kept them held low. Few of them dared look directly at Lord Colgath, instead focusing their anger on Dad.

'Would you have accepted our charter if you'd known?' Dad asked.

It was the wrong tone to take with the captain, who growled dangerously. Her wings gave a single beat which slapped the air.

Taggie was sitting at a table with Jemima, who was carefully stroking Favian's long ice-cuts. As her finger moved over each slash, it would slowly close up, the skin knitting back together. Taggie was helping as best she could, dabbing the dried blood away with a cloth. Favian kept sighing in relief as the pain was vanquished. 'My shoulder, Lady Jemima?' he said hopefully. His muscles there had been badly torn as he clung to the sail. Jemima smiled and lay her hands on his shoulder.

Several of the crew were standing round the table, watching in wonder as Jemima tended to their friend. They'd left their daggers in their scabbards. Taggie was pretty sure where their sympathies lay. She stood beside Dad and confronted the captain. 'It was Lord Colgath who killed the loxraptor.'

'And they all saved me,' Favian said. 'See what Lady Jemima is doing now.' He moved his shoulder again. 'I will not forget my debt.'

Captain Rebecca gave Taggie a troubled glance, then tossed her head at the Dark Lord standing silently at the back of the room. 'What kind of Karrak would do such a thing?'

'Yo, Captain,' Earl Maril'bo said, a warning tone in his voice. 'Be nice, now. This is the brother of the Grand Lord.'

The members of the crew drew their breaths as one. Those with daggers gripped them a little tighter.

'Not helping,' Taggie told the elf.

Captain Rebecca raised her arm. She was holding a thin cutlass with a single green stripe of enchantment glowing along its length, which lined up on the Dark Lord. 'You leave my ship. All of you! Take your chances in the sky.

There will be some dark fallen angel who will comfort you out there.'

'You're overreacting,' Dad said in his best reasonable tone. 'You can't win a fight against us. Come on. You saw what Agatha alone can do.'

The cutlass shifted round to Taggie. 'And you hellbound swine cannot sail this ship without us,' Captain Rebecca said. 'I would rather die than help you unleash your evil on Banmula.'

'We're not unleashing evil anywhere,' Taggie said irritably.

'Sorceress deceiver!' Captain Rebecca shouted furiously. 'Every word from your mouth is a lie.'

Maklepine slowly put his hand over the captain's, pushing the cutlass down. 'Captain. Enough. That is no way to speak to the Queen of Dreams.'

Taggie wasn't terribly surprised by his intervention. The deep blue eyes of the shipsmage hadn't left her since he came into the wardroom.

'What?' Captain Rebecca gave the shipsmage a crazed

129

look of disbelief. 'What say you?'

The crew were now staring at Taggie in amazement.

'The Queen of Dreams.' Maklepine bowed slightly, and turned to Jemima. 'Which, I believe, makes you the First Realm's Blossom Princess. And as their father, you must be Prince Dino. So then this is Sophie, Lady-in-Waiting of Piadro's flock whose endeavours in London have been the talk of Air's taverns this last week. And you, Felix, are quite plainly a Weldowen. Which I think just leaves you, Prince Lantic, son of the War Emperor.'

'What?' Captain Rebecca moaned incredulously. 'The Queen of Dreams . . . This cannot be.'

'It is,' Taggie told her simply. 'I am.'

'What?'

'You might be better served asking why we are here,' Lord Colgath said in his deep bass voice.

Captain Rebecca glanced at Maklepine, who shrugged. She brought the cutlass up again, but it was a half-hearted gesture. 'Why?'

'We're trying to prevent the war, to stop thousands of people from being killed,' Taggie said.

'What?'

'You mean *how*, actually,' Lantic told her kindly.

'How?'

'By finding Mirlyn's Gate, and letting those who do not belong here return to their own Universe,' Dad said.

'Wait – you're the son of the War Emperor?' Captain Rebecca asked. '*You?*'

'Er, yes.' Lantic coughed.

'And you're the brother of the Grand Lord?'

'Yes.'

'And this is our quest,' Taggie said. 'To reach Banmula in order to find Mirlyn's Gate. After that, we will happily leave the *Angelhawk* and find another ship to carry us further.'

The cutlass was lowered. 'Further, where?' the captain asked.

Taggie tried not to smile at the curiosity she could see burning so brightly in the captain's face. 'All I know is that Mirlyn's Gate was brought to the Realm of Air through the Great Gateway Forilux. Our hunt will begin at Banmula.'

'And you.' Captain Rebecca addressed the Dark Lord again. 'You mean us no harm?'

'No. The Queen of Dreams has my pledge to help her.'

'You killed the loxraptor,' Captain Rebecca said as if she'd only just realized it. Her stiff hair grew looser, the strands coiling up and waving round.

'Captain?' Maklepine asked tentatively.

'And you say that after Banmula you will voyage through Air to find Mirlyn's Gate?' Captain Rebecca asked.

Taggie proudly held her head up. 'We will.'

The cutlass was slowly pushed back into its sheath. 'No matter where it is hidden?'

'No matter where,' Sophie said.

'For a voyage like that, you will need a good ship. The very best, in fact. With a fearless and loyal crew.'

'That we will,' Taggie said.

'There are none better than the *Angelhawk*.'

'So I've heard.'

Captain Rebecca's smile was greedy enough to scare a loxraptor. 'A voyage that will be talked about in every port-park tavern for uncounted generations,' she whispered, not looking at anyone. 'A ship crewed by heroes that saved two universes. Will you sing about it, too, elf?'

'For time evermore,' Earl Maril'bo assured her.

'Then it is agreed: the *Angelhawk* will take you to Mirlyn's Gate.'

'Thank you,' Taggie said, feeling unbelievably relieved.

'Of course,' Captain Rebecca said as she turned to Dad. 'Such a charter will not be cheap.'

12

ISLE HO!

It was barely another two days' sailing before they finally arrived at Banmula. The old capital isle was a much larger and rounder than Tarimbi, though it was nothing close to spherical. *More like a potato*, Taggie thought as the *Angelhawk* approached the old capital.

The lush vegetation that covered most of the isle was a relief after a week voyaging. Leaves that shone with a multitude of green shades rippled in the light breeze, flowers of every hue speckled the ground, vying with ripe glossy fruit for variety. She hadn't realized how wearying a monotony of blue could be until she'd been immersed in it for so long.

Captain Rebecca was at her customary place on the upper deck, shouting orders as the ship drifted in towards the three towers of Banmula's port park. Taggie was having to grip the net to keep herself secure as gravity faded along with the ship's movement.

'Furl the tipsails!'

'Do you think she'll keep her word?' Sophie asked quietly.

Taggie did her best not to glance in the captain's

direction. 'She has no reason not to.'

'And every reason to keep it,' Lantic said. 'She's seen the damage your destruction spell can inflict.'

'I'm not threatening people to make them do what I say. That's not what I am,' Taggie told him. She felt her feet leave the decking as the last sails were furled and the *Angelhawk* was finally becalmed.

Felix made his way along the net above their heads. 'We have a far more effective weapon than violence to use against the captain.'

Taggie grinned up at the white squirrel. 'Money.'

'True,' Sophie said knowingly. 'Its loss is a pain like an enchanted dagger in her heart.'

'You're forgetting her hunger for fame,' Lantic said. 'She wants her exploits to be sung about in a thousand years' time.'

'Oh, Heavens,' Sophie muttered. 'Well I'm not singing that ballad.'

'Make it your opening number,' Felix teased cheerfully. 'That way you get it over and done with.'

'Fly out the landing cable,' Captain Rebecca shouted at Jualius.

The bosun slipped through the elasticated hole in the upper deck netting. He flew up to the prow of the ship, and pulled the end of a thick cable out of its big reel. Sophie watched him tug it towards an empty wharf.

'I do love the First Realm,' she said. 'But this is a life I could easily live. Sailing between isles, carrying cargoes, making deals with merchants, fighting loxraptors.'

'Getting slashed to ribbons by ice flakes,' Lantic said. 'Getting smashed to pieces by continent storms. Being eaten by loxraptors. Being harpooned by pirates.'

'Those scars still hurting?' Sophie jeered back at him. 'Is that's what making you so tetchy?'

'Hey, I healed him properly,' Jemima protested.

Lantic's hand went halfway to his face before he managed to stop it. 'Next time I'll animate my tunic armour,' he admitted.

'I think we'll all be buying hoods, goggles and gloves in this town,' Taggie said.

'What's that?' Jemima asked. She'd been watching the isle closely ever since she came out of her cabin.

Taggie looked where her sister was pointing. On the side of the port park furthest away from the town were four thick pillars of wooden beams almost half as high as the tower they were approaching. Their tops were uneven, with broken, rotting beams jabbing up into the sky. Clearly, they had once been a lot taller.

'It's like they're stumps,' Felix said.

'Of a giant's docking tower,' Lantic concluded.

He was right, Taggie thought. 'Captain!' she called. 'What is that structure?'

Captain Rebecca's grin showed off her gold teeth again. 'Ah, those there ruins, my young Queen, are all that remains of Exator's Folly.'

'What's that?' Taggie asked, wondering just how

much she would regret the question.

'Exator was a skyman who married the Highlord Piaffelo's sister. He was either a visionary, a hopeless dreamer, or a lunatic – it all depends who you ask. But he had a fierce ambition driving him through life; so much so, that he started off as a simple galley boy when he was eight, and by the time he reached his nineteenth birthday he owned his first ship. By twenty-eight he had one of the biggest merchant fleets in the Realm of Air. But that accomplishment was nothing more than the start of his dream. So with all that money and the Highlord's support he set to building the *Lady Silvaris* – named after his wife.'

'And that was his folly?' Jemima asked.

Captain Rebecca sucked down air as she regarded her eager audience. 'Depends how you look at it, Blossom Princess. The *Lady Silvaris* was one of a kind, and we will never see her like again. She was the greatest ship ever made, so big she needed her own special tower just to be built – that's what those ruins are. They say a whole forest in France was cut down to supply the oak for the tower, and imported from the Outer Realm at fabulous expense. Then another forest followed for her hull. She carried a crew of two hundred and fifty souls. When her sails were finally unfurled, they cast a shadow across half of Banmula.'

'Where did she go?' a rapt Jemima asked.

'Ahh . . .' Captain Rebecca exhaled happily. 'That is the most fantastic part of Exator's obsession. The *Lady Silvaris* was built to sail past the darkward ice isles that mark the boundary where the true coldness begins.'

'The true coldness?'

'Air that is so cold, it burns when you breathe it in. And, that, Blossom Princess, extends all the way out to the Heavens. You see, it was Exator's mad dream to visit the angels themselves. He believed that us skyfolk weren't just brought here by them at the start of the First Times, but that we are directly descended from them. He wanted to acquaint himself with our distant family.'

'Gosh,' Taggie blurted.

'Amazing,' Lantic said in admiration.

'Now that's the kind of voyage I'd definitely go on,' Sophie said wistfully.

Taggie grinned at her friend's enthusiasm, and turned back to study Banmula. Jualius had reached the wharf, and the towerhands waiting there slowly reeled in the cable, bringing the *Angelhawk* carefully to the tower. As they drew closer, more skyfolk took shorter mooring ropes over, and the ship was secured to the wharf.

Taggie studied the other boats docked at the towers. It seemed as if all their crews were fully occupied getting them ready to sail. She guessed everyone was preparing to chase the comet.

Dad glided up the ladder to the upper deck. 'Everyone ready?' he asked.

They waited for Captain Rebecca to pay the docking fee to an assistant portmaster, then set off down the tower.

'Where are we going first?' Earl Maril'bo asked.

'The Great Gateway site,' Jemima said. She was back in her blue dress, which covered her armour. 'That's where they came through. I'll see what I can sight there.'

As they walked into town, Taggie looked around in curiosity. The buildings were all a lot larger than those of Tarimbi, and looked Tudor-ish with their black wooden frames and tiny lead-lined widows. Every roof seemed to have a rotunda mounted high, with arched openings where skyfolk could come and go. But time had made them sag and shift so there wasn't a straight wall anywhere to be seen.

Gateway Square was in the middle of town. Ancient covered markets occupied two sides of the square, while a

stone guildhall formed the third side. The elaborate stone frescoes and statues that once covered the façade were cracked and broken. A mishmash of buttresses held up the walls now, clearly added later, themselves under siege from vines and weeds.

'All the damage here is the same,' said Earl Maril'bo. 'It has to be the destruction spell the Grand Lord struck Forilux with.'

The last side of the square, where Forilux had once stood, was now a row of shops and timber yards. They looked very shabby compared to the older buildings. The enormous fountain basins of the square itself had also suffered devastation. Where elaborate jets of water used to play dainty patterns now festered big muddy craters where bedraggled marsh plants grew wild.

Jemima faced the ramshackle line of shops with an expression of dismay. 'There's nothing left at all.'

'It was a long time ago,' Taggie said comfortingly. 'Have a go anyway. We've come a long way to get here.'

Jemima reluctantly took out her little purse of rune stones. With one hand gripping Prince Salaro's letter, she threw the rune stones and let them fall to the ground. A puzzled frown crossed her face as she studied them. 'He was here so briefly. The trail just . . .' She looked upwards at the empty sky. 'Goes away.'

'But it is a trail,' Felix told her encouragingly. 'We're another step closer.'

Jemima gave him a grateful smile.

'So what's our next step?' Sophie asked.

Dad turned full circle, taking in the whole square. 'This was the heart of the town. Somebody must have seen them.'

'Yeah, but dude, they wouldn't necessarily know what they were seeing,' Earl Maril'bo said thoughtfully. 'The best way to hide something is right out in the open. Man, I'll bet you some serious coinage they would have come through looking just like all the other ragtag bands of soldiers heading home after the battle.'

Dad nodded in agreement. 'And the first thing they did was leave Banmula. Jem just confirmed that.'

'So they took a ship,' Lantic said, speaking quickly as his thoughts formed. 'And we know the date they came through.'

'There will be records,' Taggie said in growing excitement. There were times when Lantic's devotion to methodical logic really paid off. She held up her hand, and he gave her a high-five. They grinned at each other.

'The portmaster registers the arrival and departure of every ship,' Sophie said.

'From a thousand years ago?' Felix asked dubiously. 'Will they still exist?'

'Governments never throw anything away,' Dad said. 'You should see what some of the vaults under the First Realm palace are full of.'

'Yes, but . . .' Taggie's good humour began to fade. *A thousand years?*

'Only one way to find out,' Lantic said briskly.

The portmaster's office was one of the tallest buildings on the edge of port park. Eight storeys high, with the very top floor looking like an elaborate glasshouse, the portmaster had his private office there, with its curving glass walls and ceiling giving him a unrivalled view out across port park and up into the infinity of Air.

It was phenomenally warm inside, with the sun beating down on the glass. Leaves on the plants that sent their shoots winding up the wooden supports shrivelled round the edges as they burned under the bright light and stifling air.

The portmaster himself was a Jannermol called Mr Howard, who enjoyed the heat that filled his domain. He stood on his four stumpy legs behind a semi-circular desk, with his sinuous arms and neck extended out from the hairy shell that covered his body.

The pincer hands on his scaly blue arm closed on a square of parchment, and brought it closer to his face. 'As I understand it,' he said to the company assembled below him, 'you wish to review our records?'

'We do, sir,' Dad said.

'For what purpose?'

'We are scholars, sir, from the First Realm. We wish to add knowledge to our library.'

'Scholars?' Mr Howard blinked his wide eyes slowly. His head, with its cap of shell, slowly moved forward as his neck curved, giving him a closer view. 'You are strange-looking scholars.'

'These youngsters are my assistants,' Dad said smoothly, 'who will take notes for me. And my elf friend is our travelling companion.'

Taggie was impressed with herself for keeping a straight face. She worried Jemima would start laughing, though.

'And which of our records do you wish to review, my friend of letters?'

'Those of the ships here when Rothgarnal was fought, and the Great Gateway destroyed.'

'I see. You wish to study the war?'

'Yes, sir. The more we learn and teach of the past, the more I believe we can avoid making those mistakes again.'

'Dear me.' Mr Howard made a gurgling noise that was his chuckle. 'You sound like you are siding with the Queen of Dreams.'

'Sir?' Dad asked cautiously.

'Apparently, she opposes the coming war. Fresh news arrives with every ship and is much gossiped over in the taverns – so I'm told. I'm surprised you don't know that.'

'Our ship encountered a continent storm. We were in port a long time undergoing repairs. We didn't hear any news.'

'Dear me, a continent storm? You must have an excellent captain to survive such an encounter.'

'She is most professional, yes, sir.'

'What an adventure for a man of letters such as yourself.'

'Yes, sir. Er . . . the request?'

Mr Howard blinked again. 'Request?'

'To study your records for our library?'

'Oh, indeed.' Both of Mr Howard's arms slid about over the desk like sluggish serpents. One pincer picked up a chit, the other a stamp which was pressed into an inkpad. The chit was duly authorized and handed down to Dad. 'My assistant will show you to the records hall.'

Dad bowed smartly. 'Thank you, sir.'

The records hall was tucked away behind the portmaster's building, looking like a warehouse. It made the palace library seem small. But every ledger was identical, with only the date, stamped in gold leaf, distinguishing between them.

An assistant portmaster, another Jannermol, led them down a wide aisle at the far end.

'This is the section you require,' he said.

'Thank you,' Dad replied courteously.

'You'd make a great spy, Dad,' Jemima said, once the Jannermol had left them. 'You were so convincing in front of the portmaster.'

'Thank you, sweetheart,' Dad said, without any conviction at all. 'But you're still not going surfing again. Now let's find what we're here for.'

'This is the decade,' Lantic called out. He was standing in front of shelving three times his height. 'The year of Rothgarnal is up at the top. I'll get it.' There was a ladder that ran on rails fixed to the shelving. He slid it into place and put his foot on the bottom rung, which promptly snapped.

'I'll get it,' Sophie told him wryly, and took off into the air. Her wings stirred up clouds of dust, but she hovered at the top and pulled out several ledgers.

'Let's see what ships left in the week following the end of the battle,' Dad said, and adjusted his glasses.

The ledger creaked as he opened it. More dust fell out.

Dad started to turn the pages carefully; more than one cracked and tore as he moved it. Then he stopped, staring captivated at the page he'd found. 'Oh, great Heavens,' he gasped.

Earl Maril'bo leaned over his shoulder, reading the list of arrivals and departures. 'The best place to hide is in plain sight,' he smiled. 'That is so beautiful, man.'

13

A LONG-AGO VOYAGE

Either Captain Rebecca no longer worried about Lord Colgath, or she hid her nervousness perfectly. Taggie suspected the latter. Whichever it was, the captain welcomed all her passengers politely as they slid into her topdeck cabin. Secured on a pedestal in the middle of the lounge was an orocompass, an impressive mechanical sphere made up of brass bands and clockwork mechanisms that helped every captain navigate through the Realm of Air. Wind charts were pinned to a wall. The wall behind her desk had over a dozen clocks fastened to it, each one keeping the time of a major isle. The array of weapons she kept in a glass cabinet was also remarkable – in a lethal way. Taggie didn't know what half of them did, though the violet glimmer of bad magic pulsing behind the glass was disturbing.

Captain Rebecca remained behind her desk, her wings quivering occasionally to keep her in place, and gave the delegation an expectant look.

'We need to know about Exator and the *Lady Silvaris*,' Dad said.

Captain Rebecca gave him a suspicious glance. 'Why? I've already told the youngsters everything I know.'

'No you haven't,' Taggie said with some indignation. 'For a start, was it successful? Did they meet an angel? How far into the coldness did it get, all the way to a star?'

Captain Rebecca gave her a very startled glance. 'Aye, you're really not from around here are you? My apologies, young Queen, everyone in the Realm of Air knows the story of the *Lady Silvaris*.'

'So what happened?' Lantic asked.

'The *Lady Silvaris* hasn't yet returned,' Captain Rebecca said in a melancholy voice. 'This isle still awaits the day she will appear out of the darkwards sky.'

'She set sail a thousand years ago,' Dad said in an accusing tone.

'About that, aye.'

'Three days after Rothgarnal was fought and Forilux was destroyed.'

'Three days?' Captain Rebecca murmured. 'I knew the *Lady Silvaris* launched in the same year as the war. But . . . are you sure?'

'We checked the portmaster's records,' Earl Maril'bo said. 'Three days.'

A look of wonder spread over Captain Rebecca's face. 'Mirlyn's Gate was on board when it launched. Of course it was! A unique ship that can take you anywhere, and a Gate that has to be hidden forever. It's a perfect combination.'

'Do you think Exator would've agreed to such a voyage?' Dad asked. 'Sailing to the stars was his life's obsession, after all.'

'He was definitely a man of honour,' the captain said. 'I doubt if he would refuse the War Emperor the opportunity to save the realms from invasion by the Dark Universe.'

'You told us the *Lady Silvaris* could withstand the true coldness of the Heavens,' Lantic said. 'Could she also sail into the sun?'

'Don't be stupid, Prince. Nothing can sail into the sun.'

'But that is one of the great theories scholars have devised over the centuries,' Taggie said.

Captain Rebecca snorted in contempt. 'Not scholars from this Realm,' she said. 'The smallest child here could tell you such a thing is nonsense.'

'Why?' Felix asked.

'There is a limit on how far sunward you can sail,' Captain Rebecca explained. 'As the ice isles mark the start of the true coldness, so the lava rivers dictate where the air ends. There is a gulf surrounding the sun where the only thing that exists is raw heat. And we've only ever seen the lava rivers through telescopes – you cannot get within five thousand miles of them, your ship would simply burn to ash.'

'Which would then be blown darkwards by the hot winds,' Lantic concluded. 'So the Grand Lord and War Emperor wouldn't do that, because Mirlyn's Gate would fly free from the ruined ship and might be found. A small chance, admittedly, but they would not leave its resting place to chance.'

'So the *Lady Silvaris* did sail for the stars,' Earl Maril'bo said. 'Mr Blake's second lesser theory was right, but not in a way he imagined. Mirlyn's Gate was taken to be guarded by angels.'

'If the *Lady Silvaris* sailed into the coldness and didn't come back, the Grand Lord and the War Emperor would have achieved what they set out to do,' Dad agreed.

'That can't be right,' Taggie blurted.

'Why not?' Dad asked. 'I know it means you can't recover Mirlyn's Gate, darling, but it would certainly explain why nobody can ever find it.'

Taggie closed her eyes and saw a lifeless ship covered in glittering frost, floating gently through the darkness between stars; her crew dead, frozen in their watch posts, in their beds, at the wardroom table . . . 'No,' she said. 'Captain, you told us there were two hundred and fifty crew on board the *Lady Silvaris*, right?'

'Aye, at least that many.'

'Just how are you going to convince two hundred and fifty people to commit suicide for a cause, however noble? Some of them might, yes – but all? I don't believe it. When the *Lady Silvaris* left, the crew must have believed they would be coming back. They knew they weren't sailing into the sun or out to the stars, they were going somewhere else. A very difficult place to reach, yes, but one that gave them a chance of returning, however slim.'

The lounge was quiet for a moment.

'Where?' Jemima asked.

'It was Exator's ship,' Taggie said. 'He might have

agreed to carry Mirlyn's Gate for the War Emperor, but he was still captain. He's the key to this. The Grand Lord and the War Emperor spent three days here on Banmula before the *Lady Silvaris* launched. We know that. So what were they doing for those three days?'

'Deciding the final hiding place with Exator,' Sophie said in excitement. 'That's all they could be doing.'

'Exator knew the Realm of Air,' Taggie said. 'Not them. They were as ignorant of it as we were. He was the one who must have given them real options.'

'Exator must have had a home here, a place he planned his great voyage from,' Earl Maril'bo said. 'We should take Jemima there.'

'I wonder if he had any descendants?' Lantic mused. 'They would surely keep their ancestral home.'

'Ha!' Captain Rebecca chortled. 'Even your mind works like a Second Realm contraption, Prince. Yes, Exator had nine children, and that was over a thousand years ago. Today, every skychild born on Banmula is related to him. That is why this isle still believes the *Lady Silvaris* will return.'

Jemima's head snapped round. 'Captain,' she said in a voice that was more challenge than question. 'Where were you born?'

Captain Rebecca laughed delightedly. 'Oh, you're good, Blossom Princess, very good. Aye, I was born on Banmula. Exator is my grandsire, twenty-seven generations removed. I grew up in the shadow of the family mansion.'

Captain Rebecca grinned all the way down the docking tower as she led Taggie and the others back into town.

Lord Colgath had decided to accompany them. 'If there are any secrets hidden in Exator's house I would like to be there when you find them,' he said. Taggie wasn't sure if he was simply bored, or if he didn't quite trust them. Either way, she didn't try and argue him out of it.

They were halfway down the tower when she saw a newly arrived ship floating close to one of the other towers; a skywoman was towing its landing cable to a free wharf. It was smaller and narrower than the *Angelhawk*. 'Who's that?' she asked Captain Rebecca.

The swirl of yellow stars in the captain's sapphire eyepatch tightened up. 'That's the *Dory Maria*, out of Tantuma. I know the captain, he's more pirate than merchant if you ask me. See how many harpoon hatches there are?'

Taggie tried, but they were a long way down the tower now. She flipped her hands against the bamboo lattice, powering herself along towards the ground.

Exator's family estate was a mansion on the edge of town. Built from some kind of reddish stone in the shape of an oval dome, it looked as if someone had buried half of an egg in the ground. Huge vertical windows ran up the curving sides, giving it long dark eyes to look over the surrounding streets. Six tall rotundas crowned the apex, with narrow door arches. There were several tarpaulins stretched over various parts of the roof. Weeds and small bushes grew from the cracks they attempted to cover, providing a shaggy green fringe to the fabric.

'Ha! Here we have my family's proud legacy,' Captain Rebecca said with thick irony as she stood outside the wide entrance gates that had rusted open.

'You grew up here?' Felix asked, standing on his hind legs to give the air a suspicious sniff. He put his purple-lens glasses on: Second Realm contraptions that could reveal enchantments.

'Over there, actually,' the captain said, pointing to a row of tall houses leaning at precarious angles. 'My seventh cousins, the Micalwaths, live in the mansion itself. But they only use seventeen of the shell chambers.'

'Oh. Why didn't you all live in it? Had you fallen out with each other?'

'No. It's just that the other two hundred and thirty-five shell chambers need repairing. None of us had the money. Still don't.'

The captain walked up the wide steps to the massive double doors that were set into the head of the dome at ground level. A whispered enchantment, and a much smaller door set in the base swung open for them.

One by one, they passed into the gloomy interior.

Taggie looked round with interest. The oval dome was a single giant space inside, filled with slender stems supporting shell chambers – fat lens-shaped rooms with circular windows on the upper surface, and an entrance-way at the rim. A number of them had collapsed. Like trees felled in a jungle, the taller ones had crashed into their neighbours as they toppled, bringing them down as well.

She heard a sharp intake of breath, and turned to see Jemima standing just inside the door, surrounded by a blaze of sunlight. Her sister looked so scared that Taggie immediately prepared a shield enchantment. 'What's the matter, Jem?'

Jemima glanced round nervously. 'Something has woken,' she said in a timid voice.

'Woken?' Captain Rebecca said scornfully. 'Not my idle cousins, it's not yet midday.'

Felix went over to Jemima and drew his sword, its blade glowing a delicate emerald. Lantic scrambled round in his bag for his own revealor glasses as his scarlet and black tunic hardened and transformed into an armour suit. Sophie tugged her crossbow from its strap at her side.

'Let's all calm down,' Dad said. 'Jemima, what did you see, darling?'

She shook her head, her face pale. 'I don't know. I just felt something really old stirring. It knew we had come.'

'Use your runes,' Felix suggested.

Jemima's face told everyone she didn't want to, but she took out the little leather purse anyway, and shook the black stones. They landed on the worn marble tiles of the floor, and she frowned. 'That's wrong. How can that happen?'

'What?' Taggie edged closer for a look. She saw the stones had all landed so their blank face was uppermost. 'What does that mean?'

'None of the stones *have* a blank face,' Jemima said. 'The runes have vanished.'

'Perhaps they're hiding,' Sophie said. 'Something has frightened them.'

'Not helping,' Felix said, as his tail swished from side to side.

Taggie gave the bleak interior of the massive mansion another nervous glance.

Captain Rebecca guffawed. 'I have never seen such a bunch of timid flowers. Can you really be the same people who saved Favian? Come on, this is my family home, I played cover-and-hunt here with my cousins when I was half your age. Every time I was victorious, my parents had to spend hours finding me – they had to bring in a seer once. And the fights we had! Aye, pirates and merchants we were, in ships made of furniture and sheets. I won every time.'

'You mean you bullied us every time,' a loud voice said from above them.

Taggie looked up to see a handsome skywoman staring down at them from the entrance of a modestly sized shell chamber on a thirty-metre-high stem. She was obviously related to Captain Rebecca, with the same thick profusion of ebony hair that coiled leisurely around her head. She wore a simple green cotton skirt and leather jerkin over a white blouse.

'May I present my cousin Penelopi?' Captain Rebecca boomed. 'Penelopi, how fare you?'

'Worse for seeing you,' Penelopi said. She spread her wings and flew slowly down. 'What are you doing here?'

'Showing my passengers the magnificent ancestral home, of course. They're rightly fascinated by Exator.'

'Your pardon for our intrusion, madam,' Dad said. 'But Exator was an amazing person. We are inspired by him.'

Penelopi's feathered feet folded up as she reached the floor and stood in front of the captain. She watched everyone as they sheepishly put their weapons away.

'So who are you?' Penelopi asked.

'Just a scholar with a few hours to spare,' Dad replied. 'I was wondering, did Exator leave a journal behind?'

'No.'

'What about papers and charts? Was there a particular star he was heading for?'

'Why do you need to know such things?' Penelopi asked suspiciously

'I am a scholar.'

'For the love of the Heavens, Penelopi,' Captain Rebecca snapped in exasperation. 'Show some manners and take our guests to Exator's study.'

Penelopi scowled at her cousin, then nodded with bad grace. 'Follow me.'

As they walked round the ground-level chambers deeper into the eyrie mansion, Taggie realized Penelopi hadn't seen Lord Colgath. His tricky concealment magic had worked well, but it would never last. The charmsward bands began to turn again, ready for the moment the surly skywoman noticed.

'So how's that lovely husband of yours, cousin?' Captain Rebecca asked merrily as they picked their way over rubble and avoided dank puddles.

Penelopi's sullen expression darkened further. 'He is away voyaging.'

'Has he finally been promoted to First Officer?'

'He is doing very well, thank you. He does not lie and cheat and steal his way across this realm.'

'Well, who does?'

Penelopi suddenly stopped walking. Her wings flapped once. 'He was engaged to *me*!'

'And you married him. Eventually.'

Jemima's jaw dropped down in astonishment at hearing such juicy gossip. She gave Taggie a secret grin. Taggie pressed a finger to her smiling lips.

'You lured him away with false promises,' Penelopi stormed. 'You broke his heart.'

'There was nothing false about them. It was just so sad that our love burned out very quickly.'

'You never loved him.'

'I loved him enough to let him go back to you. Happy landings all round, eh?'

Dad made a show of clearing his throat. 'Uh . . . ladies, the study?'

Penelopi glared at Captain Rebecca. Her arm thrust

out, pointing to a heavy door in the circular chamber she had stopped beside. 'Here! This is the very heart of our family. You may look, but you are to touch nothing. Understand?' Penelopi said sternly as she opened the door.

'Absolutely,' Dad said.

Exator's study was in much better condition than the rest of the mansion. A ring of blue-green lightstones shone from tiny nooks halfway up the concave walls. Below them, the inevitable bookcases contained shelf upon shelf of thick leather-bound books, complemented by innumerable pigeonholes stuffed with parchment scrolls. Several elaborate orocompasses stood on plinths, protected by glass covers. There was a family portrait hanging above the mantelpiece: Exator and his wife Silvaris standing in a pleasant garden, surrounded by their children – nine sons and two daughters, the youngest a mere infant, her wings nothing more than buds. Taggie smiled to herself, Silvaris had the same exuberant black hair as Captain Rebecca.

Jemima gasped, struggling for breath. 'It's here!' she rasped.

'Jem!' Dad held her close, worry in his eyes. 'It's all right, Jem.'

'What's here?' Penelopi demanded. 'What can you see?'

'It is a guardian seal,' Lord Colgath said in surprise. 'But not a kind I have encountered before.'

Penelopi turned round slowly, and her eyes finally found the Karrak Lord. She opened her mouth to scream.

Behind her, Captain Rebecca was smiling maliciously

as she raised a leather cosh loaded with lead balls, ready to beat her cousin unconscious.

'*Wonfi al turon*,' Taggie chanted quickly.

Penelopi closed her eyes with a surprised expression, and crumpled on to the floor, fast asleep.

'Did you do that?' Captain Rebecca complained.

Taggie ignored her. 'What is it?' she asked Lord Colgath.

The Dark Lord swept into the study, and turned a full circle. 'It is very faint, but still active. Can you not feel it?'

'No,' Taggie admitted with mild annoyance. She thought she could sense all types of magic these days.

'You must be able to!' Jem said. She was clinging to Dad for comfort.

Felix was looking round with his revealor glasses, as was Lantic.

'Something is concealed here,' Lord Colgath said. 'Not by strength, but by skill. The guardian seal is elusive. I only see it because the magic is disturbed somehow.'

'Disturbed?'

'I believe the Blossom Princess is right. It awoke.'

'Jem,' Taggie said benevolently 'I know this is hard, and you're scared, but do you know where this guardian magic is?'

Jemima gave her a resentful look from inside the circle of Dad's arms. 'It feels as if it's beneath us.'

Everybody looked at the floor. It was marble, old and worn with many tiny cracks. Blue, black, and dark-orange tiles made up an elaborate mosaic, with what Taggie assumed was the family crest in the centre – a pair of wings with an archway of stars above them.

'Why would it wake now?' Sophie asked.

'Because of us,' Lantic said. 'There is something about us that stirred it. Probably Lord Colgath. I don't suppose there have been any Karraks in Banmula since the Grand Lord set sail.'

'Some of us have been,' Lord Colgath said. 'Many brethren have searched for Mirlyn's Gate since Rothgarnal. I would be surprised if this place had not received a quiet visit from one of us.'

'All right,' Lantic said. 'So it has to be something else about us that is fairly unique.' He looked round at his companions and thought for a while. 'Ah! Perhaps it is in bloodlines! Lord Colgath is the son of the Grand Lord. I am the descendant of the original War Emperor. It may be that the guardian magic recognized the combination. Together we can make a claim to see whatever it is shielding.' His gaze went to the wings and stars crest. He knelt down beside it and put his hand on it. His lips moved as he uttered an opening spell.

The lightstones flickered, sending odd-shaped shadows slithering across the walls.

'My lord,' Lantic called.

Lord Colgath knelt down beside Lantic and pressed his hand on the crest. His rings started to glow brightly. The air grew colder, and the shadows quickened their flight.

'It's working,' Lantic cried. 'I can feel it now. The

enchantment is looking at us.'

Then the lightstones steadied, and the weird shadows began to retreat.

'What's wrong?' Sophie asked.

'It's not enough,' Lord Colgath said. 'The enchantment lacks something.'

'Exator was also part of choosing the Gate's hiding place,' Taggie said. 'Captain, you're one of Exator's heirs!'

Captain Rebecca's grin was inordinately smug as she joined Lantic and Lord Colgath, pressing her hand on the crest on the floor.

The lightstones went out. The tiny marble tiles of the crest began to glow from within. One slid down, then hurriedly shunted sideways, it was followed by another, a third . . .

THE HEIRS

They all stood around the crest, watching as its tiles rearranged themselves. Before long they were staring at a hole in the middle of the floor. With her heart pounding in excitement, Taggie peered down, but it was pitch black. She held out a hand, palm downwards. '*Falavor.*'

The illumination spell lit up the deep shaft below the study to show a crude set of stairs carved into the naked rock.

'Who goes first?' Lantic asked, clearly waiting to be told he should be the one.

'That'll be me, dude,' Earl Maril'bo said. 'It's what I'm here for, to fend off trouble.' He walked past a suddenly sulky Lantic, and started down the stairs. Felix drew his sword and scurried down behind the elf.

'It is my family's home,' Captain Rebecca said half apologetically to Lantic as she flew over the hole, and dropped down, keeping level with the white squirrel.

'Yay!' Sophie followed her.

'Go on, Lantic,' Dad said with a knowing smile.

The prince hurried down, animating his tunic's armour just in case.

Taggie followed Lord Colgath as he descended silently, his smoke cloak rippling over each step.

The chamber they found at the bottom was a smaller version of the study above, but not nearly as well preserved. It was cool and damp, the air smelling like wild mushrooms after the rain. Consequently, the wood of its bookshelves was mouldy and rotting. Most of the ledgers had turned to a soft mush that was merging into a single mass of pulp. Taggie thought it was mainly the spiderwebs that were holding everything together.

'There's no magic down here,' Lord Colgath said. 'Not of my father's, nor any of yours, I feel.'

'I think you're right,' Taggie said, depressed by the decay surrounding her.

'This is where they decided, though,' Lantic said, oblivious to the state of the secret chamber. 'They spent three days here arguing where to take Mirlyn's Gate. There must be some clue. Jemima?'

Jemima reluctantly cast her rune stones. She shook her head at the result, and threw again. 'I can't see anything of them. It was too long ago. Sorry.'

Taggie gave the opening in the chamber roof a shrewd look. 'Then why did they leave the guardian shield behind?'

'For the three heirs to find,' Earl Maril'bo said. 'There is something here for you.'

Taggie gave the chamber another exasperated look. 'There's nothing. All we know is that they made the decision here.'

'Perhaps that is what the guardian shield is telling us,' Felix suggested.

'Why, though?' Lantic asked. 'The odds of the three heirs turning up together are ridiculous.'

'Ridiculous,' Taggie repeated with a growing smile. 'But not impossible. Jem, show me the prince's letter.'

Jemima fumbled in her purse and produced the parchment.

Taggie squinted at the faint writing. 'Somewhere at some time the folk of the Realms and the people of the Dark Universe must sit at the same table and learn to live in harmony,' she read, then looked round at everyone. 'Prince Salaro said that was the hope of both the Grand Lord and the War Emperor. They hid the gate because of the threat of invasion in *their* time, so that when trust was finally reborn, Mirlyn's Gate could be re-opened without either side fearing invasion.'

'And the only way the three heirs would ever come here together would be in a time of peace,' Lantic concluded.

'Well, that didn't happen,' Felix said glumly.

'We're too early,' Sophie said gloomily. 'We should have waited another thousand years.'

'No, we're right on time,' Lantic said. 'Because the three heirs are here, and peacefully. It's everyone else that's the problem.'

'But this place isn't telling us anything.'

Lantic massaged his forehead as he concentrated. 'As you said, it tells us they made the decision here. So . . .

what did they use to make that decision? Captain, are those books and charts in the study the ones Exator used when he was planning his voyage?'

'Aye, of course,' Captain Rebecca said. 'It's his original library.'

'Then that's where the answer is,' Lantic said. He started up the stairs in a very determined manner.

Taggie and Sophie exchanged an amused glance at his behaviour, and followed him up.

'They used the knowledge on these shelves to find the location where they would hide Mirlyn's Gate,' Lantic continued when everyone was back in the study. 'So we use the books to make an identical list of possibilities. Captain, what would you suggest?'

She grinned approvingly at the prince. 'The obvious thing is to sail beyond the isles we know. Aye, maybe just keep sailing all the way around the sun, and hand the task down to their children who would be born on board. That would keep the Gate safe, yet ultimately it would become available again.'

'Er . . .' Jemima said.

'Just shush for a moment, darling,' Dad told her. 'Captain, how long would it take to sail around Air?'

'Centuries at least – not that anyone has ever done it.'

'Daddy.'

'All right,' Lantic said. 'That's one possibility. Now what else—'

'Hey!' Jemima stomped her foot. 'They're different!'

Everyone stared at her.

'What's different, Jem?' Taggie asked.

Jemima pointed down at the crest on the floor which had re-formed when they all left the secret chamber. 'The stars.'

Captain Rebecca barged past Sophie and Earl Maril'bo to examine the archway of stars that curved above the wings. 'You know, she's actually right. I think they are a little different.'

Jemima glared at the captain.

'In plain sight,' Earl Maril'bo said, and smiled in admiration.

'That's our clue?' Sophie asked.

'Oh!' the captain exclaimed. 'It might be more than a clue. If it's accurate . . . Let's see. That's definitely the Wingedwitch constellation, and I think that's The Axe, though it's an odd alignment. H u m m. Easy enough if that's truly the star pattern you can see from your destination and you know your navigation.' She lifted the glass case off the biggest orocompass in the study, a fine spherical apparatus of brass bands, each with precise measurements engraved beside complex astronomical markings. Its interior was packed with a globular clockwork mechanism. There were graduated dials set on the axis shaft protruding from the top of the shell of bands, which the captain turned like a safecracker, constantly referring to the new pattern of stars in the crest.

Taggie wanted to yell at her to hurry up. Didn't she understand they were close to finding out where the gate was? Didn't she understand the importance?

The captain began turning the bands around the outside, adjusting the small pearl arrow-shaped regulators that slid along each one. Finally she depressed a key on the very top.

All the cogwheels at the heart of the device began to whirr and buzz, regulator levers rocked about. The bands started to click round. Tiny wire indicator-hands slid along the measurement notches of the three largest bands.

Captain Rebecca let the orocompass run, and went over to the bookshelves. Her hand went along a shelf of large leather tomes.

'Here we go,' she said in satisfaction, and pulled one out.

'What's that?' Lantic asked.

'A star almanac.'

Taggie was practically hopping from one foot to the

other she was so excited. When she glanced round her friends she could see how eager they were. The tension was awful.

The captain slapped the almanac down on the desk and turned just as the orocompass mechanism finished its run. She bent over to read the numbers on the bands where various indicators had stopped, and ran her fingers down the columns, finding a number. 'Aye, this is it.' Her finger ran along the line.

Taggie was watching her face, so she saw the shock register. The captain's features were suddenly blank as the colour left her; even her coiling hair held still. 'Thundering Heavens,' she whispered.

'What is it?' Dad and Lord Colgath asked simultaneously.

'They were insane,' a badly frightened Captain Rebecca said. 'Rothgarnal must have pushed them into madness to agree to this.'

'Where was Mirlyn's Gate taken?' Taggie asked, keeping her voice unnaturally calm.

The captain looked at her with the pain of someone carrying news of a bereavement. 'Wynate. They were going to take Mirlyn's Gate to the isle of Wynate.'

Which meant absolutely nothing to Taggie. She wanted to cry out in annoyance.

'Oh no,' Sophie groaned in dismay.

'What is Wynate?' Jemima shouted for all of them.

'An isle sunwards from here,' Captain Rebecca said despondently. 'Its location is of little importance. Wynate is infamous as the foremost nest of the paxia. Their capital rock, if you will.'

'The paxia?' Taggie asked.

'The foulest, most vicious, flesh-eating vermin of the skies,' Captain Rebecca said. 'No one knows if they are animal or just barbaric folk. If you encounter a flock you *do not* stop and ask questions – you're too busy fleeing for your life. I've seen them strip the meat off a volpas in less than ten minutes.'

'And they took Mirlyn's Gate there?' Felix asked in alarm.

'Aye,' Captain Rebecca said with an angry gesture at the archway of stars in the crest. 'They never hid Mirlyn's Gate, they left it guarded by exiles from the Hell Realm. No wonder the poor *Lady Silvaris* never came back.'

Taggie exhaled loudly. She was delighted they probably knew where Mirlyn's Gate was now, but it was a joy sorely tempered by that very same location. Still, she wasn't about to turn back now. 'How long will it take the *Angelhawk* to reach Wynate?'

Every strand of hair on Captain Rebecca's head straightened out and stiffened. 'By all the stars in Heaven, young Queen, you have got to be joking.'

'I'm most certainly not.'

'Uh-oh,' Sophie said. Her head was twisting about in alarm.

'Did you not listen to a word—' Captain Rebecca began.

'Where's Penelopi?' Sophie asked.

Everyone looked around the study. Penelopi was nowhere to be seen.

'Jemima! Where is she?'

'Uh . . .' Jemima stared at the rune stones she held in her hand. 'Not here. It looks like she's somewhere in the town.'

'Busy telling everyone the *Angelhawk* brought a Karrak Lord to the isle, no doubt,' Felix said.

'We need to leave,' Dad said. 'Now.'

'Wait,' Captain Rebecca said. She was giving the ancient orocompass a forlorn look. 'Destroy it,' she said wretchedly.

'What?' Taggie asked.

'Orocompasses record up to fifty of the settings keyed into them. Heavens forgive me, it belonged to Exator himself.'

'Allow me,' Lord Colgath said. He held his hands on either side of the orocompass. After a few seconds the brass began to blacken, then glow. Molten droplets started to splatter down on the marble. The whole mechanism sagged and collapsed inward like an Easter egg thrown on a bonfire.

'Captain, you need to fly back to the *Angelhawk* and get her ready to launch as soon as we arrive,' Dad said. 'We won't be long. Jemima, you're going to have to run.'

'I know.'

'Fly with the captain,' Taggie told Sophie quietly. 'Make sure she doesn't launch before we get there.'

'Got it,' Sophie said; she patted the crossbow she carried.

They all raced out of the eyrie mansion. Captain Rebecca and Sophie took off, streaking over the rooftops towards the port park, quickly gaining height.

Taggie started to jog through the streets, keeping up with Dad. From the start, Earl Maril'bo was in front, a position which apparently cost him no effort to maintain. People swayed out of the elf's way without really realizing what they were doing. Then they turned to watch the rest of the strange company run past. Some of them saw Lord Colgath, some did not. It was easy to tell which was which. Erratic screams followed them all the way through town.

They burst out of the last street on to the grassy expanse of the port park, red-faced and out of breath. Taggie saw five small armoured figures standing at the foot of the tower where the *Dory Maria* was berthed. Their scarlet armour was horribly familiar. 'Oh no,' she groaned.

The Rannalal knights noticed them. Protective enchantment runes flared across their armour, and they moved forward to intercept.

Taggie stopped and took careful aim. '*Droiak.*'

A wide patch of grass in front of the knights erupted. Soil and withered grass fountained through the air, leaving a big crater in the ground. The knights dived for cover.

A couple of lightly armoured skymen were flying in fast and low. They raised their crossbows. Taggie spun a shield around herself. She saw Lantic's tunic turn black and harden.

But both crossbow bolts with their gleaming tips were aimed at Lord Colgath. The Karrak Lord slithered around nimbly as his smoke cloak's rippling slivers of colour began to darken, turning ember-red. Somehow the crossbow bolts missed him. Taggie could have sworn they swerved at the last minute.

The skymen swished away, curving above the taverns and warehouses that lined the port park as they reloaded their crossbows. Another joined them. Four more armoured figures emerged from an alley.

'What do we do?' Jemima yelled.

They were less than thirty metres from the tower where the *Angelhawk* was docked.

'Get up the stairs,' Dad shouted. 'All of you.'

Taggie opened her mouth to argue – but never got a word out. Dad's ancient green oilskin coat was doing exactly what Lantic's tunic had done. The fabric darkened to black, and flipped over, hardening. Dad was wearing armour! He drew his sword. 'I'll hold them off,' he announced.

Six Ethanu stepped out of the base of the *Dory Maria*'s tower. Taggie groaned in dismay. *Where did they come from?*

'*We'll* hold them off,' Earl Maril'bo called. In one hand he held the semi-circular dagger elves favoured, while his other drew a firestar from his pouch. Strange light swirled round his rainbow hoops, and he became extraordinarily difficult to see.

'Daddy!' Jemima cried frantically.

'Go, Jem! Taggie, get her up to the *Angelhawk*.'

Taggie grabbed Jem's hand. 'Come on!' They started to run up the stairs. Within seconds they were bounding high each time a foot slapped on to a step. Gravity had deserted them by the time they reached the top of the tower leg. From behind came the metallic clash and clang of swords as Dad and Earl Maril'bo defended the entrance to the stairs. Shield enchantments sizzled. They could hear angry shouting.

Taggie pushed off hard, sliding sleekly along the tube of bamboo lattice that ran up the centre of the tower. As she flew up, she looked through the gaps to see another bunch of people pouring across the port park. This time it was the portmaster's guard in their yellow-and-grey uniforms.

A crossbow bolt went *thunk* into the bamboo lattice, barely a metre from her face. A skyman was flying level with them, reloading his crossbow.

Taggie made a fist and pulled her arm back. '*Israth hyburon*,' she snarled. Orange light erupted from her arm. On the other side of the lattice, the air warped into a translucent fist. Taggie punched her arm forward. The air fist smashed into the skyman. He screamed as he was flung backwards, flipping over and over.

A minute later they reached the wharf, with the bridge leading over to the *Angelhawk* stretching out ahead.

'Come on,' Sophie cried frantically from the lower deck.

Taggie saw the tipsails were already unfurled, causing the *Angelhawk* to strain against her mooring cables. She started to haul herself along the tubular bridge.

'Now!' Captain Rebecca shouted.

The crew cut all the mooring ropes.

Maklepine was chanting protective enchantments. Magic flowed along the hull runes. Taggie reached back and pulled Jemima on to the lower deck as severed mooring cables writhed through the air around the ship.

'Daddy!' Jemima wailed.

The *Angelhawk* began to slide away from the wharf. Taggie twisted round in mid-air; she could see a mass of people around the entrance to the tower's stairs. A firestar flew out of the melee and struck one of the Ethanu. Skymen were hovering overhead, tussling with each other. She could just make out a figure in dark armour fencing with a knight.

'He's all right,' she shouted at a crying Jemima. 'Jem, Dad's OK. Use your sight if you don't believe me.'

The *Angelhawk* began to pick up speed. Taggie felt her feet pressing into the deck as weight returned. They were starting to head up away from Banmula, but their course would still take them close to the *Dory Maria*. Her crew must have realized that at the same time. Harpoon hatches around the ship's lower deck started to hinge open.

'Mainsails,' Captain Rebecca demanded.

'Who are they?' Felix asked, staring at the *Dory Maria* as he clung to the net.

'One of my brethren is on board,' Lord Colgath announced. 'I feel him.'

'What?' Taggie cried in dismay. 'That's no accident. How could the Grand Lord possibly have known where we were?'

A harpoon whistled out across the gap. It struck the *Angelhawk*'s middle-deck hull. The runes flared brightly, and the harpoon tip bounced off with a loud clatter. The runes darkened where it had struck and Maklepine hurriedly cast enchantments to reinforce them.

Jemima burst into tears.

'Jem, it's OK,' Taggie said. 'I can hold them off. We'll be all right, really. Now get into the cabin.'

'You don't understand,' Jemima wailed.

'Get into the cabin, now!' Taggie snapped.

'She's launching,' Captain Rebecca warned.

Taggie saw a Karrak Lord emerge from the *Dory Maria*'s upper deck. He extended both hands. A scarlet fireball zoomed out towards the *Angelhawk*.

Up on the top deck, Lord Colgath flung his own fireball. The two flaming spheres rammed together between the ships in an explosion that flung Taggie to the decking. The *Angelhawk* bucked violently in the blast. Captain Rebecca cursed madly as she fought to keep the ship on track, spinning the helm wheel round in a smear of speed.

Another harpoon thudded into the lower deck hull, five

metres below the helm. It trailed a wire which began to pull straight as the *Angelhawk* slipped ahead of the *Dory Maria*.

'Shipsmage, you are useless!' Captain Rebecca snarled. 'Everyone, brace yourselves, we'll have to pull free.'

Lantic bent over the rail and thrust his arm towards the harpoon, eyes closed, face scrunched up with effort. Slender streamers of emerald and turquoise radiance leaped from his fingers as he incanted urgently. The length of the iron harpoon became soft, and wiggled like a fish spine. Its barbed tip prised itself out of the *Angelhawk*'s hull plank where it was embedded. The tough metal cable undulated as if it was a whip that had just been slashed, pulling the harpoon back across the gulf.

'Nice animation, Prince,' an impressed Captain Rebecca said with pursed lips as the *Angelhawk* began to leave the port park towers behind.

Sophie and several skyfolk crouched on the upper deck, to send a volley of crossbow bolts at the *Dory Maria* as she started to leave her wharf in pursuit. Taggie took careful aim. '*Droiak!*' The destruction spell smashed into one of the *Dory Maria*'s masts, just above its deck mounting. The huge length of wood started to spin wildly through the air, canvas flapping as it began a long curve down towards the port park.

Undaunted, the Karrak Lord on the *Dory Maria* flung another fireball. Lord Colgath countered with his own. Their collision explosion was deafening. The *Angelhawk* juddered badly again, shunting sideways. Several parts of the sail tail mechanism splintered and buckled.

Taggie was slammed into the net, which gave alarmingly before springing back and throwing her the other way. She gripped the rail and steadied herself. *'Droiak!'* The destruction spell hit another of the *Dory Maria*'s masts. A lethal barrage of smouldering splinters sprayed out from the impact point. It took a moment, but the top of the mast started to bend over. Then it snapped. Some of the rigging snagged, and the broken mast section was dragged along by the ship, which was now pitching alarmingly.

Standing on the upper deck, Lord Colgath watched keenly for another fireball. No more came.

'Midsails,' Captain Rebecca ordered.

With her full set of sails unfurled, the *Angelhawk* caught the fast, lightwards wind, and soared cleanly away from Banmula.

INTO THE FOURTH REALM

The city of Morath'ki shimmered in the heat cast by the Second Realm's fierce blue-white sun. Its white towers and canvas-covered streets were nestled in the wide valley at the northernmost end of the Lulrol mountains.

Just outside the city, the War Emperor stood before the Great Gateway Olatha which was a placid oasis of clear water in the rocky ground of the valley. Tall palm trees surrounded the water, their long fronds swaying gently in the warm breeze.

Ten warriors of the Morath'ki Sentinel regiment stood across the road which led to the water, guarding the entrance to the Fourth Realm as they had done proudly every day and night since the Battle of Rothgarnal. Their silver armour was polished to a mirror shine, gleaming in the bright sun, and possessing shield enchantments strong enough to resist a charging Zanatuth.

The War Emperor faced them in his own resplendent scarlet and gold armour. Behind him, the Kings and Queens of the Gathering were arranged in close ranks, while behind them, stretching away into the distant haze, the vast combined army of the Realms stood silent and ready.

The War Emperor raised his arm in a respectful salute. 'Men of the Sentinels, through all these long centuries you have never faltered from the noble task you were set to guard us from invasion through the Great Gateway. This realm owes you a debt which can never be repaid. But on this day, you may finally stand aside. On this day we take the first step towards purging our Realms of darkness.'

'Well said,' Queen Judith murmured.

The captain of the Sentinel watch saluted back, and shouldered his pike. His whole squad followed suit. They marched away to one side, leaving the road to the oasis open.

The War Emperor marched up to the edge of the water. 'Great Gateway Olatha, I am Manokol, King of this Realm. I am the anointed War Emperor of all the Realms. And I ask you provide passage for my armies into the Fourth Realm.'

'Are you truly the War Emperor of every Realm?' the musical voice of Olatha asked, carrying a hint of mockery.

The War Emperor flicked a glance at the Kings and Queens around him. 'All these armies you see here today are under my command.'

'I see no army from the First Realm.'

'I am here,' Taggie's mum said in a clear voice.

'Are you an army?' Olatha asked.

'Do you judge an army by its size, or by its ability?'

Olatha simply chuckled, a sound that merged with the breeze and was soon lost. The air above the water began to shimmer, distorting the view of the valley behind the oasis.

Strange shapes began to weave through the wobbling air which was turning silver. The mirage gradually calmed into a perfect mirror above the water. The War Emperor stared at his own reflection, which showed his immaculate white and gold armour with a red cloak flowing to the ground. He admired the colourful pendants of the regiments fluttering in the breeze. In the air above the endless ranks of soldiers, olri-gi, pegasi and skymen flew in wide circles, so many of them they resembled the spinning streamers of a hurricane.

'Welcome to the Fourth Realm,' Olatha said.

The War Emperor would have dearly loved to be the first to cross, but even he accepted that wasn't realistic. 'General,' he called. 'Send the scouts through.'

A squad of Second Realm battlemages in thick armour walked towards the mirror, backed by a line of towering soldier gols. As they reached the rim of the water, they released a flock of tiny bird contraptions made from thin metal, with leather wings, animated by the magic the Second Realm specialized in. Their jewelled eyes sparkled as they darted forward to slip straight through the unnatural mirror with the tiniest ripple.

'Nothing lying in wait on the other side,' the battlemages reported as the bird contraptions sent their vision back. 'Advance,' General Welch called to the Ninth Realm cavalry. The giants urged their snarling rinosaurs forward. Pegasi of the Second Realm air cavalry swooped low, and flashed through the Great Gateway above the spiked iron helmets of the giants.

One by one, the immense troop columns waiting in the sweltering dry heat of the valley moved forward through the Great Gateway.

It was an hour before the word came back that the land immediately beyond the Great Gateway had been made safe, and no spies or assassins lurked nearby. The War Emperor mounted his horse, and rode forward eagerly. In his zeal he barely noticed that the hoofs of his horse walked on top of the pool's water, never even forming a ripple.

Then he was through the ghostly mirror, and into the cold, grey desolation of the Fourth Realm. A single dreary cloud had been stretched across the entire sky, from which fell tiny flakes of snow. Somewhere above the cloud the invisible sun cast a melancholy radiance that seemed to drain any colour from the frozen land. A frigid wind blew constantly from the west, instantly turning the War Emperor's breath to frosty mist. His horse shook its head and became skittish at the

strange suspended environment.

General Welch had already set up a command post in a series of circular tents on the edge of the ice-covered rubble which had once been the city of Torislis. The War Emperor joined him, and gratefully accepted a mug of tea from a young squire. 'Any sign of the enemy, General?'

'No, sire. But our early scouts have always maintained that this part of the Fourth Realm is uninhabited.'

'My finest seer sorceresses have already sighted the Grand Lord,' Queen Judith said. 'As we speak, he marches at the head of an army that travels to Rothgarnal.'

'Rothgarnal?' the War Emperor whispered the name as if it belonged to a forbidden deity.

'Indeed.'

'How long until all our forces are through?' the War Emperor asked.

'Two days at the earliest, sire,' said his aide-de-camp, Lady Jessicara DiStantona.

'Very well. Organize a rear guard to hold this Great Gateway. We march on Rothgarnal in two days' time.'

When Taggie walked into the captain's lounge she was fairly sure Captain Rebecca had been drinking again. The skywoman lolled in her low-back chair behind the desk, regarding her visitor with a mixture of belligerence and worry.

'We're not going to Wynate,' the captain said with a

slight slur to her words. 'That's final. Did you have anything else to say?'

'I have to go there.'

The captain's fist hit the desk. 'My ship! I give the orders.'

'We have the chance to stop the war.'

'We don't because we'll be dead. There is no chance.'

'You said yourself, you've seen them attack a volpas, so you must have outrun them to escape.'

'I . . .' The captain grimaced as if she was in pain. 'I've heard of ships outrunning them.'

'It can be done, then?' Taggie pressed.

'No.'

'I don't expect you to land there. Just take me as close as you can.'

'Ha! What use is that?'

'I can shapeshift. I'll fly over to Wynate and see if Mirlyn's Gate is there.'

'You're as crazy as Exator was.'

'It has to be done. Do you know of another captain who could get as close as you and the *Angelhawk*?'

'Oh no you don't. Don't you try that kind of talk on me, young Queen. I don't have a death wish.'

'Just get me close. That's all I ask. You've seen what Lord Colgath and I can do. We can hit a paxia flock hard.'

'You know what? I'm betting this is exactly what the old Grand Lord and War Emperor told Exator down in that secret cave. And where are they now, huh?'

'That's what we have to find out.'

The captain's hair thrashed about. 'Arrrgh! I curse the day I took your coins.'

'Seriously. If you won't do it, you have to take me to a captain who will. That is my charter! You took our money.'

The captain spent a long moment getting her breathing under control. Her hair calmed and her wings stopped their slow aggravated flaps. 'When you're a bird, how far can you fly, exactly?'

Taggie tried not to smile too much.

The morning after the dramatic fight at Banmula's port park a cluster of unexpected shadows began to slide over the isle's ancient neglected town. Startled residents looked up into the blue infinity to see a full squadron of the Highlord's frigates holding position directly above them. The sleek three-deck ships with conical prows and hull planks aglow with protective runes had their prodigious collection of harpoon hatches open. A flock of seven imposing olri-gi were flying escort duty, looking down on the isle the way vultures regarded a fallen beast.

None of the frigates wasted time mooring at the port park towers. Instead, skymen in light armour flew down to the town. Those with the keenest eyes saw they were accompanied by a large black eagle.

Penelopi showed Katrabeth into Exator's study. The teenage sorceress dressed in a plain aquamarine dress was an unnerving figure, though Penelopi couldn't quite work out why. The girl was certainly pretty enough, with auburn hair combed back neatly. It was perhaps something about her intense brown eyes, which seemed able to look through anything solid. Then again, it could be the uncanny resemblance to the younger sorceress girl Rebecca had brought into the eyrie mansion a day earlier.

'You say the little girl sighted something in here?' Katrabeth asked as she circled the molten remains of the orocompass, regarding the tarnished lumps as she might a poised scorpion.

'Yes. I don't know what. That was when I saw the Karrak Lord.' Penelopi shivered at the memory.

'Go on.'

'They enchanted me, and I fell asleep. When I woke there was an opening in the floor where that crest is. I never knew it existed! I could hear them talking down there. Naturally I flew to alert the portmaster's guard.'

'Naturally.' Katrabeth knelt down and put one hand flat on the middle of the crest. She clicked her fingers. Nothing happened. She gave the crest a warning look, and clicked her fingers again. Several cracks split the mosaic tiles. Then they started to move, expanding to reveal the dark shaft.

'How did you do that?' Penelopi asked, startled.

Katrabeth showed her a blank smile and walked down the steps. Penelopi watched the young sorceress prowl round, casting enchantments into the decayed bookshelves and crumbled furniture. 'There's nothing here,' Katrabeth announced, and made her way back up to the study.

When the floor had closed up again, Katrabeth examined the two remaining orocompasses in their glass cases, then gazed thoughtfully at the molten remains of the third. 'What makes this orocompass different from the rest?' she asked.

'Not a lot. They were all commissioned by Exator. The family have maintained them ever since. The one they destroyed was the largest and most elaborate, hence the most expensive to preserve. It's also the most accurate. I can't believe the sorceress girl did this. It's wicked vandalism.'

'She didn't,' Katrabeth said stroking a finger along a buckled brass band. 'This is Karrak wizardry.'

Penelopi shivered again.

'They must have used it,' Katrabeth said. 'But why do this?'

'Orocompasses record the settings they are loaded with. It's a quick way of checking your course on a ship, especially in a storm when you get blown about. I'd say they didn't want anyone else to know what course Rebecca was calculating.'

'Ah,' Katrabeth said. She walked over to the desk, and ran her fingers over the thick almanac. 'How do you find your location with an orocompass?'

'You just need to load in the star positions, and it gives you the precise coordinate.'

'And if you have the star positions for your destination?

You just load them in as well?'

'Well, yes. Obviously.'

'I see. And once you've correctly loaded the star positions of that location, the coordinate which the orocompass gives you can be checked in –' Katrabeth waved her hand casually over the desk – 'an almanac such as this one?'

'That's right,' Penelopi said. 'What did they come here to look for?'

'Why don't we find out?' Katrabeth said with a sweet smile. 'Oh Nursy,' she called.

Penelopi flinched as an ancient woman in a black dress limped into the study. The way the light fell on the gauzy fabric prevented her seeing anything but the simplest profile.

'Nursy is the best seer in the Third Realm,' Katrabeth explained to Penelopi. 'That makes her quite valuable. It's the reason I just can't bring myself to let her go.'

'The *Angelhawk* is hidden from me now,' Nursy said in a thin voice.

'Why is that?' Katrabeth asked with a hint of cold anger in her voice. Penelopi instinctively took a step back.

'Since she realized who I am, the Blossom Princess has cast a powerful wardveil around it.'

Katrabeth's lips turned up in a humourless smile. 'No matter. My dear cousin looked something up in this book. Would you sight what it was for me, Nursy, there's a dear.'

Penelopi watched in fascination as the old woman began to stroke the book with fingers that were gnarled and knobbly from arthritis. 'Not your cousin, sweet thing,' Nursy said. The veiled head was jerked in Penelopi's direction. 'One of her kind used it last.'

'Rebecca,' Penelopi snarled in barely controlled fury.

'Cousins,' Katrabeth said brightly. 'Can't live with them. Not allowed to execute them in public.'

Nursy opened the almanac, leafing slowly through the thick pages with their charts and extensive tables. 'Here,' she said eventually, her pointed yellow nail resting on a line. 'This is the last thing they looked at.'

Katrabeth examined the line Nursy had sighted. 'And what exactly is Wynate?' she asked.

Penelopi couldn't prevent the moan of profound dread escaping from her lips.

16

BETRAYED

Taggie left Captain Rebecca in her cabin. A fair breeze was blowing across the upper deck as she walked round to the ladder. The *Angelhawk* was making good time in the wind current they'd caught; already Banmula had vanished into the infinite blue. She could see several crew dangling on ropes halfway down the lower hull, clustered round one of the damaged tail sail mechanisms. Jualius and Patrina were hovering even further aft, hammering another sail tail's jammed tip.

Lantic was waiting for her outside the wardroom hatchway. 'What did she say?'

'She's plotting a course to Wynate for us.'

'Uh-huh. I wonder how she'll break that to the crew?'

'The captain will deal with them,' Taggie replied, with more confidence than she felt. Right now all she could think about was Dad. 'Are you OK?'

'I'm fine. I was coming to find you. Jemima is inconsolable.'

Taggie sighed and squared her shoulders. *Time to be the perfect big sister again*, she told herself. 'Where is she?'

Jemima was sitting at one end of the wardroom table

sobbing uncontrollably, her face all red and blotchy. Sophie was on one side, stroking her between her shoulder blades. Felix had both her hands in his forepaws. None of the reassurances they crooned made the slightest difference.

'Hey there,' Taggie said gently as she slid on to the bench beside her distressed sister. 'Dad is going to be fine.'

'It's all my fault!' Jemima wailed.

It was all Taggie could do not to laugh. 'I think that's an exaggeration, Jem. We knew the Grand Lord or the War Emperor would find us eventually.' Though some part of her mind was puzzled by how the *Dory Maria* had found them so fast.

'You don't understand,' Jemima said. 'I betrayed you.' She looked round at her friends. 'I betrayed all of you. I didn't mean to. I'm sorry, really truly I am. I thought I was helping. She said I would be.'

'Jem?' Taggie said cautiously. 'What are you talking about?'

'I let her see through the wardveil. She sighted us here.'

'Who?'

Jemima gulped down some air, and in a miserable voice told them about the old woman she'd met in the dream, how she claimed to be Mum's old nurse, and how there was a cure for Felix on its way.

'I saw her in Tarimbi,' Sophie said. 'She was in the wharf as we left.'

'You sighted her, most like,' Lantic said.

Jemima started crying again.

'Please stop, Jem,' Felix said. He stroked her cheek with a forepaw.

'I can't,' Jemima said, gulping down air between shudders. 'There is no cure for you. The Grand Lord's brethren know where we are. Dad's a prisoner. Everything is ruined, and it's all my fault.'

'Jemima, look at me,' Felix said with quiet insistence. 'You have ruined nothing. Everybody in every Realm is looking for us, every spy, every mage, every seer. It was only ever a question of which one was first. I'm sorry the old woman tricked you. But there is absolutely no dishonour in being deceived by evil. She exploited your good nature, that's all. That's all evil ever does. And because you're so good natured, they could really take advantage in a despicable way. But I'm proud of you for being that person. And I thank you from the bottom of my heart for trying to help me.'

'Really?' Jemima asked in a tiny voice.

'Of course. But you're not to worry about my curse again, OK?'

'All right. If you're sure.'

'I am.'

Taggie wanted to say she couldn't believe Jem had been so stupid, that anyone could see the woman in black was obviously lying and trying to manipulate her. But despite all she'd seen and done over the last year, Jemima was only twelve. *And my sister*. 'It's over now,' she said. 'And we know where Mirlyn's Gate is. There's nothing they can do about that, no matter how treacherous that horrible woman is.' She was pretty certain the old woman must have been acting either for Queen Judith or Katrabeth, but didn't say it. Jem was miserable enough at being fooled already.

'We destroyed the orocompass,' Lantic said. 'So they don't know where we're going. They're back to square one with nothing to show for it.'

Thank you, Taggie mouthed to him over Jemima's head. Lantic blushed slightly, but looked happy enough.

'And we know they're out there now,' Sophie added. 'They've completely lost the element of surprise. How do you think the Grand Lord is going to take the news that we escaped them? I almost wish we could be there to see the old woman explain it to him.'

Jemima attempted a smile.

Mr Marcus came over from the galley hatchway. He rocked slightly as his four stumpy feet walked over the planks.

'You drink this now, and cheer up,' he told Jemima and put a tall glass of lemonade on the table in front of her. 'No more crying, please. You're too young to be crying like this. You're breaking my heart.'

'Thank you.' Jemima took a sip. 'Oh, how do you get it so cold? It's lovely.'

'You think you're the only ones who can work magic?' The Jannermol chuckled.

'*Heartbreakers!*' Sophie tasted the name. 'That's us.'

'Could be,' Taggie admitted.

'I like it,' Jemima said, looking up with red-rimmed eyes.

'I suppose it's a start,' Felix muttered.

'I can live with it,' Lantic said.

Jemima finished her drink, and wiped her eyes one last time. They all went outside on to the deck, and leaned on the rail, looking out across the endless blue sky with its smattering of small isles in the distance.

'How many isles are there in this Realm?' Lantic asked.

'Millions probably,' Sophie said. 'But most of them are small and uninhabited, only birds use them. In the part of Air we know, the Highlord's domain covers about two thousand inhabited isles.'

'Finding who else is out there would be a real voyage,' Taggie said, and tipped her head back, content to let the wind blow her chestnut hair about. 'I wonder if I could persuade Dad to let us go and do that?'

'We could sing in every port-park tavern in the realm,' Sophie said wistfully.

'Aye, you sing too, do you?' Captain Rebecca said, slipping down the ladder from the upper deck.

'We're the *Heartbreakers*,' Jemima told her proudly.

'Really, my little warrior maid? So what do you sing?'

'I haven't finalized the group's musical direction yet,' Felix said.

'Direction!' The captain snorted. 'You're not plotting a ship's course, Weldowen. You sing from the heart, whatever the moment needs. Every time. I know, because I have a fantastic voice. I've sung in half the taverns in the isles. The lads beg me for more every time I get up there on the piano.'

'You sing?' Sophie asked in surprise.

Lantic gave her an uncertain look. '*On* the piano?'

'Aye, Prince, I stand on the piano. Where else in a tavern? I might let you join in with me next time we hit a port park. *The Captain's Heartbreakers*. Yes, that's definitely got a ring to it. You'll be my backing vocalists.' She held up a scroll. 'Right then, I have plotted our course. I'll instruct the helm.'

Jemima blinked as the captain walked round the curving hull. 'I don't want to be her backing group,' she complained.

'What sort of songs does she sing, do you think?' Lantic asked.

Felix tilted his head to give Lantic a long glance. 'I doubt they've ever been sung in your palace, Prince.'

Clouds were scudding along with the *Angelhawk* now, tenuous white streaks, tens of miles long carried by the same vast current of air that was pushing them steadily sunwards. The *Angelhawk* was tacking several degrees eastward and northward which occasionally pushed them through the vapour. The encounters would leave the hull and decks soaked in water. It was more like fog than rainclouds. Thankfully there'd been no hail yet.

The ship began to change course, the prow slipping

several degrees lightwards. Taggie sighed. It meant they were heading even further from Dad.

'He'll be all right,' Sophie said, reading Taggie's mood. 'Remember when we rescued him from the palace dungeon? That was much worse.'

'I suppose.'

'Earl Maril'bo was tackling the Ethanu most effectively when we launched,' Felix said from his perch on the net above them. 'At worst the Prince Dino will be sitting in court with a good lawyer, getting bored while the local magistrate tries to work out what to do with him.'

'Do you think so?' Jemima asked eagerly.

'You just have to use the runes,' Sophie said.

'I have. They don't say much. Just that he's still on Banmula.'

'But he's alive,' Felix said reassuringly. 'That's the point.'

Taggie gave her sister a curious look. 'What about Earl Maril'bo?'

'I don't know. I can't sight him at all.'

'Nobody can sight elves if they don't want to be sighted,' Sophie said.

'You know what?' Lantic said. 'I bet Prince Dino is far more worried about you and Jemima than you are about him.'

Taggie grinned without much humour. 'You're probably right.'

'And we know where Mirlyn's Gate is,' Sophie said, her long strands of red hair stirring vivaciously. 'The first people in over a thousand years of searching! Us! You're going to stop the war, Taggie!'

'Well,' Taggie said, trying to sound modest, but actually feeling very satisfied about that. 'Yes. I hope so.'

'What do paxia look like?' Jemima asked just as Captain Rebecca made her way back from the helm.

'Aye, you'll not be worrying about them now are you, little warrior?' the captain exclaimed, clasping a small brass telescope in one hand.

'You're the one that keeps saying how awful they are!' Jemima said crossly.

'That's because I don't want you to lower your guard. Like goblyns with wings, they are. Half of their head is a mouth, with a ring of fangs that can slice clean through a hull plank. They live like sloths, sleeping for months at a time. But when they waken – ah! That's the danger. Their ravenous hunger drives them mad, so that they'll fall on anything living without mercy. Even themselves, so I've heard survivors say late at night in the taverns when they tell their fearsome tales.'

'Urrgh!' Jemima pulled a face. 'They're cannibals?'

'Good for us, though,' Captain Rebecca said. 'Maybe they've all eaten each other.'

Taggie nearly started to tell the captain to stop scaring Jemima. But actually anything that made Jemima more cautious was probably a good idea.

'Anyway . . .' The captain's hand came down hard on Lantic's shoulder, making him wince. 'I've found something of interest for you all. Take your young minds off the terrible perils ahead, hey?'

She handed the telescope to Taggie, and pointed aft. 'There.'

Taggie put the tube to her eye, and followed the captain's directions. Under magnification the darkward sky appeared as a lush deep purple where stars twinkled. One of them glowed like an ember. But it was blurred, as if there was some kind of smear on the lens. She lowered the telescope and peered at that section of sky. Her eyes could just make out a tiny ruby-red glimmer.

'What is it?'

'The comet.' Captain Rebecca smiled.

Suddenly everyone wanted to use the telescope.

'Looks like it was an omen after all,' Lantic said after he'd had his turn. 'It can't be coincidence that it appeared when we found the location of the Gate. The Heavens are smiling on our quest.'

'Do you know where it's going?' Felix asked the captain.

'Only in general terms,' she told him. 'Comets don't hold steady. As bits of them fall off and they jet out gases they dart about like crazed fish. But it is coming down in this direction, that's for sure.'

'How many ships will come after it?' Taggie asked.

'As many as can afford to; aye, and plenty of those that can't, too. Captains will risk much for a hot nugget of *athrodene*.' She gave Jemima a pointed look. 'So you'll be seeing at least a hundred ships chasing after it, nerving themselves up to dash through the tail.'

'Rock ho!' came the cry from the upper deck watch.

Captain Rebecca snatched the telescope from Sophie who was using it to track the comet. She looked up, and gasped in dismay.

They didn't need a telescope to see the large dark boulder drifting gently along. It was emerging from a cloud swirl not two hundred metres ahead of the prow.

'Southwards!' Captain Rebecca bellowed at the help.

Favian, who was at the wheel, spun it hard. The *Angelhawk* didn't seem to respond at all.

'More!' the captain said, flying fast along the deck.

But Favian had turned the wheel as far as it would go. 'The tail sails are still jammed,' he said desperately.

Taggie peered over the rail. The crew working on the damaged tail sails were shouting wildly at each other, trying to shift the stubborn mechanisms.

'Can you break it?' Jemima yelped.

Taggie gave the rock a desperate glance. It was almost as big as the *Angelhawk*. And only a hundred metres away now. The ship was starting to turn, but oh so slowly.

She flung her arm out. '*Droiak!*'

The dazzling bolt of magical lightning struck the rock. It juddered. Several smaller chunks came whirling out of the impact point.

'*Droiak!*'

This time a larger splinter fell free, along with several globs of lava.

Fifty metres away. And the *Angelhawk*'s prow was still turning sluggishly. A sliver of clear sky was growing between the ship and the rock.

'To me,' Taggie called to her friends, and spun her strongest shield as they huddled close.

The rock descended on the *Angelhawk* like a fist from the Heavens. Taggie tensed, ready for the terrible strike. But then the *Angelhawk* was somehow slipping past the craggy rock, almost close enough to reach out and touch. Taggie could make out individual patches of spongy moss mottling its surface. She gasped in shock. *We're going to make it!*

A vicious splintering sound filled the air. As the rock

slid past the hull, it caught one of the *Angelhawk*'s masts. The tough wood snapped as if it were nothing more than a matchstick.

The *Angelhawk* gave an almighty judder as if in pain. And the rock was aft, starting to dwindle away. The broken mast tumbled off into the blue vastness of the sky, its sails flapping loosely.

'Another mast gone!' Captain Rebecca yelled furiously. She shook her fist darkwards. 'You vile angels, why do you hate me so?'

'Everyone all right?' Taggie asked. Her friends nodded and murmured they were OK. Together they looked out miserably at the shattered stump of the mast.

17

A NEW ALLY

Visibility was no more than a few metres in the cool clammy mist which surrounded the *Angelhawk*. Mr Marcus, the ship's cook, was moving steadily through his battered galley, recovering pans and crockery from the piles that had been strewn across the floor during the collision. Jualius had climbed down a rope to supervise repairs to the tail sails. Captain Rebecca sent seven crew out over the masts to re-rig their remaining sails in a fashion to restore their balance. Even so, the *Angelhawk* was flying at a pronounced angle.

Once they got under way, Captain Rebecca asked Taggie and Lord Colgath into her topdeck cabin. 'We'll have to dock at an isle,' she told them. 'We need a new mast, and to make proper repairs to the tail sails.'

'But we're moving,' Taggie complained.

'Aye, but barely, and we manoeuvre with the grace of a harpooned loxraptor. This is no way to fly. We need all three masts for any long voyage. And we're still a good fortnight out from Wynate – that's with a good wind.'

Taggie gave Lord Colgath an uncertain glance. 'People are going to be looking for us.'

'Aye, I know. We'll steer clear of the major isles. Guatigua isn't far from here, maybe a day's sailing at this speed.'

'And how long will it take to replace the mast?' Lord Colgath asked.

'If the shipyards have the right timber in, no more than a day.'

'We can probably risk that.'

'We don't have a lot of choice.' Captain Rebecca glanced over at the wind current charts pinned to the lounge wall. 'I'll start plotting a course to Guatigua.'

Guatigua was surprisingly verdant, with a thick forest of tall sturdy trees forming a collar round a rocky pinnacle which protruded from the end of the isle like a mountain peak. The town was small, and sprawled like a three-limbed starfish in the hollows between steep ridges. There were two other ships berthed at the port park's single tower when the *Angelhawk* arrived.

Taggie asked Jemima to cast her rune stones, but there was nothing questionable about the ships. So Taggie and Captain Rebecca went to see the isle's lone shipwright, an enterprise run by an old skyman called Hoolonde.

'I'd like the work, of course,' he said them as they stood in the middle of his high workshop, surrounded by carpentry benches. 'And the tail sails are easy enough to fix. But I haven't got the timber for a mast. It's the comet, you see. I fitted three new masts last week for captains who have sailed to chase it.'

'When's your next load due?' Captain Rebecca asked.

'The *Gollarie* normally brings my wood in from Rorbotha or Kanaba. She should swing by in another month or so.'

'Another month?' Taggie exclaimed in dismay. 'But there are hundreds of trees in the forest here. I saw them when we approached. Can't we chop down one?'

Hoolonde sucked down a breath. 'That's olri-gi land,' he said. 'They like to keep the forest for birds to nest in. There's all sorts of parrots and turkeys and dodos and swans and cockooahs, even some geese.'

'Why do they want them?'

'To eat, of course. Takes a lot to fill an olri-gi's stomach.'

'Oh,' she said, dispirited. 'There has to be some other timber, somewhere.'

'If there was, I'd be able to buy it for you,' Hoolonde said. 'Sorry, but you'll just have to wait for the *Gollarie*.'

'This is ridiculous,' Taggie said as they walked away from the shipwright. 'Do you think I could ask the olri-gi for a tree? I know they used to help humans in the Outer Realm against the Karraks. And the War Emperor was talking about calling them to help his war. Perhaps if I told them how important this flight was?'

Captain Rebecca shrugged expressively. ''Tis a beautiful folly, young Queen. But I suppose we have nothing to lose.'

Half an hour later, Taggie was picking her way across the isle's small fields towards the forest beyond, with

Jemima tagging along beside her.

'Any of these would probably do,' Taggie said as they walked along a narrow track in the forest. Big trees towered overhead, their wide branches casting thick shadows across the ground. Birds were flying everywhere, warbling and squawking. The vines that webbed the trees were already showing off a multitude of brightly coloured flowers. Now with the Blossom Princess herself walking among them, even more buds burst open in welcome. The sunlight shining past the leaves slowly transformed into a glorious rainbow dapple.

As they carried on through the forest, Taggie's nerves did strange things to her stomach. It wasn't just that their voyage depended on getting one of the trees. These were dragons they were going to talk to; fire-breathing creatures that were notoriously short-tempered.

'They'll give us a tree, I'm sure,' Jemima said confidently. As soon as Taggie had announced she was visiting the olri-gi, Jemima had pleaded to come with her. 'To see real dragons,' she'd said delightedly.

Maklepine and Captain Rebecca had both winced at that. 'You're not to call them that,' they insisted. 'They really don't like it. Really. *Don't.*'

The forest ended, giving way to a broad expanse of naked rock.

'This way,' Jemima said without hesitation.

Taggie followed her sister, knowing better than to question. They were walking towards the isle's pinnacle. It was hard going, the rock had many deep narrow gullies and awkward snags. Eventually, about quarter of a mile from the apex, Jemima stopped outside a cave entrance wider than a train tunnel back in the Outer Realm.

Taggie stood there, looking into the darkness with growing tension as she waited to see what would emerge, her imagination bringing up all sorts of unwelcome thoughts.

Soon enough, she heard a rustling sound from inside the entrance. Shadows moved inside the darkness. Taggie forced her legs to stay put. Those were *big* shadows.

An olri-gi emerged out into the light.

Taggie knew what dragons looked like. Everybody did. They were lizards the size of elephants, with a crocodile-shaped head, and leathery wings sprouting from their shoulders.

But this creature . . . Taggie's mouth dried up and she took a step back, partly from confusion and partly from shock. An olri-gi, she thought, was like a manta ray reborn as a fighter jet, a sleek long aerodynamic triangle. Its head was a simple wedge, with golden multi-faceted eyes on top, and a wide curving mouth underneath.

Most worrying were the two long tails that extended from the rear just above the hindlegs. They were segmented, bending like springs, and tipped with the most lethal-looking stings she'd ever seen – longer than swords, sharper than razors.

'The skyfolk are right,' Jemima said in a very tiny voice.

'That is *not* a dragon.'

The apex of the olri-gi's head halted a couple of metres from Taggie. Unnerving golden eyes regarded her solemnly. All Taggie could do was stare up at the nostril slits that were pointing at her, wondering if she'd see the fire as it came shooting out . . .

'Your Grace,' Taggie said, just remembering in time the correct form of address.

The olri-gi sniffed. 'Human royalty,' it said in a voice that was like the rumble of a storm's first thunder. 'You are royalty.' The giant head shifted round to Jemima, whose lower lip was trembling. 'As is this little one. Never in my drove's history has one human royal visited this isle. Now two, in the time of the largest comet in a generation. Your kind talk of omens. They may be right.'

Taggie bowed. 'I am the Queen of Dreams, and I thank you for seeing us.' She looked from the olri-gi's nozzles to the stings. If it could breathe flames, why did it need stings?

'And I am Canri, drove leader.'

'I have a request, Your Grace. My ship's mast is broken. The shipwright has no timber. I need a tree and will be happy to pay.'

Canri's head withdrew. A ripple moved slowly down the length of his sinuous body. 'Your coins pay for comforts we cannot fashion for ourselves, and such exchanges help our kind to live harmoniously. But most of my drove have left. They answered the call of the Highlord, who himself answered the call of the War Emperor. They fly to war, Queen of Dreams, they hunger for the taste of rathwai in their teeth. I do not fly with them. I am shamed because of a simple fight with a loxraptor flock. One ill-judged turn left my hindleg damaged. None but the stoutest and most able should fly against rathwai being ridden by the Dark Lords and Ladies.'

'I'm sorry about your leg,' Taggie said. She noticed the back of the olri-gi's hindlegs had a membrane stretched between them and the underbelly, which gave it twin tailfins for stability in flight. One of them was badly torn, and Canri limped when he walked on it.

'And I am sorry about your tree. But I have no appetite for your coins while I await to hear the fate of my children. Ships will come. They will bring timber from another forest for you to make your new mast.'

'We've got to have a tree, Your Grace,' Jemima blurted. 'We're going to stop the war.'

'Jem,' Taggie warned.

'But it's true!'

'How would you stop the war?' Canri asked. 'It is the command of the War Emperor.'

'I believe him to be wrong,' Taggie said. 'Thousands will die, including olri-gi. And all for nothing.'

Canri shuffled his front feet, and looked straight at her. 'How will you stop the war, Queen of Dreams?'

The sheer force of the olri-gi's demand made it difficult for Taggie to return his golden stare. He had a dignified presence that was truly awesome. 'I know where Mirlyn's Gate is,' she said carefully. 'If we can open it, the Karrak Lords and Ladies will be able to go home.'

'I see your valour, young Queen. But that is an impossible dream. They would never leave.'

'Yes they would,' Jemima said. 'One of them is helping us.'

Canri exhaled and Jemima jumped in fear. 'Don't burn us,' she squeaked. 'We're trying to stop people from dying.'

The olri-gi raised its head. 'What do you mean, burn you?'

Jemima gave Canri a puzzled look. 'Well, you're a . . . You breathe fire. I thought.'

Canri's laugh was like a boulder crashing down a rock face. 'You believe I breathe out fire, little royal?'

'Well . . . Don't you?'

'I don't exhale flame, I expel it!'

'Er, what's the difference?'

Canri blinked. 'Are you a good runner, little royal?'

'Yes. I'm in the hundred-metres relay team at school.

We made it to the national finals.'

'Next time you run: spit.'

'What?'

'Spit when you're running. Then tell me where it lands.'

'Well, it would just hit my face, of course,' Jemima said indignantly.

'Indeed. And if you breathed flame out of your mouth when you're flying, where would the flame go?'

'Oh yes.' Jemima scrunched her lips up as she considered the dilemma. 'But you just said you do expel flame.'

'I do, when I need to. But not forward.'

Jemima tilted her head to one side and regarded the huge olri-gi curiously.

With growing alarm, Taggie could see her sister's thoughts working. Realization began to shine in Jemima's delighted eyes.

'Jem!' she growled threateningly.

'You mean . . .' Jemima's smile widened to show her teeth.

Taggie made urgent zipping motions across her mouth.

'You mean . . .' Jemima started to giggle. The giggle turned into a hysterical laugh. 'You mean you *fart* flame?' Jemima broke up, shrieking helplessly.

'I expel my flame behind me,' Canri explained with phenomenal dignity. 'Yes.'

That set off another round of giggling.

'I apologize for my sister, Your Grace,' Taggie said angrily. 'She has a simple mind and doesn't realize when she's being extremely rude.'

'Fart flame,' Jemima sniggered.

Taggie wanted the ground to open up and swallow Jemima whole. The charmsward obediently began to make those particular spells available. It was very tempting.

'Your culture is different,' Canri said. 'And she is a child.'

'Thank you for your understanding,' Taggie said, red-faced. 'And thank you for your time.' She started to turn away.

Jemima stopped giggling. She saw Taggie's lowered head, and knew exactly how crushed her sister was. They desperately needed that tree.

Her humour turned to anguish. *I've done it again*, she realized. *I've let everyone down*. A few seconds ago she'd been laughing uncontrollably, now she thought she might cry. She was so angry with herself, almost as much as she was ashamed.

'Wait,' she blurted. 'Before we go, I want to help you, Your Grace.' *Then at least I'll have done one thing right today*.

The olri-gi's head lined up on her. 'How can you help me, little royal?'

'Your leg,' she said. 'I'd like to try.'

Jemima hurried round to Canri's hindleg, suddenly very conscious of the segmented tail curling above her. The membrane was badly tattered, flapping like one of the *Angelhawk*'s loose sails. She laid her hands on the leg, closing her eyes so she might feel the warm skin, which despite looking so smooth was actually quite rough to the touch. And through her questing fingertips she could somehow feel the torn tendons, the fractured bone, the scabs along the membrane where loxraptor claws had torn. Somewhere in the distance the olri-gi's mighty heart thumped reassuringly.

As always when she touched an injury, something stirred inside her. She guided that strange, gentle force out, sending it to soak into the olri-gi's bruised and hurting flesh, easing and soothing. An ethereal balm that cooled inflamed tissue and encouraged the huge creature's flesh towards recovery.

Jemima shuddered, suddenly feeling cold and tired.

'Find yourself the finest tree in the forest,' Canri said. 'And use it for your new mast.'

A weary Jemima looked up at his great golden eyes. 'I didn't do it for that, Your Grace,' she said.

'I know. And that is why the tree is my gift, also freely given. There is enough dishonesty and selfishness in this universe, Blossom Princess. Kindness should always be encouraged, especially in one as young as yourself. I would hate your character to grow disheartened from exposure to greed and deceit.'

'You are most kind, Your Grace,' Taggie said, feeling enormously relieved. 'Your gift will allow us to reach the isle before it's too late.'

'Which isle are you sailing to?' Canri asked.

'Oh, we're going to Wynate,' Jemima said. 'That's where

Mirlyn's Gate is hidden.' She paused. 'We think it is. Well . . . hope, really.'

Another ripple ran along Canri's body, straightening the tails. 'You do know what awaits you there, don't you, young Queen?'

'Yes,' Taggie said with a sigh. 'We do.'

'And why is it you alone that seeks Mirlyn's Gate to prevent the war?' Canri asked.

Taggie settled down on the rock, and told him the whole story.

Hoolonde was better than his word. Spurred on by a shortage of work, and Taggie's promise of a hefty bonus, one team of his carpenters took seventeen hours from cutting down the tree to fashion it into a mast and fit it to the lower deck. Another team repaired the *Angelhawk*'s tail sails in a mere eight hours.

The speed of the turnaround was probably for the best. The whole town was extremely interested to know more about the young girl who'd convinced Canri to let her cut down one of his trees, and the sister with the gift of healing. Many people were finding excuses to visit the tower, hoping for a glimpse.

'How did they know?' a puzzled Jemima asked as she watched from the lower deck as another group of people were politely turned back from the base of the tower.

Felix tipped his head towards the captain, who was currently harassing Patrina and Ormanda as they carried new supplies to the galley. 'Guess. Who's the biggest teller of stories onboard?'

'She wouldn't tell anyone about our quest, would she?'

Felix chittered his teeth. 'Well, she hasn't yet. That's got to be good.'

With the repairs finished and fresh stores onboard, Captain Rebecca gave the orders to make ready.

'Currents are slow,' she said, studying the way distant clouds scudded through the sky. 'But no worry, there'll be a pressure surge or a storm drift we can catch. One thing's always for certain in this beautiful Realm, the sky is never still.' She smiled happily, and took the helm wheel.

'Captain,' Maklepine called. 'We have visitors.'

'Huh?' Captain Rebecca spun round.

Floating inside the net of the upper deck, Taggie felt herself tense, the memories of launching from Banmula and what it cost them were all too fresh. She heard the crew gasp in delight, and twisted until she was facing the forest end of the isle. Three black triangles were approaching. A slow smile broke out on her face as she saw how fast they moved.

Canri's lithe body seemed to ripple as his wings undulated with a steady beat. The two sting tails waved from side to side, complementing the sinuous way he powered through the air. Then his wings were curving back, and he slithered to a halt. A few small ripples ran down his body, which manoeuvred his head right up to the net around mid-deck.

'My greetings to you on this new day, young Queen,' he said.

Taggie smiled at the great golden eyes on the other side of the net. 'Your Grace.'

'Blossom Princess, your healing power is a beautiful blessing. My leg hurts no more. I thank you for that.'

'You're welcome,' Jemima said, feeling immeasurably proud.

'And the tree makes a sturdy mast, Your Grace,' Captain Rebecca said respectfully. 'We should catch some fine winds.'

'Wind alone may not be enough for the young Queen's compassionate quest to succeed. I am here to offer myself and Flencen and Loarva from my drove as your escort.'

'Thank you so much,' Taggie said, beaming at the gigantic olri-gi.

'Many peoples have helped you this far,' Canri said. 'I feel it is now the turn of the olri-gi to share some of the burden.'

'We need a good wind from darkwards, Your Grace,' Captain Rebecca said.

'And we will find you one,' Canri said. 'Make sail, and I will accompany you while Flencen and Loarva find your current.'

With Captain Rebecca shouting her orders at the crew, the *Angelhawk* launched effectively from the tower. Tipsails caught the breeze, pushing her away from the wharf. Midsails quickened her pace. They steered in a wide curve, soaring over the town, then straight up away from the isle. Glancing darkwards, Taggie glimpsed the comet with its long tail shimmering red against the starry dark blue sky. It was a lot brighter than it had been just a couple of days ago.

Canri matched the ship's manoeuvres with barely a flick of his wings. Flencen and Loarva shot off ahead with astonishing speed, and were soon lost amid the infinite blue.

18

THE SEA GLOBE

On the third day out from Guatigua Taggie saw the olri-gi feeding. They were passing wide of a small isle, no more than a mile wide and covered in a thick coat of trees and bushes, when the three dark shapes suddenly darted away from the *Angelhawk*.

As always, the air around the little isle was thick with flocks of birds, like multi-coloured clouds forever shifting about. The olri-gi approached them from the sun, accelerating fast with their wings rippling into a blur of speed. Just as they hit the outer fringes of the birds, their mouths opened wide, and the birds were simply scooped up. The flocks scattered, of course, flapping madly, heading for the safety of the vegetation smothering the isle. The olri-gi spun and turned as if they were performing some elaborate dance, ploughing through the densest congregation of the fleeing birds, gulping them down.

'They must be eating a hundred each,' Lantic said in fascination. He'd borrowed Captain Rebecca's small telescope to observe the awesome creatures. Most of the crew were standing on the mid-deck below, watching the same spectacle.

The bird flocks were now contracting round the isles. The olri-gi performed one last skimming manoeuvre just above the tree tops and streaked away.

Taggie borrowed the telescope and pointed it aft down the hull until she was looking at the comet. It had grown from a star-point to a small circle. The red light it emitted was strong, and constantly fluctuating. When she lined the telescope up on it, she could see small curving fountains erupting from the surface; none of them lasted for more than a few minutes before blending back into the long hazy tail. She started to wonder how far away it was.

'It looks like it's chasing us,' she remarked.

'Let's hope not,' Lantic said. 'We've got enough odds stacked against us already.'

Canri slipped elegantly through the air to manoeuvre close to the *Angelhawk*. 'We think there's a sea globe in the clouds half a day ahead,' the olri-gi said.

Captain Rebecca took the telescope from Taggie and scoured the sky above the prow. Vast streamers of white and grey cloud drifted slowly across the sun, meandering into shallow curves that wound round a distant eye-shaped swirl. 'How big is the sea globe?' she asked.

'There's a lot of cloud ahead, so it'll be a large one,' Canri replied.

'Can't we just go round those clouds?' Taggie asked.

'This wind current will be drawn to the sea globe,' the captain told her. 'So we can go the long way round, outside the clouds, but it will add at least a couple of days to our voyage. We'd have to find a decent wind current on the other side as well.'

Taggie examined the clouds ahead. 'So what happens if we follow the cloud streamers in and fly over the sea globe?'

'It's very cloudy on the other side,' Favian explained. 'With the sun shining on it all the time, the sea gives off a lot of water vapour. We'll be flying blind for a while.'

'So, young Queen, how quickly to you want to get to Wynate?' Captain Rebecca asked.

Taggie didn't like the idea of flying blind through this Realm, but she was starting to worry about how long it was taking them to reach Mirlyn's Gate. The War Emperor would be leading his armies into the Fourth Realm by now; it wouldn't be long until the first battle began.

'Just how risky is flying above the sea globe?' she asked the captain.

'Barely any risk, especially with the olri-gi flying scout for us.'

Taggie saw the expression of dismay cross Maklepine's face, but then it seemed to be his place in life to worry. 'All right,' she said. 'Let's take the shortest course we can.'

After a couple of hours' sailing the *Angelhawk* reached the edges of the long streamers of cloud. They began to trace a gentle curve through the air, following the drawn-out tatters of vapour in towards the sea globe.

'Water ho!' the forward watch called.

Everyone looked up. There was a large blue-grey sphere far beyond the prow. The sky beyond it boiled with pure white cloud that was rushing away from the sea globe's sunward side, not that they could see the sun any more. The white cloud was too thick.

'That is one big sea,' Lantic said, looking up with growing concern at the immense sphere of water. Right at the centre of the darkwards' surface the water gleamed red under the comet's escalating light.

'This?' Captain Rebecca said scornfully. 'The olri-gi exaggerated, young Prince. Why, I've seen some sea globes big enough that it would take a week to fly round them.'

'Taggie.' Jemima was pulling on Taggie's sleeve, her face turning an unhealthy white.

'What's up?'

'I don't like this. Tell the captain to steer the long way round. Please?'

'What's there?' Taggie asked. 'What can you sight?'

'I don't know. I just know there's something bad in that sea.'

'Captain?' Taggie asked. 'What lives in the sea globes?'

'Nothing that can hurt us, Blossom Princess, don't you worry. I know what I'm doing.' The swirl of stars in her jewelled eye contracted. 'That is a lot of cloud on the other side, though,' she admitted. 'We could be heading into a bit of a storm.'

Jemima's sullen expression became a little more satisfied. 'See?'

'I'll ask the olri-gi to take a look,' the captain said. She put her head back, and emitted a high pitched airsong.

Taggie watched the hulking black triangle of Loarva dwindle away into the thin mist that was building around the *Angelhawk*. Visibility shrank by the minute as the ship rushed onward. She could see the great curving streamers of foggy cloud they were following start to wind up tightly. As the seething vapour streaked down to the sea globe it grew narrow, turning to a torrent of rain which lashed down on the darkward side.

Both Sophie and Felix were pressed against the lower deck net, looking aft. 'That comet is going to come close,' Sophie told Taggie. 'We've been watching it. It's heading almost straight for us.'

Taggie didn't need to use the telescope any more. To the naked eye, the comet was now a tiny ball whose surface seethed as if it was an agitated living thing. Big jets of glowing pink gas were firing out at random, expanding to tattered puffs that stretched out for miles and miles behind it.

'They never hit sea globes,' Maklepine told them. 'We're in the safest place, trust me.'

'They must hit them occasionally,' Lantic said stiffly. 'It's sheer probability.'

'If they were natural phenomenon, aye,' the shipsmage said. 'But you forget, young prince, these are the bodies of angels.'

Jemima came out of the little cabin she shared with

Taggie and Sophie, wearing her armour. Even after a year, it remained oversized for her; she had to roll the sleeves and legs up.

'Are you still worried?' Felix asked.

Jemima shrugged. 'I know something bad is waiting up ahead,' she said. 'I can sight that much.'

'What?'

'I don't know. All right?'

Taggie scoured the sky ahead. The surface of the sea globe was now barely twenty miles away, and so great it was starting to resemble a flat sea just like any of those in the Outer Realm.

Something rose up from behind the northwards curve of the sea globe, exactly the same colour. A sphere that raced above the surface extremely fast. It was as if the sea globe had a tiny moon.

'What is that?' Jemima squealed fearfully.

'Jem,' Taggie said, starting to get annoyed at her little sister's panic. 'You need to get a grip.'

'Aye, calm you down, little Princess,' Captain Rebecca said with a grin. ''Tis just a globelet. Most sea globes have a few.'

'Globelet?' Felix asked.

'Aye. They're thrown off by the surface every now and then. Mostly they just evaporate into more cloud, but some fall back with an almighty splash. 'Tis quite a sight.'

Taggie was watching the globelet in astonishment. It really was like a moon. She tried to work out how big it was; several miles in diameter at least, with its own choppy waves clashing all over it.

'I don't like it,' Jemima whined.

'Give it a rest,' Taggie snapped.

'Here we go!' Captain Rebecca spun the helm wheel again, altering their course slightly so they were flying parallel to the water, perhaps fifteen miles above it. For the first time, Taggie began to appreciate just how fast they were sailing. The tiny white crested waves below were flashing past.

Something moved just under the surface, gliding along under the breakers. Something dark grey and large.

Felix gasped, and scurried down the net to the handrail. 'Did you see that?'

'Relax, squirrel,' Captain Rebecca laughed. 'There are many pods of pearlwhales living in the globe seas of this realm. They can't fly. You're perfectly safe. Sweet heavens, for a group anxious to visit Wynate you're all badly nervy.'

The *Angelhawk* spent three hours flying over the water. Her passengers spent the whole time staring down at the surface. They saw more of the great pale shapes of pearlwhales slipping through the depths. And other, smaller creatures that moved quickly. The waves battled each other constantly. Then there were the whirlpools. Huge spinning funnels of water, whose tapering craters reached down twenty or thirty miles to a blackness which hid their true extent. Another globelet came racing round the sea globe, its sunward hemisphere a bright grey-blue while the darkward hemisphere shone a dull scarlet under the light of the expanding comet. Just like the *Angelhawk*'s sails, Taggie noticed, which shone from the two different lights that now dominated the sky above the sea globe.

Once, Jemima and Sophie yelled in amazement and the others turned just in time to see a massive geyser of water powering miles up into the air from an exceptionally choppy section of water. The crest began to curve downwards again. Though they could all see several tiny spheres of water break free and hurtle into the distance. Taggie thought that must be how the globelets were created. She didn't like to think how big one of those geysers would be, nor what caused it.

'What is down there?' Lantic exclaimed with a frown, clearly considering the same thought.

'Something powerful,' Lord Colgath said, his deep voice for once subdued with caution.

Maklepine joined them at the rail, staring down at the turmoil of water far below. 'Sailors of this Realm claim that the sea globes are the prisons of fallen archangels cast down from the heavens during the war of the gods before our First Times,' the shipsmage said with a spark of delight in his eye. 'And that they are held in place only by the weight of water on top of them. Every wave you see, every whirlpool and geyser, is caused by them twisting and turning as they struggle to be free.' He touched his forehead with his finger, and walked off round the mid-deck.

'Gosh.' Taggie gulped, and turned back to watch the shrinking geyser again. Her hand went to the bag hanging round her neck, feeling the shape of the dark gate it contained. Just in case . . .

'A fallen archangel,' Jemima said, pale-faced. Her hands gripped the rail so hard her knuckles were whitening. 'Taggie, I just want to go home.'

Taggie put her arm round her little sister, and cuddled her tight. She felt more than a little overwhelmed herself after listening to Maklepine. 'We will, Jem, very soon now. I promise. But you know we can't turn back, not now. Still, at least you know what was troubling you.'

Jemima gave a reluctant nod, and sniffed hard.

They flew across the sea globe for another twenty minutes. All that time, the red light of the comet grew brighter and brighter aft of the *Angelhawk*. When Captain Rebecca finally spun the helm wheel again, taking them up away from the waves and whirlpools, it was as if a second sun was shining behind them. A sun that blazed scarlet and sent flickers of crimson shadows across the hull.

Ahead of the prow, the cloud that rose from the sunward side of the sea globe was like a fluorescent pink wall stretched right across the Realm. The temperature of the air gusting over the deck began to rise again.

'Where's Loarva got to?' Felix muttered anxiously as the ship raced towards the cloud. He stuck his tiny damp nose through the net and sniffed hard. 'She

should have been back by now.'

Captain Rebecca gave him a sharp glance, betraying how she was thinking along similar lines.

Taggie stared at the unyielding pink mass ahead with growing unease. Cloudbusting was the oldest magic she had; when she was younger she'd often chased rainclouds out of a summer sky. Not that she had the strength to shift anything like this massive barricade of shining vapour. Not in its entirety. But all they needed was a clear passage.

'Go away,' she told it, and clicked her fingers.

A blemish appeared in the uniform sheet of pink. Strands of darker cloud slunk up to the surface, and curled round as if someone was stirring them like foam on a coffee cup. The blemish bowed inward and began to expand, like an iris opening.

All around the deck, the crew began to cheer.

Captain Rebecca steered them into the centre of the vast tunnel which pushed up through the cloud. The *Angelhawk* sailed along the immense passage of clear air, with its escort of two olri-gi flapping lazily at her side.

Everybody on board felt it at the same time as Jemima cried out in shock. It was as if they'd passed through a curtain of magic. Magic which disgustingly licked every part of them and the ship. Even the olri-gi spun in agitation.

'What in the sweet heavens was that?' Captain Rebecca demanded. The air around the *Angelhawk* remained perfectly clear, she could see for miles and miles along the tunnel of slow-spinning pink cloud.

'We have been sighted,' Lord Colgath boomed. The slivers of iridescent colours within his cloak all turned a sickly orange while his head turned from side to side, as if he was trying to find the source of the magic.

Along both decks the crew were immobile and silent, scouring the blank sky of pink cloud enveloping them.

'It's *her*,' Jemima wailed, staring at the rune stones in her hand.

'Who?' asked Taggie. 'Who is it, Jem?'

'The old woman in black. She's found us.'

Taggie gave Lantic and Sophie a frantic glance as her charmsward bands started to slip round silently. Sophie was already reaching for her crossbow, while several of Lantic's rings were starting to glow brightly. The only noise was the wind in the *Angelhawk*'s sails.

'Oh, Jem, I'm so sorry,' an aghast Taggie said. 'It wasn't the archangel you sensed.' She could have kicked herself, she'd always suspected who the old woman was working for.

'Ships ho!' came a cry from the forward watch.

Taggie craned her neck back to stare up past the prow. Her breath caught in her throat. Five miles ahead of the *Angelhawk*, three ships were sliding out of the curving pink cloud which lined the side of the tunnel. *I'll bring the clouds back*, she told herself, and raised her hand ready to click her fingers.

Two more ships emerged from the cloud up ahead. With them was a shape she knew was an olri-gi, though not one of their escort.

Five ships! Sweet Heavens. The War Emperor must be desperate to stop me.

Taggie could feel spells as powerful as her own being added to her original cloudbuster enchantment, strengthening the tunnel of clear air.

And there was only one person she knew who had a magic that equalled her own. *Katrabeth!*

Another four dark specks appeared, along with several more olri-gi.

'Frigates,' Captain Rebecca growled, baring her teeth in defiance. 'So the Highlord has sent his finest against me, has he now? But they'll be no match for my *Angelhawk*, you see.'

Taggie, Lantic, Sophie and Lord Colgath all turned to stare in disbelief at the captain.

'What?' Captain Rebecca challenged. 'Bring the cloud back, young Queen. We'll soon outrun them amidst that veil. And they'll not follow where we go. They wouldn't dare.'

Two more frigates sailed out of the cloud.

Taggie let out a groan of trepidation. 'It's not the Highlord,' she said miserably. 'It's the War Emperor who sent them. And they will pursue us all the way to the Hell Realm if they have to.'

'Is the War Emperor here?' Captain Rebecca sneered. 'No! He sits in his fine castle drinking wine and lets others do his dirty work. They haven't the fire for this fight.'

Canri came gliding in towards the *Angelhawk*. 'That is Meaor's drove with the Highlord's ships,' he said. 'I wasn't expecting to confront my own kind. Olri-gi do not fight among ourselves.'

'I would not ask you to,' Taggie said.

'How did they find us?' Lord Colgath asked. 'I thought Jemima's new wardveil was sufficient to shield us from their seers.'

'I expect it was Penelopi,' Captain Rebecca spat. 'If the navy commander knew we were heading for Wynate, he'd know we would sail past this sea globe.'

'Damn my father!' Lantic stormed, thumping his fist

down on the rail. 'Taggie, you know we have to try to break past them.'

She gave him a melancholy smile, thinking back just a few short weeks to the timid, browbeaten prince who had greeted her that first time in Shatha'hal. And now here he was, ready to take on an entire navy – single-handed by the look of him.

'I can animate the *Angelhawk*'s firestars,' Lantic insisted, 'And you and Lord Colgath can—'

'Yes!' she held up a hand. 'I get it. And . . . thank you.'

Lantic's smile was one of pure admiration directed at her.

It was hard for Taggie to look away – but when she did scan the sky ahead there were now eleven ships visible, and seven olri-gi. She took a breath. 'Captain?'

'Aye, young Queen?'

'There's another sorceress somewhere on those frigates. My cousin. And she wants me dead, very badly.'

'She'll have to catch us first. If we can just get ahead of them, then we stand a chance.'

19

BATTLE STATIONS

Standing on the bridge of the Highlord's frigate *Intrepid*, wearing a long grey silk dress which comet light was staining the colour of blood, Katrabeth watched the *Angelhawk* keenly.

'Whatever is she doing?' she asked.

Several miles ahead of the *Intrepid*, the *Angelhawk* was changing course, curving through the remarkably clear air to line her prow up on the squadron. One of the olri-gi accompanying her was flying directly in front while the other . . .

'It's pushing her,' said Ohola, the frigate's commander.

'What does she hope to achieve?' Katrabeth asked, and put her hands on her hips like a teacher dealing with a problem child.

'I think . . .' Commander Ohola hesitated, as if he couldn't quite believe what he was witnessing. 'She might be trying to outrun us.'

'But we're ahead of her,' Katrabeth said.

'Yes. But we have to manoeuvre to match her.' His eyes narrowed. 'That might be difficult. Given the circumstances that's a smart move. At that speed, she'll be past us in another ten minutes.'

'The War Emperor himself assigned me to deal with the Queen of Dreams,' Katrabeth said. 'And I intend to carry out that instruction to the letter. Send the olri-gi over to wreck her masts. That should allow you to harpoon her easily. I'll lead the boarding party over.'

Commander Ohola's wings gave a single slow flap. 'They might prove reluctant to approach while Canri is so close. Olri-gi do not fight olri-gi.'

Katrabeth tapped a foot in disapproval. 'Heavens, dragons are useless animals.'

Commander Ohola's delicate skin turned red at the slur. 'The olri-gi are *not*—'

'Yes, yes,' Katrabeth said impatiently. 'At least see if they'll lower themselves to hindering the *Angelhawk*'s course somehow. We need to slow that ship down.'

The commander inclined his head. 'My lady.'

'Idiot,' Katrabeth grumbled vehemently after the skyman left the bridge to talk to Meaor. She looked at the *Angelhawk* again. It was considerably closer.

'Take care,' Lantic said as he ducked into the hatchway on the lower deck. The ladder inside led down to the *Angelhawk*'s harpoon deck. Several crew were already down there, opening the hatches. When Lantic joined them he would animate the ship's various weapons, making them do things the frigates wouldn't be expecting. Hopefully.

'And you,' Taggie replied, feeling she ought to say more but not knowing what exactly.

They exchanged a nervous smile. Then she and Lord Colgath climbed up on to the crown of the *Angelhawk*'s top deck. The ship's prow was a simple circle of planks, broken by the glass dome of the watch officer, and two windows for the captain's cabin where she could look ahead.

'Careful up there,' Felix called from the net just below the rim.

With the wind ruffling her hair and shirt, Taggie suddenly felt a sensation like vertigo run down her legs. There was no net up here, no rail around the edge.

'Yes,' she murmured, realizing how precarious the position was. Even though she could shapeshift to a bird, it was a big sky to get lost in. 'Felix, throw a rope up for me, please.'

'Make that two,' Lord Colgath said as he stepped off the top of the ladder. 'Without my rathwai to ride, I seem to be developing a fear of heights.'

She flashed him a tentative smile. 'It's not the height; it's the fall that's the problem.'

'I haven't done anything like this for six hundred years,' he said in his resonant voice.

Taggie looked up. The frigates were flying into a wide ring formation. And the *Angelhawk* was aiming right for the centre of them. 'How long do Karraks live?' she asked, suddenly curious. According to Dad, members of the First

Realm royal family could expect to last almost a hundred and fifty years.

'I was born two hundred years before my father brought us through Mirlyn's Gate. Some of my brethren here are over three thousand years old. They tell us of Karraks alive in our own universe that had lived ten thousand years.'

'I'm not sure if that's a blessing or a curse,' Taggie said.

'We don't live as long here. The nature of this universe is as ill-disposed to our life magic as it is to all our aspects.'

'You mean you live for so long because of an enchantment?'

'Partly. We live a long time anyway. Legend says our first lore masters studied our very nature, and used their power to enhance various traits. But such a spell is part of our inheritance now – we don't even have to cast it on our children. They are born with it.'

'Do you have children?' she asked. It wasn't something she'd ever thought of.

'Only thirty-two, of which twenty-eight are sons. This universe does not favour us with daughters. Their birth here is rare. We guard them jealously, for they are so precious.'

'Thirty-two children? *Really?*'

'Indeed.'

'Gosh.'

Felix stuck his head up above the topdeck's rim. 'Ropes,' he announced. 'I've secured them to the hull down here. Catch.'

Taggie tied the rope round her waist. When she finished, the enemy frigates were a lot closer. Three olri-gi were hurtling towards the *Angelhawk*.

'Get ready!' Captain Rebecca yelled gleefully.

As soon as the *Intrepid* hoisted its signal flags, Katrabeth stood on the bridge, watching in satisfaction as they curved round into a giant ring formation. The *Angelhawk* would have to pass through the centre of them. When she did, fifty harpoons would stab out for her. Even if only five hit and held, it would be enough for them to haul her to rest and the boarding troops could fly over.

She heard Commander Ohola give the order for the harpoon launchers to be readied. Hatches around the *Intrepid*'s lower hull opened, and the metal tips slid out. A quarter of the launchers were loaded with firestars. Meaor and three of his drove flashed past the *Intrepid* to harass the olri-gi helping the *Angelhawk*, and hopefully slow the ship.

'Olri-gi ho!' called the upper deck watch.

Katrabeth turned to see another of the superb black shapes come arrowing out of the cloud tunnel's wall, heading right for Meaor and his drove. The mighty creatures broke formation half a mile distant from the *Angelhawk*, twisting and spinning in confusion as they sought to avoid collision with the newcomer. Then the *Angelhawk* launched a barrage of firestars.

'Why are they doing that?' Commander Ohola asked.

The firestars didn't seem to be aimed at anything. Then he gasped in shock.

Katrabeth watched in dismay as the firestars started to curve round in the air. 'Lantic,' she whispered angrily. Somehow the prince had managed to animate the firestars.

The spinning firestars chased after the tussling olri-gi, expanding into flaming discs as they went. Meaor and his drove scattered in earnest now. And the *Angelhawk* powered onwards.

'Full sails,' commander Ohola bellowed. 'Interception course!'

Taggie and Lord Colgath stood on the upper deck as before, hunched against their increased weight as Canri pushed the *Angelhawk* along at an unheard-of speed.

The first batch of firestars launched, and started pursuing the startled olri-gi. Lantic had consulted with Canri before animating them, assuring the olri-gi that they would never actually hit any of Meaor's drove. The first batch were used to scare and confuse only.

Taggie saw the navy frigates change course abruptly, heading in for the *Angelhawk*. And one of the Highlord's olri-gi with more nerve than its fellows dived round under the *Angelhawk*, screaming furiously as a firestar followed it. Canri's answering screech was loud in her ears. Then the *Angelhawk*'s acceleration dropped off sharply, and she saw the two giant creatures flying away together, almost but not quite touching as their wings rippled in powerful undulations. Like three-year-olds squabbling in a nursery, she thought in bitter amusement.

Frigates were rushing in from every direction.

Taggie clicked her fingers. The sides of the cloud tunnel heaved in torment. Vast foaming bands of thick mist tore loose and jetted into the clear air. The tip of each one was directed at a frigate, like a giant spear of fluorescent pink fluff. She felt Katrabeth's spells frantically trying to counter her own, and smiled mercilessly at how ineffectual her cousin was at this particular magic.

'Second barrage,' Captain Rebecca ordered. 'Launch.'

Nine firestars zoomed away from the *Angelhawk*. This time they ignored the olri-gi and arched round to head for the frigates. Somewhere aft, Lantic was laughing like a maniac.

'I hate that little brat,' Katrabeth snarled as more firestars shot out from the *Angelhawk*. One of the expanding discs sliced round to head straight for the *Intrepid*.

The frigate's helmsman swung the wheel frantically, but it made no difference; the firestar kept coming for them like a demented homing pigeon.

'Brace for impact!' the forward watch screamed.

Katrabeth stood on the mid-deck and glared at the deadly spinning flames hurtling towards them. '*Gathoiak!*' She clicked her fingers, and the flames burned black for a second before breaking up into a puff of cinders.

The crew's shouts of relief mingled with their cries of

gratitude. Katrabeth ignored them all. 'I can't waste my time on this nonsense,' she declared. Her fingers clicked again.

The air around her seethed and darkened. Her silhouette writhed energetically and there was a big black eagle standing on the deck. The protective netting above the vicious-looking bird burned to ash, and it flew away through the hole.

Three frigates struck by firestars floundered. Flames started shooting out of the rents torn through their hulls. But still they managed to manoeuvre to shoot back in retaliation. Four of the undamaged frigates added their weapons to the barrage. Seventeen firestars spread out along the *Angelhawk*'s course.

Taggie blasted four of them apart. Lord Colgath nailed two with his fireballs. The rest passed by without any danger. Luckily the navy didn't seem to have an anamage with them.

The *Angelhawk* was drawing level with the ring of navy ships, and the intact frigates were looping round and closing fast. Lord Colgath flung fireballs at them as they drew nearer.

Around everybody, the pink clouds were tossing about in chaos, and still contracting. Winds churned at random through the shrinking gulf of clear air, making steering a real challenge. Angry, shrieking olri-gi darted about in a tight tangle, antagonizing each other, but not venturing near the ships.

Taggie sensed Katrabeth approaching, a malevolence that made no attempt to shield itself from her. She hurriedly untied the rope. 'She's coming,' Taggie yelled in warning, before diving cleanly off the topdeck.

The *Adrap* shapeshift spell seethed around her, transforming her form to a pure white snow eagle. And Taggie stretched her superb wings wide to greet the rushing air. Baleful comet light shimmered cerise off her feathers.

Ahead, Katrabeth came rushing towards her. A death spell lanced out. Taggie swatted it away with a shield enchantment and veered sharply southwards. As she passed the b l a c k eagle she let loose a death spell of her own – the first time she'd ever used one. Katrabeth parried with diabolical skill, and launched a needle-plume of dazzling white fire.

Her heart pounding, Taggie veered away. *Doesn't anything work against her?* she thought. This time she sent a lump of solid air to strike at the terrible eagle. Katrabeth simply soared round it, squawking mockingly.

Taggie braced herself fearfully for the next spell, spinning her protective enchantments as strongly as possible. That was about all she could think of now – to hang on grimly and hope for some outside intervention. If it wasn't for what Katrabeth would do to all her friends on the *Angelhawk*, she might even have turned and flown off into the infinite blue.

Death spells struck her in quick succession. Taggie hauled in firestars, and sent them streaking at the black eagle – timed with her own destruction spell so Katrabeth might be overwhelmed. But Katrabeth avoided them all.

Then the acute whistle blasts began.

Crews on every ship stopped what they were doing to watch the titanic battle of the sorceresses. They shielded their eyes from the incandescent blasts of lethal magical lightning as the two birds wove their deadly dance though the air. Even the olri-gi stilled their feints and glided round to observe.

Lantic hurried round the mid-deck, desperate to keep the two protagonists in view. Lord Colgath was still slamming out fireballs at the frigates who retaliated by launching a barrage of firestars at the *Angelhawk*. And Captain Rebecca was smiling manically as she steered them through the tightening knot of navy ships, dodging harpoons and firestars.

'We have to help Taggie!' Sophie yelled at him. She pulled her crossbow round, enchanting the mechanism ready to fire.

'No,' Lantic yelled back. 'Don't fly out there. Katrabeth will attack you. Taggie can't defend you as well as herself, it's tactical suicide.'

Sophie slammed a fist down on the rail in frustration. 'What about the harpoons? Can you animate them to chase Katrabeth?'

'I can try.'

'Then do it! Don't wait for—' She broke off in shock as the whistle blast sounded, the one piercing note she had been taught to fear from birth. 'Oh no,' she groaned in horror. Already the shout was going up among the skyfolk on the *Angelhawk* and the navy ships alike.

'Rathwai! Rathwai are coming!'

The Karraks flew their formidable beasts out of the thrashing clouds in a wide V-formation. They swept in gleefully towards the beleaguered *Angelhawk*, crying out challenges as they went.

Lord Drakouth urged his rathwai on towards the ship carrying Lord Colgath. Until now he hadn't realized how much he missed war. But *this* – this made him happy to be alive, even if it was in this wretched Light Universe. Around him the Highlord's frigates burned, trailing long smears of thick black smoke. The worrying shapes of the olri-gi were massing beyond the frigates, which made his mount nervous. Firestars slashed about between the ships. And the two vile sorceresses battled in mid-air, sending out intense torrents of lethal magical energy. Then the whistle came – he'd been expecting that, he'd heard it so many times over the centuries: the alarm call of the skyfolk.

He saw them take flight from every ship, the nasty little winged people, holding grimly on to their cherished bows, tips of bad magic glimmering. And the olri-gi were abruptly heading in towards the rathwai, their stingers curling up ready to jab. After four hundred years of creeping about and launching pitiful raids on the other Realms, Lord Drakouth was about to do proper battle again. It was a truly glorious feeling.

The V-formation split into three streams, and peeled apart, heading for their respective targets. Lord Drakouth raised his arm and bellowed in delight as his rathwai caught his own battle frenzy and strained forwards. His smoke cloak flowed out behind him, spreading along the rathwai's back like an ethereal serpent. A burst of purple-white magic crackled around his upheld fingers, and he flung the deadly power at the flimsy wooden ship ahead.

As soon as the whistles sounded, Taggie and Katrabeth abandoned their fight to search round. Taggie saw the terrible formation of rathwai come racing through the dwindling channel of clear air towards her. There must have been eight or nine Karrak Lords and Ladies sitting astride their diabolical creatures, whose wings were pumping away urgently. Ferocious sword-sharp beaks snapped in anticipation even as they extended their talons to rip her from the sky.

'Such a shame,' the black eagle taunted as she flew a slow circle round Taggie. 'Now we'll never know who was the fairest of them all, will we, cousin?'

Taggie eyed the approaching Dark Lords fearfully. The brutal magical fight with Katrabeth had already left her feeling drained. Behind the approaching rathwai she saw spells and enchantments flare in the air round the *Angelhawk*. The tiny figure of Lord Colgath stood on the prow, defiantly hurling fireballs and death spells at the four Dark Lords on their rathwai who were closing on him. A firestar struck the *Angelhawk*'s lower deck, blowing out a shower of debris – flames licking at the edges of the rip. One of the frigates that was pouring out smoke suddenly exploded as the flames reached its store of firestars.

'Here she is,' Katrabeth called to the approaching rathwai. 'The Abomination herself. I have isolated her for you. Have fun, everyone.'

'Er . . .' Taggie mumbled in puzzlement. The incoming Karrak warriors weren't slowing down, nor did they seem to be paying any attention to Katrabeth. Taggie spun her strongest protective shield around herself. The charmsward bands turned, and she chanted the absorption spell she'd devised a year ago.

The three Karraks in the lead raised their hands. Sharp blue wizard light flashed out from their fingers. Two of the death spells struck Taggie, turning her shield a dangerous rosy gold before the charmsward sucked in their power and held it. One death spell smacked into Katrabeth.

'*What!*' Katrabeth shrieked in utter outrage, her voice rising higher than the peals of the skyfolk alarm whistles. 'I am allied with your Grand Lord, you fools!'

Taggie was almost sorry she was in eagle form; having a beak meant she couldn't grin.

'And he bid you banished to the Hell Realm,' one of the Karraks sneered. He sent another death spell flashing through the air at Katrabeth.

Her mad scream split the air. She hurtled at the rathwai like a back-feathered meteorite. Her own death spell shot out and slaughtered the big creature in an instant. Grey, greasy smoke burst from its beak and slithered off its rigid wingtips like a sickly contrail. The Karrak riding it tumbled off into the air. Katrabeth fell upon him, clawing wildly with her talons, her curved beak jabbing repeatedly. A mantle of blazing scarlet magic engulfed the pair of them as they spun end over end.

Then the scarlet light popped like a soap bubble. And the black eagle came streaking out to chase vengefully after another rathwai. Behind her, the Karrak Lord's broken body floated aimlessly through the sky, his smoke cloak dissolving like frost in summer sunlight.

With the rest of their attackers turning tail, Taggie performed a sharp curve and headed back to the smoking *Angelhawk*.

'They're coming back!' Jemima yelled in warning as four circling rathwai pirouetted neatly and shot in towards the poor *Angelhawk*. There were jagged holes in the decking she had to be careful not to fall through, and smoke was still billowing out of the firestar rent in the lower hull. A couple of sails were smouldering. Another fireball engulfed one of the masts, which Lord Colgath countered with some kind of glittery black mist. Yet Captain Rebecca was still at the helm, steering them onwards, and desperately trying to avoid the pursuing frigates. Harpoons shot past the hull.

Lord Colgath pitched more spells. One of the approaching rathwai writhed as if it had struck something solid, its cries so loud Jemima had to cover her ears.

'Lantic, fire something at them, curse you!' Captain Rebecca bellowed.

A harpoon shot out, twisting sharply as soon as it left the hatch, and pierced the injured rathwai clean through its body, the wicked tip only narrowly missing the Karrak Lord riding it.

'Fresh meat tonight,' Captain Rebecca yelled.

Jemima heard several crew cheering at the same time as something crashed into the *Angelhawk*'s mid-deck cabin bulkhead amid a sound of tortured, splintering timber, and she went sprawling. A rathwai's claws thumped down beside her shattering the deck planks, and she screamed, trying to roll away.

'Get her!' a terrible voice ordered.

The rathwai moved its leg, and the black curving talons closed around Jemima. The pressure they exerted was awful, but her *athrodene* armour hardened to protect her. Then the beast's leathery wings were beating and she was yanked away from the decking. Jemima wailed in horror as she saw the ship starting to shrink away beneath her.

Felix was on the mid-deck rail when the rathwai landed clumsily on the *Angelhawk*, its great wings flapping chaotically above him. The whole ship lurched from the impact, and Felix clung desperately to the rail. Somewhere behind him, Jemima screamed. He whipped round to see the rathwai's big curving talons closing round her. The *athrodene* armour shone a pale silver, preventing her from being torn apart. Then the Dark Lord's beast crouched, preparing to leap clear.

'No!' Felix yelled, and sprinted hard along the rail towards the rathwai.

His voice must have penetrated the thunderous confusion surrounding the ship, for he saw the rathwai's eyes flick round to glance at him for a second. He – insignificant lump of white fur – obviously meant nothing to the huge beast, for it ignored him and jumped, pulling its wings back for the first proper downsweep that would carry Jemima away.

Felix flung himself after it – soaring across the gap, limbs spread wide, willing himself to complete the desperate leap. He landed on the top of the rathwai's beak, directly between the two nasal slits.

Gripping the slit edges hard with his forepaws, he dug his sharp little claws in. On either side and above him, the rathwai's dark eyes widened, first in surprise then at the discomfort of the sting where the claw tips gripped such a sensitive place. Felix looked past them at the Karrak Lord on his saddle, whose skeletal face was regarding the squirrel in disbelief.

'A Weldowen,' the Dark Lord growled in loathing. He raised a hand, the rings on his bony fingers pulsing with light – then hesitated, for Felix was crouched on the nose of his rathwai, and any death spell that hit Felix would also kill his mount.

'Oh yeah,' Felix taunted, 'You got that right.' Then he scampered away, his agile furry body snaking round the side of the rathwai's head, claws on all four paws gripping tight to the stiff dark scales like a miniature mountain climber. He slunk out of sight under its body.

The Karrak Lord snarled in frustration, and leaned over, trying to see where Felix had gone.

Felix scuttled down the underside of the rathwai's neck and saw Jemima still clamped in the beast's talons. Long tough muscles flexed under the scales as the rathwai's wings beat steadily. The stern of a frigate flashed past, belching out smoke.

'Felix,' she whimpered.

'Don't worry, I won't leave you.'

'Not worried,' she promised through her tears. 'Not now you're here.'

He crawled across the rathwai's flank until he was behind the shoulder, where the foreleg merged with its body. Carefully, he drew his sword, smiling at the brightness of its green runes, as he clung on with his remaining three paws. 'I'm going to make it let go,' he told her. 'There's skyfolk and olri-gi everywhere. They'll pick us up.'

'OK.' She nodded.

Felix stabbed his sword down into the rathwai's scaled hide. The beast roared in pain and fury as its dark blood gushed out. It wasn't a lethal wound, but it *hurt*. Wings slapped at the air as the rathwai juddered about, trying to shake loose the infuriating pest clinging to it. Felix shuffled along a bit, and stabbed again.

Jemima screamed as the talons squeezed her in reflex. Her *athrodene* armour creaked.

Felix continued stabbing. There was so much of the foul blood squirting out from the deep cuts, it was smeared all over his fur, and made the scales very slippery. He slid down the leg, and cut into the thinner flesh around the beast's ankle.

'It eased off,' Jemima shouted above the rathwai's colossal roars of pain.

Felix thrust the sword in again, just as a nearby frigate exploded. The blast punched the rathwai violently across the sky. Felix's claws tore loose, he flung himself at Jemima, who had one hand out towards him, her face crumpled in anguish, brown hair surging wildly. For one beautiful second he thought his forepaw would touch her – but the now fatally wounded rathwai spasmed, and she was snatched away.

'Jemima!' Felix fell freely through the cloud-plagued sky. Flaming debris from the exploding frigate whirred dangerously around him.

Suddenly something grabbed his hindleg. 'Gotcha!' Sophie cried.

'Jemima!' Felix yelled again, and pointed frantically at the tumbling beast with its necklace fountain of dark blood. 'The rathwai's got Jemima.'

'I know,' Sophie said. And she surged forward, curving steeply so they approached the Karrak Lord from behind. They were level with the rathwai's trembling wings when he turned in the saddle and hissed hatefully at the skymaid. His silver-tipped teeth grew out around his slim lips to give his mouth a crown of fangs. Formidable wizard light seeped out of his rings to coil around his fingers.

Sophie snicked a small lever forwards on her crossbow, aiming it at the Dark Lord's head.

'Fly away, useless little bird-thing,' the Karrak growled at her. 'Or I will take you back with me to the Fourth Realm as well as the princess. The rathwai will feed on you for a week while my magic keeps you alive.'

'You have my friend,' Sophie replied. 'Let her go.'

'Do you seriously believe your bolt will even scratch me?' the Karrak asked in scorn as his dying rathwai gave another pathetic judder beneath him.

'Not one bolt, no.' Sophie grinned. She pulled the trigger. The superb mechanism crafted by battlemages of the Second Realm fired all seventeen bolts in the space of a second and a half. The protective enchantments the Karrak Lord had woven around himself were strong enough to fend off the first eleven. The remaining six bolts shot clean through him.

'Let's go get her,' Sophie cried. She reached round to her quiver for fresh bolts.

Then a powerful wind rose from nowhere, and the very air itself started to vibrate in torment.

20

MONSTERS OF AIR

Lord Drakouth landed firmly on the *Angelhawk*'s prow, and his smoke cloak folded itself neatly around his body once more. Lord Colgath turned to face him.

'My lord,' Lord Drakouth said, bowing slightly. 'For someone who has renounced violence, my congratulations on your vehemence.'

Lord Colgath's mirror eyes regarded his brother's emissary contemptuously. 'I have not renounced violence,' his deep voice announced. 'Only stupidity.'

'Your brother bids you return.'

'So he can once again imprison me in a tower for eternity? I thank him for his gracious invitation, but feel I must decline.'

'It wasn't a request, my lord. And I have a hostage.' He indicated the rathwai holding Jemima as it shot away from the *Angelhawk*. 'The one thing seers can never see is their own death. But I daresay once the Blossom Princess is handed over to my brethren she will understand how her predicament will eventually end.'

'That was unwise of you, my lord,' Lord Colgath said. 'How so?'

Taggie landed behind Lord Drakouth, and transformed back into her normal shape. 'Your Grand Lord named me the Abomination, I believe?' she asked in an icy tone.

Lord Drakouth tried not to show any alarm at just how close she was. He watched the young human sorceress raise her arm. The magical bracelet of which so much had been fearfully whispered throughout the Fourth Realm circled her wrist. Its symbols glowed with a malevolent orange light.

Just beyond the *Angelhawk*'s smouldering mast, a Karrak Lady slung a disruptive spell into the ship's lower deck. Sturdy planks ruptured. Taggie clicked her fingers, casting a spell powered by the Karraks' own magic stored in the charmsward. The Karrak Lady flared into a ball of white light, and was no more. Her terrified rathwai flew away, screeching in dread.

'Good choice of name,' Taggie told Lord Drakouth. 'Now, I believe you were about to return my sister.'

'This is who you entrust our fate to?' Lord Drakouth asked Lord Colgath scathingly.

'Our fate is shared. All of our fates.'

'No,' Lord Drakouth said. 'And you, Abomination, do what you will with me. The Grand Lord will take your realm and all those who dwell in it.'

'No he won't,' Taggie said. 'Because we know where Mirlyn's Gate is. I offer you the road home, my lord, back to your own Universe. A free offer to you and your family.'

'You lie, Abomination.'

'My brother is concerned he has chosen the wrong path,' Lord Colgath said. 'That is why he sent you. Drakouth, you have my word that in another week we will have Mirlyn's Gate. How do you think the Congress of Lords will react to that? Come, now, how long have we known each other?'

'Long enough, my lord.'

'Then join me and the Queen of Dreams. Bring Mirlyn's Gate with me to my brother, show the brethren there is a way home again.'

'I cannot do such a thing.'

'Don't you think it's strange that your Grand Lord and our War Emperor *both* wish to stop us?' Taggie asked. 'Doesn't that make you question their judgement?'

Lord Drakouth's smoke cloak swirled as if a cyclone were building within it. 'The Grand Lord said you were capable of great bewitchment. I see he was right.'

'You should at least raise this with the Congress of Lords and Ladies,' Lord Colgath said. 'Do you wish your children to remain in this Universe forever when a way home exists?'

'This is not the place for such matters . . .' Lord Drakouth began.

A wind suddenly started to blow across the *Angelhawk*'s prow. Within seconds it had grown so strong the three of them could barely stand.

Taggie crouched down, her charmsward bands spinning round so she could refresh her shield enchantments. But this wasn't magic, she realized. On the decks below, the crew were shouting in panic.

'What is it?' she called. 'What's happening?'

Then the sound began that could surely only come from moons colliding, a bass rumble that was louder than thunder, stretching on and on. She could feel the ship's planks vibrating, threatening to burst apart. A hurricane took hold of the *Angelhawk* and propelled her onwards, plunging her into the boiling clouds. Sails began to rip. Flames streamed out behind her from the gashes in the hull where malign spells had struck.

All Taggie could do was drop to her knees and cling to a jagged split in the cabin roof as the *Angelhawk* careered along with the blast of wind. She hung on grimly, waiting for the madness to end.

A wheezing Lantic stumbled up the ladder from the harpoon deck, smoke billowing round him. As he tried to suck down clean air, Captain Rebecca was shouting orders that were instantly obliterated by the crushing waves of sound battering the ship. Nobody could hear a word, yet somehow the crew were leaping round to obey. Sails were hauled in, tipsails were simply cut free. Favian and Ormanda crouched down at the mounting of the burning mast (the tree from Canri's forest, Lantic realized) and tugged a lever on the decking above it. Whatever they did released the mast, it fell away, thrashing away in the unruly wind.

The *Angelhawk* soared through the sky as fast as

she'd ever gone, buffeted callously by the hurricane that gripped them. Without sails, all Captain Rebecca could do was steer as best she could to try and keep them from tumbling – which would have broken the weakened ship apart as surely as if they'd hit a rock.

After a frightening age the noise eased off slightly.

'What is that?' Lantic choked out.

'A volpas!' Captain Rebecca cried. 'A volpas is inhaling us!'

Lantic spun round to see four olri-gi charging past, their stings curled round in readiness. And something strange was happening to the clouds, they were merging into giant rivers to pour along in the same direction as the ships. He peered cautiously over the rail.

When the awful noise started to ease, Taggie heard someone cry out: 'Volpas!'

'Well that settles everything,' Lord Drakouth declared. 'My lord, come with me. I carry my family's gate. You will be safe.'

'No,' Lord Colgath said. 'We are close now, and I will not abandon my friends.'

'That sound,' Lord Drakouth said. 'It is death. You know that.'

'I am alive for now. While there is life, there is hope. And the Queen of Dreams is right; we have to offer our people a choice. I have come to believe that is what my father wanted in the end.'

'Madness!'

'Perhaps. But tell my brother what has happened, tell him Mirlyn's Gate waits for all of us at Wynate. Tell him if you dare.'

Taggie turned round in time to see Lord Drakouth holding out a gold and silver ring, almost identical to the one she carried in a bag round her own neck.

'Come with me, I implore you,' Lord Drakouth said.

'I thank you for your kindness, but you understand I have to try.'

'I . . .' Lord Drakouth faltered. 'I do.'

'Good luck,' Taggie said.

Lord Drakouth dipped his head a fraction. 'Farewell, Queen of Dreams.' Then the centre of his gate was showing a bleak grey land that Taggie was all-too familiar with. It swelled out of the gate like a bloated wave to envelope him. After a second it shrank to nothing, taking Lord Drakouth with it.

'Others will know now,' she said as the wind whipped her hair and dress about. 'That's a good thing.'

'Let us hope so,' Lord Colgath replied.

'You know I won't let us get eaten by a volpas, don't you?' She gripped the bag, feeling the comforting shape of the ring.

'I know. But . . . Jemima?'

'Oh no,' Taggie gasped, and looked at the torrents of cloud that were rampaging past the ship. All the clouds for miles around were draining out of the sky, faster than her cloudbusting magic could ever achieve. And at the bottom of the vast gulf they'd emptied she finally saw the volpas.

'So it wasn't the frigate squadron Jem was scared of, either,' Taggie murmured.

After all that had been spoken of the great monsters that lived in the Realm of Air, Taggie was startled to see beauty not horror awaiting them. The main body of the volpas was the size of a small isle, yet incredibly flimsy, nothing more than a translucent white sack of flesh, with a circular orifice at each end. Dozens of tentacles sprouted from the flesh on the upper half of the body sack, thin white jelly-like strands that she reckoned must have been up to five miles long. Small flickers of lightning zipped around their tips as they waved about in slow undulations.

As Taggie watched the denser lip around the front orifice began to expand, and the hollow body gradually

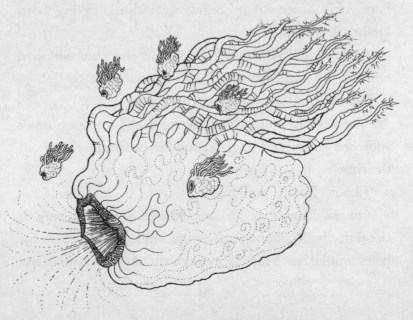

inflated as it inhaled. Rivers of cloud close to it were sucked in towards the widening milky circle, along with anything solid caught by the hurricane. Then the volpas exhaled through its rear orifice. *It's jet propelled*, she realized.

As if that wasn't bad enough, the massive volpas wasn't alone. Five much smaller volpas were orbiting around it, jetting themselves along in the same direction, their tentacles moving a lot quicker. The tips flared and flashed, creating a halo-smear of thin lightning bolts around themselves.

Lost somewhere amid the huge cluster of debris whirling crazily ahead of the frigates, heading for the volpas orifice, was Jemima. Taggie whimpered, tears for her lost sister stinging her eyes.

A few hundred metres away, a sparkling red vein of air was stubbornly fighting its way against the terrific hurricane.

'Sophie!' Taggie yelled.

All over the *Angelhawk*, the crew looked round. They shouted encouragement to the skymaid, begging her to keep flying. Far below her, the volpas continued to draw another breath, sucking in more air. The hurricane's speed began to increase.

Sophie pushed her wings to their limit, clawing her way against the hurtling blast of wind. She could see her friends leaning over the *Angelhawk*'s deck rails, urging her on, beckoning frantically. It was all she could do just to hold her position now as the air flooded against her like a solid force. Felix was hanging on to the hem of her tunic.

'You'll make it without me,' he said.

'Shut up,' Sophie grunted through gritted teeth. The wind grew even stronger, pushing her down and away from the ship. She knew the captain should be hoisting her sails so they could tack their way sideways out of the terrible hurricane. It was a slender hope, but the only one the crew had. They couldn't afford to waste a second.

Then she saw the *Angelhawk* launch a harpoon. The metal shaft arched wide, then suddenly curved round as Lantic's animation guided it towards her. It slowed, straining on the end of its cable an enticing metre away. Sophie lunged forward and grabbed it.

Even through the howling wind she could hear the cheering above. The *Angelhawk* crew winched her in and she was hauled in through the harpoon launcher hatch just as the unbearable noise of the volpas inhaling reached the ship once more. The planks started vibrating as she lay there on the floor panting as if she'd been holding her breath for a week. Felix crawled away, his blood-matted fur leaving foul dark streaks on the wood. 'I failed,' he moaned. 'I failed her.'

Taggie arrived at Sophie's side and hugged her hard.

'I couldn't get her,' a distraught Sophie wailed through her near-hysterical tears. 'I just couldn't. The volpas breath carried her away. I'm so sorry.'

*

Jemima fell through the Realm of Air.

At first she'd screamed. But the deafening sound of the volpas inhaling meant she couldn't even hear herself. She stopped screaming – there was simply no point, and it hurt her throat. A weird calmness claimed her. Lengths of ship's planking spun and gyrated past. A mangled stove flipped end over end, its oven door flapping like an iron wing, spitting out glowing coals as it went.

Then she saw a pair of olri-gi in the far distance as she rolled round and round in the wind. They were attacking one of the young volpas, dodging in past the gaudy halo of lightning to strike the soft pale body with their stingers. Whatever poison they had, it was clearly working. The volpas tentacles spasmed then slowed, and the gaudy band of lightning faded away. That made her smile.

When she closed her eyes she saw a vast army marching across a frozen landscape, and knew she was sighting the War Emperor's forces approaching Rothgarnal. Midway along the vast columns of troops the War Emperor himself rode on a splendid white horse. Clustered round him were other grand figures in impressive shining armour; Jemima recognized Lady Jessicara DiStantona whose black armour had been polished to a gleam. And there near the back of the procession was one woman in a fur coat, who suddenly looked round and up, staring straight back at Jemima. She smiled and winked.

'Mummy,' Jemima moaned.

She opened her eyes just as the big volpas inhaled

again, eager to get to the morsels it could feel in the air. Jemima saw she was barely a mile away from the gruesome front orifice now. The noise struck once more, and she jammed her hands in her ears – not that it made any real difference. It was hard to see any of the frigates now, nor the *Angelhawk*. The three ships she could make out far above her were tacking frantically across the hurricane, trying to escape its clutches before they reached the volpas itself. More cloud was clearing from the sky, sucked into the big rivers that poured down alongside her.

Then Jemima saw the comet in the clear air above. Its warm rosy glow shone down on her, and she stared up at it, entranced. It was huge now, and moving fast. Its pale, insubstantial tail stretched out behind, surely reaching halfway back to the stars from where it had come. Darker, thicker gases boiled fitfully out of its bulk, creating unsettled spectral shapes around it.

Jemima gazed, feeling bizarrely contented, at the strangely attractive patterns formed by the swirls, and gradually realized they were surging into the shape of a face. There was no doubt about it. The red-flare blemishes were congealing as a mouth and eyes, the tail was revealed as streaming hair.

The angel.

Jemima grinned in delight at the apparition, who was the most beautiful person she'd ever seen. The angel grinned back. A finger of ephemeral gas beckoned.

Jemima pointed at herself. 'Me?' she mouthed.

The angel smiled and nodded.

Suddenly, Canri slid across the face of the comet. Jemima was almost cross.

'Found you,' the olri-gi called. His powerful triangular wings rippled as he manoeuvred close, and Jemima was abruptly spread-eagle on the back of his head.

'You'll need to hold on,' Canri yelled.

'OK,' she shouted back, and her hands discovered some knobbly ridges in the sleek black skin. Less than a mile beyond his nose, the volpas's front orifice was starting to open again, its translucent body expanding. The hurricane force began to pick up.

'I didn't want to die alone,' Jemima shouted. 'I'm sorry you're here, but I'm glad, too.'

'For a seer you make a bad optimist, young Princess,' Canri roared.

The noise of the volpas inhaling began, making Jemima's bones tremble. She knew they couldn't escape, not now; they were too close to the orifice. Not even an olri-gi could fight its way across the formidable hurricane in time.

'Grip tight now.'

Jemima did as she was told, pressing her face against his lovely silky black skin. It was almost a bedtime comfort hug, the kind Mum and Dad used to give her. And the angel's smile lingered warmly in her mind. Jemima was curiously content.

Canri the olri-gi expelled his flame.

Jemima yelled in shock as their speed quadrupled

in seconds. She risked a glance back, to see a splendid blue-white flame searing out between the olri-gi's two stingers. And she was abruptly weeping as she laughed uncontrollably. 'You were never dragons, you're rockets!' The words were lost in the hurricane and flame roar. *Maybe I'm not going to die after all*, she thought.

Canri rode his flame with impeccable skill, powering sideways across the hurricane, rolling to slice neatly through the waving gaps between the tentacles and emerging into the churning air outside the main plume of the wind.

'That was incredible!' Jemima cried as the blue flame shrank away. 'Even better than rainbow surfing.'

'After we've stung the volpas we have to elude their tentacles somehow,' Canri explained modestly. 'They thrash about afterwards. Even we aren't always quick enough.'

'Can you kill this one?'

'I could, but even if I sting it now, something this size would take a month to die. And we need to get you back to the *Angelhawk*.'

Jemima nodded in understanding, and held on tight as Canri soared away from the volpas, turning round on to what seemed a collision course with the comet.

As soon as her crew hauled Sophie and Felix on board, Captain Rebecca ordered the half tipsails to be rigged on the lower arms of the remaining two masts.

'And hurry,' she told Jualius, 'Else we'll be joining

our ancestors before the hour's out.'

Sure enough, the *Angelhawk* responded immediately to the small triangles of canvas, straining their rigging hard. Captain Rebecca tacked them at a precarious angle, fighting against tipping the ship over.

Three times the volpas inhaled while the *Angelhawk* careered sideways across the hurricane. There was nothing anybody could do except wait and see if the ship would shoot them free before they reached the tops of the tentacles. Taggie even got everyone to gather round her, ready to use her gate if they didn't make it. All the while, the comet grew and grew in the opposite side of the sky from the volpas.

Then finally the *Angelhawk* passed half a mile over the glaring, fizzing tips of the tentacles and the wind lessened to a mere gale.

'Prepare to rig the midsails,' the captain ordered. She gave the radiant crimson comet a fearful glance as it loomed frighteningly large darkwards of the *Angelhawk*. It seemed as if half of the sky was now obscured by its rampaging crimson gas fountains. What a terrible irony it would be to escape an inhaling volpas – which so few captains managed – only to be swatted by a comet.

Sophie's arm suddenly shot out. 'Look! That's Canri!'

Sure enough, the olri-gi rose from sunwards to fly level with the ship, then he slowly rolled over. Delighted cheers rose above the sound of the volpas as everyone saw Jemima clinging to his back.

Even as the olri-gi manoeuvred close enough for Jemima to scramble over, Captain Rebecca had tipped her head back to call out in the realm's airsong language, imploring Canri to push them clear.

Taggie ran to her little sister and hugged her so tight the *athrodene* armour was on the verge of stiffening up protectively. 'I thought I'd lost you,' she said through her sniffles.

Felix bounded along and just flung himself at Jemima, clinging to her chest, his tail rigid. 'You're alive,' he said in a voice that was close to cracking. 'I was so afraid you'd gone. I failed to protect you, I failed so badly.'

'Dearest Felix,' Jemima said, stroking the short soft fur on the top of his head. 'Without you, that rathwai would still be holding me as we were sucked into the volpas together. You saved me.'

A beaming Sophie gave Jemima a hug and ruffled her hair. Lantic actually kissed her, then turned bright red. Even Lord Colgath said: 'I was worried. Welcome back, Blossom Princess.'

It was as though the very air itself was turning scarlet, the comet was so close, when Jemima disentangled herself from her friends and went over to Captain Rebecca. 'We have to follow the comet,' she said.

'*What?*' the captain snarled.

'Follow it. The comet will take us to Wynate.'

'Blossom Princess you might be, young lady, but that is insanity. We'll do no such thing.'

'Taggie!' Jemima implored.

'But, the *Angelhawk* . . .' Taggie said weakly. 'She's broken, Jem. We'll regroup and come straight back to Wynate, I promise.'

'No!' Jemima said. 'It has to be now. I've sighted the War Emperor's army, he's almost at Rothgarnal. We have to save all those poor soldiers, Taggie, and Mum's there, too. The *Angelhawk* will be fine, I know it.' She tipped her face to one side and smiled at the vast ball of seething red light that was consuming the sky. 'The angel will take care of us. I saw her, Taggie, and – oh – she was so beautiful. She's going to take us to Wynate. She wants us to follow her.'

'The angel told you that?' Taggie asked sceptically.

'She showed me, yes.'

If it had been anyone else –*anyone* – Taggie would have just walked away. But it was Jem. Her very own sister, who was blessed and cursed to see things others never could.

Everybody was holding their breath, waiting for the Queen of Dreams to speak.

'Captain,' Taggie said slowly. 'Set a course that'll take us after that comet, please.'

Captain Rebecca let out a groan that was almost a wail of dismay. 'Never again will I take a royal charter! Do you understand? Never! Shipsmage, write that in the log.'

'Aye, Captain.'

'All hands,' the captain shouted at the top of her voice, 'Brace yourselves.' And she spun the helm wheel round fast.

Crew and passengers alike tied themselves to the mid-deck hull, with rope and anamage spider gossamer and harpoon cable. Whatever they could lay their desperate hands on.

Canri nosed up gently into the shattered planks and twisted hull ribs of the stern, and began to push the *Angelhawk* round, slowly increasing speed until the captain yelled to hold.

The comet's sheath of glowing vapour spewed out great cascades of gas in all directions as it ploughed its way through the sky. Seconds after it passed the sea globe, it ripped through the volpas hurricane, and smashed into the monster itself, incinerating it instantly. Onward it fell, deeper and deeper into the Realm of Air towards the sun.

In its wake, a tiny wooden ship pushed by a labouring olri-gi slipped into the howling turmoil of its wake. Long tongues of steam and smog licked round her hull like infernal chains, and drew the ship in. The olri-gi backed away, and the *Angelhawk* was pulled along in the comet's mighty slipstream, heading wherever fate and the angels decided.

WHERE NOBODY WANTS TO BE

Silence was the king of Rothgarnal now.

Since the cataclysmic battle which razed the city to the ground, ten centuries of cold had soaked into the rocks. The rows of the burial mounds, as high as houses, were the only structures remaining, where the dead of both armies were entombed in frozen earth, lying side by side and unmarked. Despite being granted the Fourth Realm, the Karraks had spurned the broken desolate land where the city ruins crumbled beneath the ice and even the frost fungus grew poorly.

As his nervous horse rode over the last crest, and the site of the ancient city was exposed to his view, the new War Emperor shivered at the dereliction revealed to him. It was almost enough to send him turning round to go back through Olatha where the welcome heat and life of Morath'ki awaited. But for one thing.

On the other side of the ancient battlefield, the army of the Grand Lord was encamped. Fires spluttered in great braziers amid the gloomy lodges. Many kinds of creatures marched across the squares within the camp, while in the dead grey sky above, rathwai wheeled about crying to each other in forlorn voices. Tall cages containing angry snuffling Zanatuth were lined up along the front of the camp.

The War Emperor regarded his enemy with cold contempt. Along the ridge on either side of him, his own massive invasion force was starting to dig in. Axes not shovels were being used to excavate pits and defensive embankments; swung by giants, their sharp points made little impression in the unyielding ground.

General Welch's command tents had been set up some way back. When the War Emperor and the other Kings and Queens arrived, detailed maps of Rothgarnal were already drawn up and spread out over the tables.

The War Emperor looked down on the two camps, separated by the long parallel lines of burial mounds.

'It would seem we will be fighting amid the dead,' General Welch said, coming up next to him.

'Nothing is sacred to those monsters,' the War Emperor replied dismissively. A finger tapped the markings of the Grand Lord's camp. 'Is this his full force?'

'Scouts and olri-gi have reported stragglers amid the foothills, some outlying sentries, no doubt alert for any attempt on our part to outflank him. But essentially yes, that is his full strength.'

'Then we outnumber him?'

'Yes, sire,' Lady Jessicara DiStantona said. 'A third of our forces have still to arrive, but the numbers are already on our side.'

'When will we be up to full strength?'

'By midnight, sire. Another six hours.'

'He will expect us to test his defences, gain an understanding of his warriors' strengths. I think we should deny him that expectation, my lady. What say you, General?'

General Welch pulled at his beard as he stared thoughtfully down at the map. 'Nobody wants to prolong this. That will lead to even more casualties. A full frontal assault is probably our best option, there isn't even that much risk attached providing we can break those forward embankments. They'll be well shielded.'

'I will leave the nature of our formations to you, General. But we attack at dawn. With the blessing of the Heavens, this will all be over by tomorrow night.'

The *Angelhawk*'s two remaining masts snapped off within minutes of the ship entering the comet's slipstream. The crew had already furled the sails. All they had left to hold them steady now were the sailtails, and the indomitable captain's skill.

Fumes plagued them, making everybody sick and listless. The noise was appalling. The buffeting intolerable. Weakened planks were worried loose and swallowed by the hostile pink spume. Plumes of brimstone smog swirled round crew and passengers alike, making their stinging eyes weep. No one dared loosen the ropes that fastened them to the ship, or the slipstream would tear them off in an instant.

Taggie lost track of time. But it felt like hours before the *Angelhawk* started to shake in a different fashion. She saw an immense plume of gas swelling out of the comet, heading for them. It hit the *Angelhawk*, which reeled badly from the blow. But the repugnant red maelstrom began to thin out, and the nauseating shaking lessened.

Ten minutes later the ship was in clear skies, with the comet's tail rushing along beside them, emitting a continuous thunder grumble that gradually diminished as they glided further and further away from it. Taggie made sure she was holding on to the warped deck railing as she cautiously untied herself. Every limb ached, and she was sure she'd never lose the acrid taste of the comet from her throat. But they'd all survived, and the skies were empty and didn't seem to contain monsters or frigates or rathwai. Right now, that was good enough for her.

'Wow,' Lantic croaked. 'We made it.'

'Made it where?' Sophie asked sullenly. Her hair was unmoving, crusted with filth from the comet, and she looked like she was going to be sick.

'Mr Marcus,' Captain Rebecca said. 'Let's have a drink and something to eat. I think we deserve it.'

Taggie thought she was about to witness her first mutiny. But the Jannermol, who had spent the whole time they were being pulled along by the comet withdrawn inside his shell, finally said: 'Aye, Captain.'

Favian and Maklepine went into the smashed-up galley to help him.

'Now what?' Lantic asked.

'We find out where we are,' Captain Rebecca said. She took off and flew across the decks to the jumble of snapped and charred timbers that used to be her cabin. After a few minutes and some hot curses she came back out with a telescope. Hovering above the prow, she slowly turned full circle, scouring the sky.

Somehow, Mr Marcus had worked his own brand of magic, and boiled water for tea, which was now handed round. Taggie took a cold sausage roll from Jualius along with a squeeze mug of tea. She couldn't remember a meal so good.

'The *Angelhawk* can never sail again, can she?' Jemima asked.

'No,' Lantic said. 'Even if we could find a forest and cut some trees down to replace the masts, there's too much damage to the hull.'

'The only way back is through the gate,' Felix said.

Taggie's hand crept up to the bag hanging round her neck, feeling the shape of the dark gate inside. The touch of it was extremely comforting right now.

Sophie glanced round at the subdued groups that had formed along the deck, drinking their tea and eating quietly. 'For us and the crew,' she muttered.

'Are you all right?' Lantic asked Taggie, who was staring forlornly at the vast red and orange streamers of the comet's tail.

'I couldn't beat her,' Taggie said. 'I tried everything I

could, every spell my ancestors know, some new ones I devised. Nothing worked. She's so strong.'

'So don't fight her head to head next time. Use a different tactic.'

'A different tactic?' Taggie spluttered indignantly.

'Yes. Outsmart her. That's one area where you've definitely got the upper hand.'

Taggie gave his anxious face a small smile, and put her hand on his arm. 'Thank you, Lantic. Captain Rebecca told me how you animated the harpoons and firestars. None of us would be here without you.'

'I think you would. But I'm glad to be by your side,' he wheezed down a breath. 'No matter where we are.'

She grinned. 'You still don't get to sing with the *Heartbreakers*.'

'I know. It doesn't matter. We're so close now. We should actually start thinking about what we do when we get Mirlyn's Gate back.'

'So we should.' Taggie glanced at Lord Colgath. 'How will your brother react if we bring Mirlyn's Gate back? You never did say.'

'Badly. He will see its return as a challenge to his entire reign. He is not wrong in that. But . . . the Congress of Lords may be more tolerant. I have some allies there. Or at least, I used to.'

'It'll be the same with my father,' Lantic said glumly.

'I'm not so sure,' Taggie said. 'He and I will have to stand before the Gathering together. He might not have everything his own way. Earl Maril'bo will speak to the Elf King.'

Sophie sighed. 'I wonder how he is?'

'And Dad,' Jemima said wistfully.

'They'll be worrying about us,' Taggie said. She pressed the handle on the squeeze mug, and gulped down some hot tea.

'What's the first thing you're going to do when we get home?' Lantic asked. 'I'm going to go travelling. I'm going to visit every place my brother went to.'

'A bath,' Sophie said firmly, raking a hand through her filthy hair.

'After that,' Lantic insisted.

'Maybe visit Tonba,' the skymaid said thoughtfully. 'I mean, I've come to this realm, which is what I always wanted to do. But I haven't seen much of it. Well . . .' She gestured at the flowing haze of the comet's tail which still obscured a quarter of the sky. 'Not the parts of it I've heard so much about.'

'Felix?' Lantic asked.

'I'm just looking forward to my job being less difficult,' the white squirrel said.

'My lord?' Lantic asked.

'I haven't seen my wife, Lady Anaquis, for thirty-seven years,' Lord Colgath rumbled. 'I miss her. It is my hope that this will allow me to see her again.'

'Jemima?'

'I want Dad back. That's all.'

'Me too,' Taggie told her. 'And he'll be there, Jem.'

'What about you?' Lantic asked.

Taggie shrugged. 'Finish school, I guess. Then move to the First Realm permanently and sit on the throne.'

'That's what you *want* to do?' Sophie asked dubiously.

Taggie grinned at her friend. 'When I dream in the First Realm, I help people. So yes, that's what I want.'

Captain Rebecca flew down to them, and gave Jemima a long look.

'What?' Jemima asked, flustered.

'I've seen Wynate,' Captain Rebecca said. 'May the angels preserve me. When the comet expelled us, it threw us on a course that's taking us straight there. At the rate we're drifting, we'll be there in another five or six hours.'

Taggie held out a hand. 'Captain, I'd like to see it.'

Captain Rebecca handed over the telescope.

The isle of Wynate had no vegetation of any kind. As far as Taggie could see there wasn't even any moss clinging to its dark-grey rock. She wasn't surprised, the surface certainly looked inhospitable. There wasn't a flat patch of ground anywhere; instead long sharp blades of rock stabbed up into the air at all angles. The whole isle was viciously barbed.

Nothing moved amid all the severe rock, though as they got closer, the telescope allowed them to see black gashes that were entrances to caves in the clefts between the pinnacles.

It was clear that the *Angelhawk* would pass close, but thankfully not crash and impale herself on the dreadful spikes. Everyone got ready to fly over. There were enough skyfolk to carry the rest across.

As they were preparing their shields and weapons, Maklepine gasped. 'Ship ho!'

Taggie's first thought was that one of the frigates had somehow followed them. But the shipsmage was pointing at the isle ahead, and his face held an expression of wonder.

It had to be there, of course. Everything they'd done, the effort and sacrifice they'd made to get to Wynate, was totally dependent on the *Lady Silvaris* being there. Nonetheless, when the isle's slow rotation gradually brought the giant ship's broken hull into view, Taggie thought she might cry – first from the joy of finding her goal, then from the state of the ship itself. The *Lady Silvaris* had been built as a labour of love by an entire generation of skypeople to sail amid the stars, only to lie fallen among desolate rock. Even now, abandoned for centuries, her vast bulk had a grandeur which remained exciting. It wasn't hard to imagine the incredible old behemoth flying smoothly past the ice isles and out into the coldness.

'We were right,' Taggie whispered, incredulous. 'We were right! This is where they came.'

Captain Rebecca shook her head in amazement. 'By every angel in Heaven, it was all true.'

'My father's resting place,' Lord Colgath said softly.

'And many others,' Felix said. 'They committed

themselves in the belief their descendants would live a
better life.'

'We will,' Taggie said in determination.

'I can't see any paxia,' Lantic said.

'They're down there,' Jemima said in a despondent
voice. 'I have sight of them. Taggie, there's an awful lot.'

Captain Rebecca gazed down on the forbidding isle,
her ebony hair coiling slowly. 'Aye, Blossom Princess, that
there will be. But sleeping. For once, some good fortune!
We may yet get out of this alive. We just have to be very
quiet, and very sneaky.'

22

THE RESTING PLACE

Taggie faced the *Angelhawk*'s crew on the mid-deck. She took the gold and ebony ring from the bag round her neck and held it up. 'This is the gate that will take Mirlyn's Gate to the War Emperor. There's not much life left in it, so we'll only have one chance to use it.' She gave Captain Rebecca a nervous glance. 'That means we all have to use it together.'

'Aye,' Captain Rebecca said. She nodded at Wynate, which was growing larger in the sky above them. 'We all know the *Angelhawk* isn't sailing anywhere again, which means we're all going to have to go down to the *Lady Silvaris* with our young Queen. So now, if you have any complaints or questions, keep them to yourself, I'm not interested. Sharpen your weapons and be ready to move out when I tell you. Above all, stick together. That way we'll be in a decent tavern by nightfall, and the bards will have started composing their songs praising us.'

Sophie lifted Taggie as the *Angelhawk* glided a quarter of a mile above Wynate's brutal spikes. They were the first. Captain Rebecca herself took Lord Colgath. The others followed in pairs. Shields were covered in cloth so as not to clank and bang, boots were wrapped in thick wool socks.

Despite the danger they were flying towards, Taggie's eyes were shining in anticipation. This was what it felt like to have a dream come true.

They landed in a narrow gully at the base of the *Lady Silvaris*'s stern. Even after hearing so many stories of Exator's ship, the sheer size of it was inspiring. She lay on her side, the planks on the bottom buckled and shattered by her fall from the sky a thousand years ago. Masts and yardarms lay around, leaning against the wreck as if they were gangplanks. There was only the wood itself remaining, along with some rusting pulleys. The ropes and sails had long since rotted away. But the good French oak from which she'd been built had hardened down the centuries, remaining intact.

With everyone on the ground beside her, Taggie's charmsward bands spun round, ready to cast her strongest protective enchantment. She walked cautiously towards one of larger splits at the foot of the huge circular stern, alert for any sign of the paxia. Everyone else kept a constant vigil over the barren rock as they followed closely. They saw several cave openings, which they took a wide path around. The silence that engulfed Wynate was so intense Taggie thought her ears had stopped working.

Eventually they were standing at the base of the ancient hull. Taggie stared at the tall, ominous fracture in the wooden wall before her.

'That didn't break open naturally,' Sophie said softly

as they peered into the gloomy interior. 'Those are teeth marks.'

Taggie examined the planks, seeing the deep gashes on every edge. Sophie was right. She gave a small shudder and crept inside.

Dust shone in the multitude of slender sunbeams that prised their way round the edges of the planks and through the jagged cracks. They created a criss-cross of thin beams that glared within the midnight black that filled the *Lady Silvaris*'s hull. The entire hull was now one gigantic empty chamber. As her eyes adjusted to the light, she saw the curving hull and protruding timbers were curiously lumpy. They were large lumps, too.

'Oh sweet Heavens save us,' an aghast Captain Rebecca whispered. The minute stars in her eyepatch gem were swirling in agitation.

Taggie peered at the closest lump. It was slate grey with the texture of leather, the surface marked by long creases. As she stared, those creases slowly resolved into the shapes of legs and arms and wing ribs. Each lump was a small human shape, crouched tight, with legs bent up, arms hugging itself, and wings folded.

It took all her self-control for Taggie not to scream as she realized exactly what had conquered the hull. Somehow she managed to stall the breath in her throat. Paxia clung to the inside of the hull, nestled along every truss and support, settled on the beam ledges, slumbered across the broken floor. There must have been thousands upon thousands of them inside the ship.

Everyone stood perfectly still as they took in the mortifying sight. Hands reached stealthily for weapons but Taggie and Captain Rebecca shook their heads in urgent, silent warning.

Lord Colgath's smoke cloak dimmed down to a subdued ember-red. Slivers of opalescence flowed swiftly along his arm as he raised a hand and pointed.

Mirlyn's Gate was indeed as he'd described it. A circle of stone, made from many smaller stones, it lay beside one of the tapering rock spires that had sliced into the ancient ship, leaning at a precarious angle. Dozens of serpents that seemed to be made of dark liquid slithered over its surface in eternal circles, their eyes gleaming a malignant purple as they wiggled across each other.

The binding enchantments, Taggie realized. And Mirlyn's Gate was less than thirty metres ahead of her. She started to study the ground between her and her goal. Not all of the paxia were pressed together. If she was very, *very* careful, she might manage to reach the gate by a winding route. She put one foot forward, making sure the ground underneath was solid before she put her weight on it. Then brought the other foot forward. Test the ground. Now – a slight turn. Another step, heart racing, sweat prickling her skin. Breath becoming ragged. Another step.

Sophie started to follow her. Then slowly the rest of the crew began to advance.

Taggie was halfway to Mirlyn's Gate when one of the

sunbeams flickered. She glanced up. It was one of those coming down from the crest of the hull curving above her. Another winked out for a second before reappearing, as if something had briefly passed through the air between the hull and the sun. Taggie stopped, her stomach knotting up to a cold ball. If anything disturbed the paxia now . . .

She waited but the sunbeams stayed constant. *All right then*, she told herself. A step forwards, then a sharp turn because three paxia were resting up against each other. One of them was on its side, allowing her the first glimpse of a face. There was practically no nose, just a smooth nub with a single nostril. The eyelids were wide, closed over a protruding hemispherical eyeball. Its circular mouth was covered by a puckered lip and its ears were small pointed shells lying flat along the side of an elongated skull.

Taggie wrinkled her nose in revulsion at the sight and took another step. Friends and crew were strung out behind her, making good progress in what had become the world's most terrifying game of Twister ever. Captain Rebecca brought up the rear.

With just ten metres to go, the dark serpents began to slow their endless slithering around Mirlyn's Gate. Narrow violet eyes were starting to show an interest in her.

Taggie gritted her teeth and took another step.

'OH TAGGIE, YOU FOUND IT. WELL DONE, COUSIN. GOOD SHOW.'

A horrified Taggie looked back. Katrabeth was standing behind them in the same gap they'd used to get inside the *Lady Silvaris*. She wore the full bejewelled robe of a Third Realm sorceress, her chestnut hair brushed to an immaculate sheen. The smile on her face as she shouted was one of pure malice.

All around the ruined hull, the paxia began to stir, limbs stretching out, heads turning to find the source of the disturbance, wings rising and rustling like a thousand leather leaves fluttering in the breeze.

Katrabeth sucked on her lower lip. 'OOOPS. TOO LOUD? So sorry.' Then she was laughing with cruel delight at the shock and dread she saw written on the faces of everyone inside the wrecked hull.

'To me!' Taggie yelled desperately as the paxia began to stand up. The charmsward symbols flared with sharp blue light. '*Ti-Hath*,' she chanted as everyone piled in round her. Felix swung his sword at the drowsy paxia next to Taggie, cutting it down. Lord Colgath's death spell blew another back through the air with smoke pouring from its mouth and ears.

Taggie's enchantment created a bubble of solid air around her and her companions. Paxia started to move towards them, slowly at first as they shrugged off their drowsiness, then with speed and purpose building menacingly fast. Their mouths opened to squawk, revealing a ring of fangs that flexed ravenously. The noise they made as they woke was phenomenal. Taggie thought the old timbers must surely finally burst from the crescendo of aggression.

'To Mirlyn's Gate,' Sophie cried. They started to run, clinging together, flinching from the paxia that had started flinging themselves at the wall of enchanted air.

The protective shell Taggie created began to stall on the sheer number of paxia bodies piling on to it. Small crude spells jabbed out of their fingers like tiny orange needles, clawing at Taggie's magic. Then they shoved their heads against the stubborn invisible barrier and began eating.

Taggie cried out in revulsion. She could feel them chewing at her magic, a sensation that was like having their wet, hot tongues licking at the skin all over her body. 'Clear a way through,' she implored the others, and relaxed the shield on one side.

Lord Colgath held both arms up, and slammed out death spell after death spell. Sophie's crossbow fired a steady stream of perfectly aimed bolts, as did the bows of the skyfolk crew. Felix stabbed and slashed with his sword. Lantic flung firestars. Captain Rebecca roared in berserk delight, and swung her cutlass triumphantly.

The paxia came in great waves. Flying and running from

every direction. Shrieking dementedly, clawing their way over each other in a frenzy to reach the new food.

Katrabeth stood beside the gap in the hull, a shadecast making her hard to see. It was her eyes which gave her away, gleaming with malicious joy as she watched the desperate struggle take place before her.

Slowly, inch by inch, Taggie and her friends were shoving their way across the floor until they reached Mirlyn's Gate. There were shattered skeletons all around it. Lantic saw the emblem of the War Emperor on a gold broach beneath his feet as he stumbled on bones.

'Father,' Lord Colgath moaned.

'Get the dark gate out,' Taggie yelled at Jemima.

She tried to reinforce the shield enchantment as Jemima fumbled at the bag round her neck. The relentless assault of the paxia made it difficult.

Jemima tugged the black and gold ring from the bag, holding it aloft triumphantly. 'Got it.'

'My lord, give us a destination,' Taggie said.

'*Eth-el' turnoch*,' Lord Colgath chanted.

The centre of the black and gold ring began to shine with a lurid light. Taggie could feel the gate's peculiar magic expanding. 'Get round Mirlyn's Gate,' she told her friends.

The paxia must have known something was happening. They hammered and scratched at the enchanted air, redoubling their efforts to break through. Taggie groaned with the effort of sustaining the spell. Then everyone was holding hands, with Mirlyn's Gate in the centre.

For a second, there was a gap in the ever-shifting wall of paxia. Taggie could now see Katrabeth clearly. Her cousin had taken a few paces into the hull so she could better watch their demise. An alarmed frown was breaking on the girl's pretty face, causing her shadecast to falter. 'What . . . ?' The paxia had seen her now as well. They began flying towards her. Katrabeth's death spells turned them to charred smouldering corpses that fell instantly to the ground. But still they kept coming. Dozens. Hundreds.

'Oh,' Taggie said, as if surprised. 'Didn't the Grand Lord tell you I have a private gate? Ooops.' She smiled blankly, and cancelled the shield enchantment so she could issue her command. '*Seseeamie.*'

The paxia rushed in. Grey light erupted around her. And she heard Katrabeth screaming: 'Wait. You can't leave me here. Cousin. Cousin, please. Nooo!'

23

ROTHGARNAL ONCE MORE

Lady Jessicara DiStantona woke the War Emperor two hours before dawn with the words: 'The Grand Lord leads his army, sire.'

Clearly, the Karrak Lord and Ladies had some excellent seers among their own kind, for three hours before dawn, a full hour before General Welch was due to issue his orders to muster, the Grand Lord's troops began to form up along the front of their camp. So in the merge-light thrown by bonfires and lightstones, cooks prepared a meal as soldiers and mages alike were roused. Tea and slices of hot ham and bread were passed round as weapons and armour was prepared for battle.

The War Emperor and the Kings and Queens of the Gathering met in the command tent an hour before dawn. Their breakfast was identical to those of the troops, on the orders of the War Emperor.

'I must face the Grand Lord myself,' the War Emperor said as he ate his bread and drank his tea.

'That's not wise,' Nicola said from the end of the table where she sat next to the King in Exile. 'We don't know precisely what we're confronting. The Karrak lore masters are destroying all the seespy birds our battlemages are sending over their camp.'

'On the contrary, we know exactly what the enemy has,' Queen Judith said, sitting next to the War Emperor. Her armour was the darkest purple, with every segment lined in gleaming *athrodene*. Black runes flowed like water across the breastplate and down the arms and legs. 'Some Zanatuth and a significant number of rathwai. The olri-gi have already agreed to sting the Zanatuth, as they did in the first battle of Rothgarnal. And the Highlord will lead his people into the air against the rathwai, as always. I say if the Grand Lord is foolish enough to march at the head of his army, then meet him head on.'

So it was that the War Emperor in his scarlet and gold armour found himself on his horse as everyone waited for dawn. Beside him, the other Kings and Queens had mounted up, all looking equally splendid in their armour. Nicola was the only exception, choosing instead her thick fur coat to protect her from the biting cold.

The Light Guard formed up around the royals in a wide U-shape, their horses three deep. Pegasi from the Fourth Realm cavalry circled overhead to provide coverage from the air in case of a rathwai attack.

'Brigades forward,' came the cry as the tiniest sliver of grey started to outline the Bernavian Mountains. The Light Guard rode slowly forward, leading the enormous army on its march out of the camp. They lined up thirty deep along the ridge that overlooked the long rows of burial mounds and the enemy camp beyond. On the other side of the field, the Grand Lord's army was already assembled in a huge triangular formation, with the elite khatu legion at the apex, their gold and blue pennants flying in the freezing wind. Right at the front of the legion, standing at the entrance to the valley between the burial mounds, the Grand Lord sat motionless astride a huge Zanatuth.

The War Emperor stared at the opposing army, and waited. But the Grand Lord didn't move.

'It was always our intention to take the fight to him,' the King of the Fifth Realm said.

The War Emperor made his decision. 'Advance,' he ordered.

Lady Jessicara DiStantona and her staff relayed the order along the massed regiments, and they began to walk down the slope. Five minutes later, flanked by his Light Guard, the War Emperor's horse entered the grim valley formed by the steep-walled burial mounds. Hoofs clattered on the hard, frozen ground. Even now, oddments left from the last battle – broken shields, arrow tips, shattered swords, scraps of armour – could be glimpsed sticking out of the dead soil.

The War Emperor's army advanced cautiously, with the giants on their rinosaurs proudly riding level with the Light Guard. Nicola glanced up at the high mounds on either side, and nudged her horse over to General Welch. 'A good place for an ambush if they could get up there unseen,' she murmured.

'Aye, ma'am,' the general acknowledged. 'That's why I have scouts on top marking us. If anyone tries to creep up the other side, they'll be in for a nasty surprise.'

'My apologies, General.'

'I took no offence, ma'am. I'm pleased you're concerned for our position.'

'Oh, I'm very aware of my position, General.'

As they approached the end of the long burial mounds, the War Emperor had to struggle against the urge to goad his horse forward. He could see the Grand Lord with his own eyes now – and almost envied his opponent's patience. The Zanatuth he sat on was as silent and immobile as him, whilst the fearsome cries of the wild Zanatuth echoed down the wide valley as their handlers struggled to restrain them.

When he was barely two hundred metres from the Grand Lord, the War Emperor drew his sword, forged by the master battlemages of the Second Realm, its mirror-silver blade shone as if reflecting the noonday sun above Shatha'hal. 'General,' the War Emperor said. 'Begin the charge.'

'Sire!' General Welch turned to his officers, ready to give the order. The giants on their rinosaurs would begin to quicken their pace, and the ordinary cavalry and mounted mages behind would follow. High above them the olri-gi would begin a fast dive to strike the Zanatuth. By the time the giants crashed against the khatu legion they would be thundering along with weight of the War Emperor's entire army behind them. A truly irresistible force.

On top of the Zanatuth, the Grand Lord stood up in his stirrups, and uttered a spell.

Something moved on top of the burial mound on General Welch's left. A chunk of frosty earth broke free and skittered down the steep slope, bouncing and rolling. It was the start of a small avalanche. All along the top, soil cracked open, then began to ripple and churn. Then the same thing started along the right-hand mound.

'Scouts!' General Welch shouted. 'What's happening up there?'

The question became irrelevant even as he spoke it. He gasped in shock as soldier gols started to rise up out of the torn earth. 'What?' He turned to the Second Realm battlemages who were in charge of the soldier gol squads. 'Who positioned them there?'

'They're not ours,' the shaken battlemage commander said.

Seespy birds swooped down for a better look. They showed the horrified watchers that these unknown soldier gols had some kind of metal weapon where their hand should be.

The scouts on the mounds ran at the threat – rising out of their cunning concealment. But swords and arrows were useless against the big clay figures. Spells had no effect. The first machine gun opened up, and cut down the fleeing scouts in a moment.

The War Emperor looked round in shock at the

unfamiliar mechanical roar. 'No!' Somewhere from the back of his mind, a terrible memory was wrestling its way out of burial. A memory of his beloved wife, her face lined with worry, pleading with him. Even now his head hurt with the effort of trying to ignore the memory. But the soldier gols were lining up along the top of the mounds, bringing their awful Outer Realm weapons to bear on his army, the thousands upon thousands of soldiers trapped in this valley which had just become certain death. The place he had brought them to.

'My daughter warned you,' Nicola said in a voice that rang clear above the mounting shouts of dismay. 'The Queen of Dreams warned you against this folly!'

'Heavens forgive me,' the War Emperor moaned. The pain in his head was so fierce he swayed about in his saddle. Riding beside him was Lady Jessicara DiStantona, whose armour had sprouted spikes as soon as the soldier gols appeared. She had to grab him to prevent him from falling.

'What orders, sire?' General Welch demanded.

The War Emperor could only groan in distress.

'Mages and sorceresses to shield what they can,' Nicola snapped. 'Now. Anyone with a weapon, aim for their guns, they'll be the most vulnerable part.'

General Welch didn't even think to question. 'Yes, ma'am.'

A thunderclap erupted directly between the two armies.

'What fresh horror is this?' the War Emperor pleaded. When he turned he saw the Grand Lord's massive

Zanatuth reeling back, along with the front rank of the khatu legion. Some kind of magical apparition was swelling out of nowhere above the icy ground halfway between the two armies. A scintillating blue and green haze that was expanding at an extraordinary rate, and breaking out into a multitude of barbs which burst open to release . . .

'What in the . . . ?' a stunned General Welch demanded. He'd never seen anything like it. The creatures that were materializing in mid-air were like half-sized skyfolk, their skin a dour stone-grey, with perilous orange magic crackling around their hands. Their mouths, opened wide to emit a savage screech, were lined with gruesomely sharp fangs. There were dozens of them soaring out of the magical storm. Then hundreds. Then . . .

'Paxia!' the Highlord of Air cried in horror. He blew his alarm whistle. A note that was swiftly taken up by every soldier from the Realm of Air.

The vast swarm of paxia fell upon their abundant new food, not caring which side the soldiers and their mounts were on. Around the tormented War Emperor, giants chopped with their huge axes. Second Realm soldier gols slung their spears with deadly accuracy. Mages and sorceresses unleashed their most lethal enchantments. Skyfolk let loose their arrows.

While rallying to their Grand Lord, the Karrak Lords and Ladies threw their death spells. Rannalal knights swung their short swords with relentless skill. Ethanu released barrage after barrage of toxic spells.

Grand Lord Amenamon let out an almighty bellow of fury and dismay as his indisputable victory was snatched from him in that one crazy instant. He let loose a death spell so potent it killed ten paxia simultaneously. It made no difference whatsoever. The vile creatures just kept coming from whatever magical portal had erupted before him. A living wall of grey wings and shrieking fangs swept towards him, blotting out everything else. He didn't even know if the War Emperor and Queen Judith had survived the onslaught.

When seven paxia fell upon his outraged Zanatuth and started to chew at its flanks it almost threw Amenamon to the ground before he smote them with death spells and mighty swipes from his sword. He dismounted hurriedly, ducking as yet more of the blood-crazed paxia flashed overhead, fangs snapping in a fever of gluttony. Warriors of his khatu legion closed protectively around him, but even they struggled to fend off the mass of paxia.

His very survival was being threatened. There was nothing for it – he ordered the soldier gols to open fire and concentrate their machine guns on the airborne menace, strafing the sky again and again, heedless that some of the paxia they killed were attacking the War Emperor's forces. That had become irrelevant now.

For half an hour the two armies defended themselves from the paxia. Finally, when the last of the ferocious grey creatures was torn flaming from the sky, silence reclaimed the battlefield. Both armies stared at each other in complete disarray. Only then did the lead ranks on both sides notice the ragtag band of dishevelled people crouched between them, sheltering under a powerful dome of enchanted air with mounds of dead paxia piled up against it. And in the dome with them was a most unnerving circle of stone. Many of the Karrak Lords and Ladies recognized it from the last time they had stood on this very ground a thousand years ago. The image was also sharp in the War Emperor's mind from the history scrolls he had studied in his youth.

'No!' he said in fury.

'No!' the Grand Lord echoed.

Taggie ended the protective enchantment with a wearied sigh. As the dome above her vanished, Sophie raised her head and gave the two livid leaders a disgruntled look. 'Oh, great! You know, just for once, it would be nice if someone was actually pleased to see us. I'm not saying it has to be the Highlord's fledgling – anyone would do.' She started loading bolts into her crossbow. 'And if they'd care to add some appreciation . . .'

'Now you're really living in the realm of wishful thinking,' Felix taunted her.

'I can sight Mum!' Jemima started waving frantically.

'Aye, now this is what I call a *dramatic* entrance,' Captain Rebecca announced in satisfaction. She glanced round. 'Did we bring everyone with us?'

'I think so,' Maklepine said.

'Ha! So now you can start writing your songs, bards. There's a lot you can rhyme with Captain Rebecca.'

'Not for the ears of young children there isn't,' Lantic muttered.

Taggie was so exhausted she could barely stand. 'Lantic, my lord, this is down to you two now.'

Lantic gripped Lord Colgath's hand, and looked unflinchingly into his eerie eyes. 'No matter where we are . . .'

'. . . no matter what we face,' Lord Colgath finished.

Then they were both striding away from Mirlyn's Gate in opposite directions.

24

TRUTHS REVEALED

'Hold, brother,' Lord Colgath said in a voice which flooded across the Grand Lord's entire army.

'Hold, father,' Lantic said, his cry amplified to reach all along the burial mound valley.

'This cannot be,' the War Emperor whispered.

'Now is the perfect time to attack,' Queen Judith told him quietly, a hand resting on his arm. 'Their ambush is broken. You can deal with the traitor Queen later.' Enchantments like tiny phosphorescent roots began to worm their way out of her fingertips, seeping through the War Emperor's armour.

'So *that's* what you used.' Nicola stepped forward. 'I think it's time the War Emperor made up his own mind, sister.' She clicked her fingers, and the enchantments shrivelled away.

The War Emperor dropped to his knees as he felt thoughts and memories burst free inside his head. *There* was the memory of his wife warning him of the bullets and guns. Clear and pure now. And the memory of Queen Judith's face in front of him, the suggestions, the insidious whispers being forced into his skull by her cunning enchantments. 'Sorceress of the Hell Realm,' he choked as the pressure threatened to burst his skull apart. 'What have you done?'

'How dare you interfere?' Queen Judith told her sister. Her escort of sorceresses backed away nervously as the dark runes on her purple armour started to glow emerald. She walked resolutely towards Nicola who stood perfectly still, wrapped in her fur coat.

'The truth is not interference, sister,' Nicola said coolly. She pushed her coat's hood back, and gave her sister a gently pitying smile.

Queen Judith's visor snapped shut. 'My truth is all that matters,' she said vehemently. 'My reign will last for eternity when this battle is over.'

'You're deluded. Nobody lives forever.'

'I can. That is my prize for victory. And you have sabotaged my rightful rule for the last time.' Queen Judith extended her arm and clicked her fingers, snarling.

An awesome bolt of magic flashed towards Nicola, who regarded the belligerent armoured form of her sister with quiet bemusement as it flared impotently around her.

Queen Judith gave a start as her sister stood there completely unaffected while the vigorous magic streamed through the air. She concentrated, pouring even more power into the death spell. Then determination changed to surprise before becoming alarm. The magic continued to stream out of her. 'No,' she exclaimed. Her fingers clicked. 'No. Stop. No.' The magic grew dimmer, and

Queen Judith staggered back. Finally the spell ended, and she pushed her visor back to reveal her tragic face. She held her trembling hand up to her eyes, staring at it, stricken. She clicked her fingers. Nothing happened. 'What have you done?' she yelled as she sank to her knees in horror. 'I have no magic. You have stolen it. I am become ordinary! Ordinary!'

'Sister, dear,' Nicola said calmly. 'You've always been that.'

Prince Lantic charged into the group, and ran to his father. 'You have to stop,' he said. 'Father, the war must not happen. Please, listen to me. Please. So many will die.'

The War Emperor looked at him as if he was a stranger. His son in the armoured tunic of the Blue Feather regiment. Smeared in filth and paxia blood. One hand holding a firestar ready to throw. His eyes wild. 'My son,' he said simply, and embraced him. 'Oh my son, you're alive!'

'Father, we have brought you Mirlyn's Gate. The Karrak peoples can go home to the Dark Universe again. There is no need for war. Please, this is never what Rogreth would have wanted. You know that. Don't you? Do you understand?'

The War Emperor slowly nodded. 'Yes. Yes, you are right. I see now. I see so many things.'

Amenamon pushed past the lords of the khatu legion to confront his younger brother. His flame teeth had turned almost sapphire they were burning so bright.

'Brother.' Lord Colgath bowed, the sparkles of colour in his smoke cloak shrinking to tiny specks.

Amenamon let out a wordless cry, and sent a burst of magic into his brother, knocking him down to sprawl on the frozen dirt. 'One minute,' he shouted down at his brother. 'That is all. One single minute more and the War Emperor's entire army would be dead. I would have been ruler of every realm in this Universe. And *you*! You appear from nowhere to snatch victory from me. Why? What have I ever done to deserve a brother like you?'

Lord Colgath made no move to get up. 'This Universe is not for us, brother, and in your heart you know this. It hates us. It punishes us for every moment we are here. This false war would have been nothing but a hollow victory. I brought you what I believe is a greater victory. You can be the one who takes us home.'

Amenamon turned to face Mirlyn's Gate with its agitated serpent bonds. Sophie, Felix and the *Angelhawk*'s exhausted crew stood round it, looking defiantly at both armies as they held up their meagre weapons.

'Father died to take that monstrosity from us, away from temptation,' the Grand Lord said. 'Its very existence is a threat to our Universe.'

'He took it away to make us safe. He knew the time was not right back then, that we had to learn how to live with those whose Universe this truly is.'

'The Abomination and her kind, you mean,' Amenamon spat.

Lord Colgath climbed back to his feet. 'Yes, I mean the Queen of Dreams. Taggie.' He beckoned.

Taggie walked over to the Grand Lord, aching in every limb and desperately weary from the magic she'd cast. 'Lord Amenamon,' she bowed.

The Grand Lord simply glowered.

'This is my friend, brother,' Lord Colgath said. 'She has saved my life many times.'

'As your brother has saved mine,' Taggie said. 'I am proud to call him my friend.'

'The reason – the only reason – we found Mirlyn's Gate where so many have failed before is the trust and respect we have for each other,' Lord Colgath said. 'Our father wished that, and together with the old War Emperor, made that possible. Only when there was peace and agreement between the two of us was the hiding place revealed. Our father knew we would have to make peace with the people of this Universe in order to make progress.'

'There is much to tell you, Grand Lord,' Taggie said. 'I would be honoured to be the one to explain what has happened, if you would agree to it.'

Amenamon looked round. Behind him, his own people were watching him intently, and he was very aware that the keenest of all were those who belonged to the Congress of Lords and Ladies. Beyond Mirlyn's Gate, he could see the War Emperor standing waiting at the head of his army. 'I will hear what you say, Queen of Dreams,' he said. And the joyful cheering started on both sides.

*

The armies waited for an hour while Taggie and Lord Colgath talked to the Grand Lord. Then the War Emperor was invited to join them. Nicola and Lantic were summoned soon after.

'What about us?' Sophie asked. 'Don't we get to tell our story?'

'In time,' Felix assured her.

Three hours after the battle, a tenuous accord was reached. In a poignant echo of what had happened once before at Rothgarnal, the War Emperor and the Grand Lord took each other's hand, pledging to honour their ancestors and end hostilities.

Four giants righted Mirlyn's Gate using hefty poles, tipping it up vertical and propping it in place. The War Emperor and the Grand Lord stood directly in front of it. Taggie and Lantic and Sophie and Jemima and Felix and Lord Colgath formed a line behind them. Next, a few metres back, was a semi-circle of the Light Guards and the khatu legion formed up like a solid wall. Behind them were the strongest sorceresses (under Nicola's command) and Karrak lore masters. Behind them, two armies were spread out over the battlefield, holding their weapons ready.

The circling serpent bonds slithered and slipped around the surface of Mirlyn's Gate as they had done for ten centuries. Every now and then, their gleaming purple eyes would flick a contemptuous glance at the colossal military force arrayed round them.

The War Emperor and the Grand Lord lifted their arms. Their rings glowed with power, and they grasped each other's hand. Together they began incanting, sending spell after spell into the writhing bonds. One by one, the fluid serpents slithered down and wiggled their way into the frozen soil until none were left.

Everyone watched the circle of naked stone. A juddering sigh filled the air, a gasp of breath for lungs that hadn't been filled for a thousand years.

'I am the anointed War Emperor of the Realms.'

'I am the Grand Lord, proclaimed by the Congress of Lords and Ladies.'

'How long?' asked an ancient voice rich with anguish. As it rumbled across Rothgarnal many were reduced to helpless tears from the residue of suffering it carried.

'Ten centuries,' the Grand Lord said.

'I saw nothing. I heard nothing. Now I am back in this place. Is there peace now?'

The Grand Lord and War Emperor looked at each other. 'There is,' they said as one.

The sigh came again, one of profound relief this time.

'Mirlyn, we bid you open to the other Universe,' the two leaders said.

'That is what I do,' Mirlyn said. 'It is what I am.' The little stones which made up the circle began to move, exposing a hole in the centre. It grew larger until it was wide enough for two people to step through side by side. A pale mist glimmered in the gap.

The armies held their breath. And the War Emperor and Grand Lord stepped through together.

Taggie looked at Lantic, then at Lord Colgath. When she checked with Jemima, her sister shrugged. 'Come on then,' she said.

Mirlyn's Gate grew wider as they approached, the little stones shuffling about busily. Taggie stepped into the Dark Universe.

The light was green. That was the first thing she noticed. Then the cold struck her. She'd borrowed a fur coat, but it seemed to have no effect at all. Her breath was coming out in white streamers, and she shivered.

It wasn't such a different place, the Dark Universe. It had a sun, like any realm. Except this one was huge, floating in the sky at least five times the size of the Outer Realm's moon. And the light it shone across the land was green-tinged. And cold. Holding her hand up to it, Taggie could feel no warmth at all.

A headache was starting as she took in the landscape. There was no snow or ice as there would be during winter in her home Universe. Yet this wasn't winter, not here. The waving grass was dark and spongy. And the trees were in full bloom. Taggie regarded them in admiration. The long valley where this side of Mirlyn's Gate emerged was planted with thousands upon thousands of trees. They were tall and thick, with leaves that were an elegant bright pink. Small silver flowers twinkled amid the boughs as if someone had sprinkled them with stardust.

'I like it,' she said. Her hand went to her stomach as she felt an unpleasant burst of nausea. 'It's strange, but kind of beautiful, too.'

'Thank you,' Lord Colgath said.

'I think I'm going to be sick,' Jemima said. 'I've eaten something bad.'

'No,' Lantic said. 'It's not that. I feel dreadful, too.'

'This is how you felt in our Universe, isn't it?' Taggie asked Lord Colgath in dismay. Her headache was getting worse.

'It is gone,' he murmured in amazement. 'The pain, the suffering. So long we lived with it. I had forgotten what it was to exist without misery.'

When Taggie looked over at the Grand Lord and War Emperor, she saw Amenamon's smoke cloak was abandoning its blackness to grow translucent.

'Brother,' Lord Colgath said.

'Brother.'

They embraced.

Taggie had to wipe a tear from her cheek. *Must be from the headache*, she told herself.

'You were right,' Grand Lord Amenamon said. 'This is victory. The most precious victory of all: peace.'

'Your victory,' Lord Colgath said. 'You made it happen, brother. You saw what had to be done, and you did not hesitate.'

'I think you played a part.'

Taggie and Sophie gave each other an incredulous look. They were listening to Karraks laughing. A harsh snarling sound, of course, but still . . . laughter!

'So what happened here?' the War Emperor asked as his gaze travelled round the beautiful valley.

'There was a battle,' Grand Lord Amenamon said. 'I remember it well.'

'Just as bad as Rothgarnal,' Lord Colgath confirmed.

'So . . . who won?' Lantic asked.

'Ask him,' Jemima said, and pointed.

Taggie saw a figure in a fur coat curled up on the grass to one side of Mirlyn's Gate. She went over and peered down curiously. An ancient-looking man was asleep, curled up around a spear. He was snoring softly. 'Who is he?'

'Mr Stimpson,' Jemima told her. 'He's been here a long time.'

'Excuse me,' Taggie tapped Mr Stimpson's shoulder. He snuffled and curled up tighter. 'Excuse me!'

'Eh?' his eyes opened, and he coughed. Then he scrambled to his feet, surprisingly fast for someone so old. His spear was pointed at Taggie, and he screwed up his face to squint, which added even more wrinkles. 'Who's that? Who goes there?'

'My name is Taggie, I've come through Mirlyn's Gate.'

'You came through what?'

'We're from the Light Universe. We opened Mirlyn's Gate.'

Mr Stimpson gulped and spun round. The spear fell from his gloved hands. 'It's open!'

'Yes,' Taggie said, smiling. 'It's open.'

'Eighty-three years I've stood guard here,' the old man said. 'Like my father, and his father before him, and . . . and all my family going back to the war. It's what us Stimpsons do. We promised everybody we would, you see, and a promise like that cannot be broken. Not by people who have standards, and without standards . . . why, you have nothing.' He lifted a tarnished brass and copper horn from his belt. 'A prince gave this to my family, it's a homecoming horn, he said, and everybody from the Light Universe would hear its call when it's blown. That way they'll know the time has come to return.'

'What happened?' Taggie asked. 'With the war, I mean. How did it all end?'

'The War of Peace? It ended as soon as Mirlyn's Gate was shut and bound. Why wouldn't it? What was the point of carrying on?'

'Yes,' Taggie said with a sigh. 'What would be the point?'

'The Princes and Princesses and the Lords and Ladies, they all sat round a table and made agreements that've held to this day. Then all the soldiers that remained, they buried their dead, and planted a cyarda tree on each grave.' Mr Stimpson's arm swept round the valley. 'Every one of those trees grew and flourished, see. An omen, everyone called it. People still make pilgrimage here, you know. They come to remind themselves about the past, so they don't make the same mistakes again.'

'So, nobody here wants to invade the Light Universe?' the War Emperor asked.

Mr Stimpson chortled. 'Invade? Naaah. I wouldn't mind going for a look, mind. That was a big part of the old agreement, see, that we would go back when the Gate opened again. It hurts for us to live here, you know. But you get used to it. Mustn't complain.'

'Well, Mr Stimpson,' Taggie said. 'I think it's finally time for you to blow your homecoming horn. Then I'd like to show you the realms of the Light Universe.'

'Very kind I'm sure, young lady. So is it peaceful over there?'

'Yes,' Taggie promised. 'It is peaceful in the realms. Now.'

25

PARTY TIME

The party had taken three weeks to plan. Mr Anatole had been disturbed by the extravagance and the always rising cost, but Taggie had insisted. People didn't argue with her so much now – apart from Mum and Dad, of course, but even they'd agreed to this. There was to be the main party in the palace – now the scaffolding was finally down in the banqueting hall. There were also street parties planned right across Lorothain. Then simultaneous parties in every town and village of the First Realm.

After all, the Queen of Dreams was only going to be fourteen once.

But it was so much more than a simple birthday party. There was also a celebration to be had. Now, a month after Mirlyn's Gate had opened, the Karrak Lords and Ladies and those who had come with them were almost all gone, returned to the Dark Universe. And after Mr Stimpson blew his horn, people originally from the Light Universe were coming home.

Taggie woke early and immediately ran over to the window to fling the curtains back and check it was sunny outside. That was the best thing about being able to magically control the weather for an entire Realm – you could always make sure it was a sunny day when you wanted it to be.

She pulled on jeans and a T-shirt ready to go down to breakfast with her friends. But strangely, her mood wasn't right, not for her birthday. She felt pensive for some reason. She sat back down at her dressing table and gave herself a brooding look in the mirror.

'Come on,' she told the reflection. 'You know what the matter is.' With a sigh she put her hand on the dresser's secret compartment and muttered the opening enchantment. The hidden drawer slid open.

The Trakal lay inside. Lord Colgath had given it to her last night.

'We will have no use for it,' he explained. 'Not back in the Dark Universe. And there is no one I trust with it more than you.'

'I'd almost forgotten about it,' she admitted.

'It was clasped in my father's hand in the *Lady Silvaris*.'

'I'm sorry we couldn't bring him back as well.'

'He rests with people of immense honour. There is no greater dignity that that.'

'You're right, of course. They all gave so much so that we could eventually find peace.'

'Which we very nearly didn't.'

'But in the end we did.' She grinned up at him. 'It was close, mind you.'

'That it was, Queen of Dreams, that it was.'

Taggie pulled a face. 'My own aunt!'

'Indeed. My brother asked me to tell you, he had agreed a bloodbond with Queen Judith.'

'We suspected as much. What was the deal?'

'For her help instigating the war, and eventual victory, Amenamon had agreed to give her the enchantment which assists us Karrak Lords to live for a long time.'

For a moment Taggie was speechless. 'Wow. He must have been desperate. He was going to make Queen Judith immortal? Her reign really would have lasted forever.'

'Would you like that enchantment, Queen of Dreams?'

'We live the lives we're supposed to,' she replied. 'I believe in that.'

Lord Colgath smiled, which even after all this time still wasn't exactly a comforting sight. She wondered if she'd ever lose her old prejudice about the appearance of the Karrak people. 'I am almost sad to be leaving,' he said. 'I think the First Realm is due to experience its next golden age.'

'You're very kind. I'm glad you are bringing your wife to the party. I've wanted to meet her ever since you told me you were married.'

'I must admit, she was also curious to meet you. But then, most of my people are.'

'What about you and her?' Taggie asked. She blushed. 'I'm sorry, that's personal.'

'We have been apart for a long time. But we were together for a lot longer before that. And now we are to start a new life together in a different universe. I believe that is a good omen for us.'

Taggie grinned. 'A happy ending. We had to have one. It's nice that it's yours.'

'I would like you to have the same opportunity. So . . .' His cold hand closed around hers, pressing the Trakal into her palm. 'Use it wisely.'

So now, sitting on her dresser, she held it up and examined it properly in the morning sunlight. The Trakal hung on a chain, a simple disc of some burnished metal, with a ring of small runes written into its edge. It didn't seem much, yet she could feel the malignant power coiled up inside. Lord Colgath had given her the trigger spell, too.

She knew she'd never use it. But if a new threat were ever to arise and endanger the realms, then the First Realm could be sealed off and made secure by a descendant.

'No,' she said to herself. Isolation was never the answer. Besides, she'd made a promise, and a true royal didn't ignore inconveniences like that. She shoved the Trakal into her pocket and went out into the big corridor, just in time to hear a commotion in Jemima's room. Her charmsward bands slid round smoothly.

Jemima's bedroom door swung open, and a boy came stumbling out backwards, not quite fully wrapped in a sheet. He was about fifteen years old, with long white hair dangling down his back. Taggie gave him a startled look. 'Felix?'

Jemima was shouting something angrily. She appeared

in the doorway, holding a sword that was almost as big as her. It wobbled about unsteadily.

'Majesty?' Felix tried to bow, and made a hurried snatch at the sheet as it slipped.

'Felix, you're you,' Taggie gasped.

'Felix?' Jemima let the sword tip drop to the floor, where it gouged several tiny flakes from the flagstones. 'I woke up and thought an assassin was in my room.' Her eyes narrowed in suspicion. 'You were creeping around in the dark.'

'I was trying to get out!' Felix said in a pleading voice. 'I went to sleep in your suite's lounge like I always do, then when I woke up, this had happened.'

Mum was striding down the corridor, dressed in her full Third Realm sorceress robes. Lantic was peering out of his room, struggling with his glasses. Sophie was framed by the doorway of her guest suite, licking her lips in enjoyment at everyone's consternation.

'Is it your birthday?' Mum asked sharply.

'Er, no,' Felix said. 'That was a while back.'

'When snow falls on oak,' Lantic said. He walked over to Felix and put on a pair of purple-lens revealor glasses to examine him closely, as if the boy was some kind of specimen in his study. 'That was your curse, wasn't it?'

'For each day outside my birthday and while snow falls on oak,' Felix said as if the words were a physical pain.

'And the curse on your family was made in the Fourth Realm, was it not?' Lantic persisted.

'Yes.'

'The Karraks have all but left the Fourth Realm,' Mum said. 'The King in Exile has already established his new court there.'

'The thousand-year winter is ending, Felix,' Taggie said kindly. 'Snow is no longer falling on oak. Not in the Fourth Realm. Spring is finally on its way.'

Felix held his hand up to his face as if he'd never seen its like before. 'It's over?' he whispered incredulously. 'The curse is finally over?'

'Yes.'

Felix sank to his knees, still staring at his hand. 'Oh sweet heavens!' He looked round at his friends in bewilderment, his eyes watering. 'What will I do?' he asked plaintively.

'You silly thing,' Jemima said, dragging the sword along as she went over to him. 'You can do whatever you want. You said you hoped your job would become less difficult once we found Mirlyn's Gate. Well, that just happened. What was next on the list?'

'I . . . I don't know.'

'The King in Exile has invited the original refugee families to return home and help rebuild the Fourth Realm,' Taggie said. 'And Jem doesn't need bodyguarding quite so much now, if you want to go.'

'Your family house looked lovely,' Jemima said encouragingly. 'I'll be happy to visit with you and wake the forests and flowers there if you'd like. It'd be a good start for a new life.'

Felix gave her an admiring look. 'You would?'

'I'm the Blossom Princess,' she said in a mock-serious tone. 'That's my job, remember.'

'I need to think,' Felix said. 'This is all so amazing.'

'Take as long as you like,' Taggie told him. She walked away from the group that clustered round Felix, and made her way out into the garden. She transformed into the snow eagle, and flew away from the palace.

The prim little canal station below the Great Gateway was the first thing Taggie had ever seen in the First Realm. It remained comfortingly unchanged as she alighted on the grass pathway behind it. She walked up to the iron-bound wooden door that was set into the hillside. It was shut, as usual.

'Arasath, I am Taggie, Queen of Dreams, and I have something for you.' She took the Trakal from her pocket, and held it up.

The door swung open, and Taggie stepped into the curving brick tunnel behind it. This time it didn't lead to the door at the bottom of the roundadown. The door she encountered was a lot older. She could hear voices on the other side.

It opened into an old hall, with little by way of elaboration. Long tables were laid out down the middle, while a big open fireplace at the far end had a grate piled high with blazing logs, throwing out a great heat. The high windows were all shuttered. Iron candelabras holding twenty fat candles apiece hung from the rafters on long chains.

All the chairs were taken by very old people, wearing elaborate robes whose finest days had come and gone centuries ago. The women had long wispy grey hair, and the men beards down to their bellies. One of them stood just inside the door, smiling in welcome.

'So this is the Universal Fellowship,' Taggie said as she looked round.

'Indeed,' the ancient man said.

Taggie knew that voice and grinned. 'You're Arasath.'

'Yes. Welcome, Queen of Dreams, to our first assembly in a thousand years.' He gave her an affectionate hug, the kind a grandfather would bestow.

Taggie held out the Trakal. 'I came to give you this.'

The hall fell silent, with all the gateway mages staring at the simple pendant in respectful silence. Arasath reached out and gingerly took it from her. The Fellowship broke into applause. Taggie blushed.

'Thank you,' Arasath said sincerely.

'I promised you I would bring it.'

'You did.' Arasath seemed to be on the verge of tears. 'You must forgive an old mage, but we grow cynical and bitter as the centuries flow past. It is both a surprise and a delight when someone acts with honour these days.'

'What will you do with it?'

'It will become unmade,' Arasath said. 'And we will rest easy once more. We have not rested easy for many years.'

'So is that what my quest was truly about?' she asked.

'We became what we are so all peoples of our Realms would be free to enjoy travel and prosperity. That is still our purpose. And now we can look to the future with hope, no longer absorbed by the past and its failings.'

'You guided me, didn't you?' she said as a lot of things suddenly became clear. 'I was your instrument from the moment I first stepped into the roundadown, even though I never realized.' She wasn't sure if she should be pleased or angry.

'You were our shining hope, Queen of Dreams. You are the proof that we were right to forge the Great Gateways. Look at you, my dear, born of parents from different Realms, raised in yet another. Such diversity brings strength in so many ways. In effect, you have become our greatest triumph.'

'Humm,' Taggie refused to be convinced by his flattery. 'And Mirlyn?' she asked, staring round the tables again. 'Is he here?'

With everybody watching, Arasath led her down the length of the hall to the seat closest to the roaring fire. She knew without having to ask further which mage was Mirlyn. He was as old as the rest, yet had a vitality that burned as intensely as the fire.

As she approached, a young woman rose from where she'd been kneeling in front of Mirlyn's chair. She smiled at Taggie. 'I am Isabel, and I thank you for freeing my grandsire,' she said, and gestured Taggie forward.

Mirlyn looked up at her with surprisingly gentle eyes for such a resolute face. 'I was unheard for so many centuries. I don't know how much longer I could have endured. And then you appeared. You are my miracle, Agatha Paganuzzi.'

'You're welcome,' Taggie replied, for once not cross that her real name was being used. 'What will happen now? Will you remain open?'

'I paid a great price for my arrogance. During the time I was unheard, I swore that arrogance would be undone. That may have been the one thing which kept me from diminishing as too many of my colleagues have done. I was the one who always wanted more. I reached into the Dark Universe, proved I was the greatest of our Fellowship. And now I see it was all for nothing, for vanity's folly. I think it is time we bade our acquaintances from the Dark Universe a lasting goodbye.'

'You're going to close permanently, aren't you?' she realized.

'This assembly is my farewell to my old friends. When the last of the exiles have crossed back, I shall become unforged. Like the War Emperor and the Grand Lord of old, I do not want temptation to stain the separate Universes. And if I continue to exist, then there is a chance it will. We must learn from our mistakes, and strive never to repeat them. So now I will say goodbye to you, the greatest Queen of Dreams. I am pleased to have met you, and seen the kindness you show to your friends and your foes. You have even shown me that hope can always flower in the darkest of places. Live your life well, my dear.'

Taggie dipped her head. 'I will,' she promised him.

The dress was perfect. A white bodice, its skirt layers of ruffles with black and scarlet bands. Its hem swirled just above her knees.

'My legs are too thin,' Taggie exclaimed in dismay as she stared at her image in the full-length mirror. 'My knees stick out.'

'Stop fishing for compliments,' Mum warned. 'You look lovely, and you know it.'

'But—'

'No! Now put this on.'

The tiara had more diamonds than a jewellery shop. But Taggie had to admit, it did look rather grand sitting on her brushed-to-a-gloss hair. She pulled a face, then grinned. 'We should go down, it's about to start.'

Mum rolled her eyes. 'Did you learn nothing from me? A lady does not arrive early, she allows expectation to build.'

'Yes, yes, but there's going to be dancing. Oh, Mum, I want to dance all night.'

'I met with the heads of the other Third Realm Sorceress houses this afternoon,' Mum said.

'Oh!' Taggie's hand flew to her mouth. 'I forgot that was today. Sorry. What happened?'

'Well! While you went mysteriously missing for several hours, we discussed the succession.'

'Mum!' Taggie squealed and clapped her hands together in delight. 'You're going to be a Queen, too!'

'Don't be ridiculous. Of course I'm not.'

'Oh.'

'When it was our house's turn to provide a Queen, we put your aunt on the throne.'

'She stole it. Everybody knows that. It's rightfully yours.'

'That was an internal house problem. Exactly the kind of thing the Third Realm gets its bad reputation from. As I didn't fight it then, I can hardly claim it was all a mistake and I should be Queen now. That would be plunging us right back into the bad old days, so it was agreed the crown would pass to Voywiss, as the duly appointed successor to our house.' Mum sighed. 'Though the Heavens know that woman is so incompetent she couldn't manage to lead a starving pig to its food.'

'OK, Mum. Well, I'm proud of you for being so noble about it.' Taggie adjusted the tiara slightly.

Mum raised an eyebrow. '*However . . .*'

'Yes?' Taggie was starting to wonder if she would actually get to dance at all this evening.

'I did agree to go back to take up the burden of leading our house. After all, someone has to keep an eye on your aunt even in her current state, and a great many changes need to be made for our house to regain its correct status.'

'Yeah, that was such a brilliant piece of magic,' Taggie said. 'Vacuuming out her power like that.'

'I don't know why she thought I would spend my whole

317

time in the Outer Realm baking cakes and driving you two about on the school run like some domestic goddess. Of course I kept up my study of the art – how else can you grow more powerful and finally defeat your arch enemy? She clearly blanked out our entire childhood.'

Taggie pressed her lips together so she wasn't smiling. There were times when Mum was just plain unbelievable. 'I'll try and remember that.'

'Quite. Come on, you're going to be late. That's a bad trait in royalty.'

'But . . . you said to arrive late,' Taggie fell silent as Mum gave her one of those 'disappointed' looks. She took a breath. 'I'm ready now.'

Dad was waiting for them out in the corridor, looking rather dashing in his new ceremonial tunic. He cocked his head to one side and smiled in complete satisfaction at Taggie. 'You look beautiful, darling.' He kissed her on her forehead.

Taggie endured her hair being slightly mussed, she was just so glad he'd come back unharmed from Banmula. Jemima was standing beside him, very content in her own satin dress – the most grown-up she'd ever had. A small crown of ocean-blue flutterseed stems was woven into her hair, with the flowers flapping exuberantly, yet never taking flight.

Taggie grabbed her sister's hand, and grinned. 'Let's go.'

'Can I have champagne tonight? Jemima asked brightly.

'No,' Mum and Dad said together.

'But Taggie's going to.'

'One glass only, and she's fourteen now,' Dad said.

'That's just not fair.'

'You can sing if you like,' Taggie said wickedly. 'The band will play any number you want.'

'By myself? No way!' Jemima exclaimed.

Lantic was waiting for them at the top of the stairs, wearing the full dress uniform of a colonel in the Blue Feather regiment. His father had awarded him the commission the previous week.

'Very stylish,' Taggie said approvingly.

Lantic held out his arm formally, and she allowed him to escort her down the stairs to the outer hall. Felix was standing at the bottom, smartly dressed in the elegant uniform of the palace guard.

'Look at this, another one who cleans up well,' Dad observed. 'Who'd have thought.'

Felix held out his arm, and Jemima accepted it, falling in behind Taggie and Lantic.

The outer hall was packed with the Kings and Queens of every Realm. Lord Colgath stood among them, with his wife, Lady Anaquis, next to him. And nobody seemed to think it was in any way odd, let alone disturbing. Taggie smiled at them as she and Lantic walked the length of the hall to the big doors at the far end, acknowledging their greetings. One by one the royal families fell in behind her so she was soon leading a grand procession. The crew of the *Angelhawk* were standing halfway along the line.

'Captain,' Taggie said, savouring the sight of the wonderful skywoman wearing a fancy new evening dress. 'How goes it?'

'Very well, thank you, young Queen,' Captain Rebecca said crisply. 'The keel of the *Angelhawk II* has been laid. I've designed a few modifications of my own, and she'll be built of the finest Fifth Realm hornash planks. It's expensive wood, but worth it.'

Taggie diplomatically ignored the pained expression on Mr Anatole's face. 'The least I could do,' she said.

'I'd be honoured if you'd perform the launch ceremony yourself. Send her on her way with a gust of good fortune, eh?'

'Of course I will.' Taggie frowned slightly, glancing round the crew. 'Have you seen Sophie?'

'Aye, over there,' Captain Rebecca said with a sly chuckle. 'Terrifying the Highlord's fledgling. He really is as handsome as everyone says, you know.'

'Ah.' Taggie saw her friend next to the skyboy who would one day be Highlord, her red hair waving slowly and sinuously above her shoulders as she pressed up close to her prey. Yes, Taggie acknowledged, he was very handsome indeed, even though his perfect features were currently marred by a nervous expression as he attempted to back away – hopeless: his wings were already squashed up against a pillar. 'I'll see you inside, then.' Taggie carried on towards the doors that led into the banqueting hall. 'I claim the first dance with you,' she told Lantic.

'What?' Lantic was suddenly as panic-stricken as the first time she met him. 'But Taggie, I can't dance.'

The doors swept open, and the orchestra struck up.

'You're only a prince,' she told him, smiling straight ahead at the sumptuous party laid out waiting for her. 'I'm a Queen. So you have to do as I tell you. Better get used to it.'

THE END

QUEEN of DREAMS
THE SECRET THRONE

PETER F. HAMILTON

Taggie and her younger sister, Jemima, are just ordinary girls living an ordinary life. Until the day a white squirrel wearing glasses turns up in their garden. The next thing the sisters know, their dad has been kidnapped!

But it seems their father has been keeping some very large secrets from his young daughters – he is, in fact, a prince from another world, and the land he *should* be ruling has been overthrown by a ruthless invader – known as the King of Night.

Can Taggie and Jemima find their way between the worlds to save their father – and just what other secrets has he been hiding?

THE FIRST BOOK IN QUEEN of DREAMS TRILOGY

THE QUEEN OF DREAMS
THE HUNTING OF THE PRINCES

PETER F. HAMILTON

Taggie has had a busy year. From finding out she's the
queen-to-be of a magical realm and learning to use magic . . .
to discovering that someone wants her dead!

Assassins have been targeting royal heirs throughout the magical
realms, and everyone thinks the Karrak invaders are responsible.
War seems inevitable – yet Taggie has just found out two very
interesting facts. Firstly that the Karraks come from a completely
different universe. And secondly that there was once a gate to this
universe – now lost in the mists of time.

If Taggie and her friends can find the gate, perhaps they
can also stop the war? But to do so they need to find a
Karrak who will take their side . . .

THE SECOND BOOK IN
THE QUEEN OF DREAMS
TRILOGY